ALSO BY AMY LILLARD

CONTEMPORARY ROMANCE

Brodie's Bride

All You Need Is Love

Can't Buy Me Love

Love Potion Me, Baby

Southern Hospitality

Southern Comfort

Southern Charm

The Trouble with Millionaires

Take Me Back to Texas

Blame It on Texas

Ten Reasons Not to Date a Cop

Loving a Lawman

Healing a Heart

AMISH ROMANCE

Saving Gideon

Katie's Choice

Gabriel's Bride

Caroline's Secret

Courting Emily

Lorie's Heart

Just Plain Sadie

Titus Returns

Marrying Jonah

The Quilting Circle

A Wells Landing Christmas

A Mamm for Christmas, The
    Amish Christmas Collection

A Summer Wedding in Paradise,
    The Amish Brides Collection

A Home for Hannah

A Love for Leah

A Family for Gracie

OTHER MYSTERIES

Unsavory Notions

Pattern of Betrayal

O' Little Town of Sugarcreek

Shoo, Fly, Shoo

Stranger Things Have Happened

Kappy King and the Puppy Kaper

Kappy King and the Pickle Kaper

Kappy King and the Pie Kaper

HISTORICAL ROMANCE

The Wildflower Bride

The Gingerbread Bride,
    12 Brides of Christmas
    Collection

As Good As Gold, The Oregon
    Trail Romance Collection

Not So Pretty Penny, Lassoed
    by Marriage Collection

CAN'T JUDGE A
BOOK
— BY ITS —
MURDER

A MAIN STREET BOOK CLUB MYSTERY

· AMY LILLARD ·

Poisoned Pen
PRESS

Published by Poisoned Pen Press, an imprint of Sourcebooks
P.O. Box 4410, Naperville, Illinois 60567-4410
(630) 961-3900
sourcebooks.com

Cataloging-in-Publication Data is on file with the Library of Congress.

The authorized representative in the EEA is Dorling Kindersley Verlag GmbH.
Arnulfstr. 124, 80636 Munich, Germany

Manufactured in the UK by Clays and distributed by
Dorling Kindersley Limited, London
001-329618-Nov/24
10 9 8 7 6 5 4 3 2 1

To Linda and Mary Beth,
thanks for being such faithful readers, beautiful neighbors,
and always having a smile for me.
I appreciate you both more than you will know!

1

THIS WAS THE LAST THING SHE NEEDED.

Arlo Stanley hurried around the building, barely missing the crumbling spot at the edge of the street. Her foot twisted, and a sharp pain shot from her toes up to her ankle. This was not the day to break in new shoes. And heels at that. Now she had a bum ankle to add to the equation. But she had already been dressed for work when the police called.

A dead body! Right there on the sidewalk! Directly in front of her bookstore!

Things like this didn't happen in their little town. Just. Didn't. Happen.

She could hardy grasp it. Yes, people died, but not on Main Street. At least not as long as she had lived in Sugar Springs. It was unthinkable.

And to make matters worse, this weekend was important to the residents of Sugar Springs and all the Main Street merchants. This weekend was the Tenth Annual All-School Class Reunion. Not many people usually came out for that sort of thing, just a few locals and whoever happened to be in the area. But this year they had a special guest, the most famous person ever to leave Sugar Springs, Mississippi: Wallace J. Harrison. Known as Wally to those who had graduated with him, he was an upcoming star in the mystery-suspense genre with ten consecutive weeks on the *New York Times* Best Seller list. Wally was a national sensation. And he was back in town.

Arlo had managed to convince Wally's assistant that he should do a signing at her newly opened bookstore. She was even going to host a special Sunday opening for the event. Now the store was currently sectioned off with bright-yellow police tape.

She picked up her pace, mincing along and trying not to grimace in pain. She needed to get to her shop as quickly as possible, but City Ordinance 52-B stated that all shop employees had to park in the alley behind their stores to allow for ample parking in the front for their paying customers. Joni, the town's petite meter maid—sorry, "traffic specialist"—was something of a stickler when it came to Main Street. So Arlo's slightly dented, vintage VW Rabbit was parked in the alley behind her shop.

Arlo groaned when she saw the crowd of people in front of her store. It might be 9:00 a.m. on Friday, but everyone was already out and about. No one was looking at the new display she had created of Wally's book along with choice murder weapons, making her window resemble an extra-large game of *Clue*. They were staring at the body. The one she could just see through their shuffling feet. Not quite a body, more a tangle of arms and legs, grotesquely twisted as if this poor soul had jumped from the third-story rooftop and fallen to the sidewalk below. Not just a death, but a possible suicide.

Arlo stumbled. A body. A real live dead body. On the sidewalk in front of her store. Goose bumps skittered across her skin. This was nothing like watching crime TV or reading about a death in the latest mystery. This was something altogether different.

There was one resident who wouldn't get to engage in the weekend festivities. Though she didn't know who it was. When the police had called, dispatch hadn't told her the identity of the person, only that it was a man and she needed to get down there fast. But Sugar Springs wasn't a big place. There wasn't any doubt Arlo would know the person who lay there on the sidewalk. Maybe she had even sold them a book. The thought was sad and sobering.

Yet she couldn't continue to stand there. She had to be professional, move forward, find out why this person felt the need to fling himself from the roof. See what needed to be done next. Keeping focus would help her handle the ordeal. At least she hoped it would.

Arlo tugged on the tails of her button-down shirt and smoothed her palms over the sides of her gray dress slacks. She pushed her waist-length, chocolate-brown hair over her shoulders and straightened her back. One deep breath in and she started forward.

"Excuse me." She nudged past Dan the grocer, Phil who owned the video store next door, Joyce the florist from across the street, and Delores the gum-smacking clerk from the jewelry store down the way. Arlo didn't bother with the niceties; she simply pushed through. She had to talk to Mads, the chief of police. She had to have him clear up this…mess? Disaster? *Crime scene.*

"Mads." She greeted him on a rush of air, then stopped when she got a good look at the body. "Is that…?"

He nodded, his normally stern face grim.

"But…" The one word was all she could manage. She looked back to the twisted form.

Wally Harrison lay dead at their feet.

....

Arlo's ears began to hum as Chief Matthew "Mads" Keller shooed everyone away from the body. "Go on now," he said.

Mads, so nicknamed from his high school football days, crossed his arms so everyone would know he wasn't budging. Most turned and trudged back to their stores, spinning around once or twice as if to make sure the scene was still the same, that their eyes weren't playing tricks on them.

"Do you think he jumped?" Jason Rogers, Mads's first officer, nudged the body with the toe of one boot.

"Would you stop violating my crime scene?" Mads growled.

Jason held up both hands and backed away. "Sorry, big-city cop."

Mads rolled his eyes.

Arlo rocked in place, staring in horror. Wally Harrison was dead. In front of her store. And dead.

"Well?" Jason asked.

Mads squatted down next to the body and used the end of his pen to lift the baseball cap from in front of Wally's face.

"The Yankees," Jason scoffed. "Of course he liked the Yankees. He left here and got all big-time on us. Too good to root for the Braves."

Mads let the cap fall back into place. Arlo knew he wanted to say something to Jason, but he was too controlled for that. One day though…one day he was going to blow. She hoped she was around to see it.

People continued to walk past, pretending to be shopping as usual, but slowing down to take in as much of the scene as they could.

The crime scene. In front of her store.

She had to get ahold of herself.

"Did he?" she finally asked. "Kill himself?"

It was a stupid question. Why would a man like Wally Harrison kill himself? He had a successful life. He was raking in the dough from his book; he was handsome. Once upon a time, he had been everything in their small town. He wasn't the geek who made it big. He was the golden boy, the one that got away. The one who would put Sugar Springs on the map if he ever admitted to being born there.

Well, Mads could have had that kind of life too, if he hadn't blown out his knee in the first game of the AFC playoffs his third season in the NFL. After that, he became a cop in Memphis and eventually made his way back home to Sugar Springs.

"Looks that way," Mads said on a breath of a sigh.

"Arlo."

She turned at the sound of her name. Chloe Carter stood in the doorway of the store they shared. Her face was a contorted mask of disbelief and horror with a little disgust thrown in for variety. After all, there was a strange past between Chloe and Wally, but that was a long time ago.

"Have you been in there all morning?" Arlo asked.

Chloe ran the "more" of Arlo and Chloe's Books & More, which included a coffee bar, cake counter, unique gifts, and fine chocolates. She had, on occasion, been known to offer flowers, but that had given Joyce at Blooming Blooms an apoplexy and so Chloe had dropped the idea before the roses even wilted.

Chloe nodded, but before she could say anything, a loud voice rang out, bouncing off the Civil War–era brick that lined Main Street.

"*Bozhe miy!*" Inna Kolisnychenko, Wally's trophy assistant approached from the end of the block. Her thick Ukrainian accent added a hard edge to every word she said. "What is going on here?"

"Ms. Kolisnychenko." Mads stood and Arlo could tell by the look on his face that he would rather be anywhere but there, anywhere but telling this woman that her employer was dead—most likely by his own hand. Arlo had to give Mads points for correctly pronouncing Inna's name though.

"Is that—?" She stopped, almost as if posing, as she stared at the body on the sidewalk, one hand on her hip as she bit her lip in confusion. She was a study in beauty.

Inna was statuesque, with dark hair and a pouty mouth, like a Ukrainian Jane Russell, but she carried herself more like a half-asleep Marilyn Monroe. Though she was much taller than most men, including her boss, she had a tendency to make them want to take care of her. There was something a little helpless about her. At least that's what Arlo thought Inna wanted people to see. Arlo wasn't sold on Inna's presentation, though she wasn't certain why.

Inna wore her deep-plum-colored wrap dress like an Amazonian queen. She had paired it with platform stilettos that gave her another four and a half inches easy. In those shoes, she was nearly as tall as Mads. Her exotic blue eyes seemed almost impossible in her face, as if they could see straight through to a person's secrets, to their soul.

She was more than beautiful, a fact Inna already knew. And

anyone who knew Wally knew Inna, the trophy assistant. Too beautiful to be much more than arm candy, Inna probably pulled in more in a week than Arlo had all last year.

The strange thing was Daisy, Wally's wife, was even more stunning than Inna, leaving the average person to wonder why Wally was fooling around. And the average person did know about his affair... or *affairs*, plural. He had all but admitted his dallying with Inna on *Good Morning America*. Everyone knew that she was nothing more than ornamentation. That much was obvious in her lack of skills, other than the savvy way she tucked her hair behind her left ear.

Wally's wife, on the other hand...

"Oh. My. Gawd." Daisy James-Harrison stood at the end of the block, fingers pressed to her mouth, but not so hard as to smudge her lipstick. Her kelly-green dress set off her blond hair and brown eyes to utter perfection.

Then Arlo remembered why the woman was there. Daisy was going to inspect the store and give Arlo the final instructions on how Wally liked his book signings set up. A job that Inna should be performing. But now...

"Mrs. James-Harrison..." Arlo breathed, completely unsure of what she was going to say. She felt like she needed to say something, but what? No one had taught her anything about this in business school.

"Is that...?" Daisy looked hard at the man lying on the ground at the officer's feet.

Arlo bit her lip and turned to Mads.

He cleared his throat. "Yes. Uh..." Mads jerked his head toward the woman, but Jason, as dense today as he ever was, didn't pick up on the gesture. Mads sighed, cast a backward glance at Daisy, then approached Inna. Arlo figured he was aware that Inna was inching closer to Wally's body. After all, there wasn't much that Mads missed.

"Is that my Wally?" Inna pronounced his name as if it began with a *V* instead of a *W*, her normally thick accent even more distinct as the truth set in.

Mads clasped Inna's elbow and tried to steer her away from the crime scene. "Jason," he called over one shoulder.

This time the officer picked up on the chief's hint and moved toward Daisy. With no one standing near the body, Wally Harrison was strangely exposed. Arlo couldn't help but stare.

She had seen Wally a thousand times during school, a hundred more these last few weeks. His face was on every publication that came across her desk. But he looked different in death. And it had nothing to do with the New York Yankees cap Jason so opposed. Yet it seemed strange to her as well. Maybe because every time she had seen him over these last so-successful weeks, he had been wearing a black turtleneck sweater—very cosmopolitan and utterly un-Mississippi, for a man at least. Still, he wouldn't have been wearing a turtleneck today. It was almost May and the heat was already starting to get to some folks. Hot enough that no one was going around in a snug black turtleneck like a sixties' beatnik.

Wally was wearing jeans, an army jacket with the collar turned up, and that baseball hat. It was nothing like what she had seen him wear during their high school years, and certainly not how he dressed in his countless interviews and media photos. But she knew as well as anyone that most writers had a persona they showed to the public, an image they wanted to portray. So he wouldn't always dress that way. Case in point, today.

But it was more than his clothes. He had a bruised look as if he had landed face-first when he fell—or jumped—from the roof. Or maybe that was because he was dead. Did all dead bodies look like that? Why would he choose to throw himself off the building as his means of ending his life? Wasn't jumping a rare form of suicide? She had no idea.

She reined in her whirling thoughts and dragged her gaze from Wally. Looking at him wasn't helpful, so she focused on the building in front of her. Her store, like every other one on the street, was made from worn and weathered brick. It gave Main Street a soft yet dependable look. Most of these buildings had managed to remain standing even during the Civil War and the siege on neighboring Corinth. Two large plateglass windows flanked each side of the double doors. Those doors were possibly as old as the building itself and wore their thick layers of paint like badges of honor. There had been some debate between Arlo and Chloe as to whether or not to replace the doors for security reasons, but sentimentality had won out. Instead, they added new locks, another coat of paint, and relied on the honesty of small-town living to do the rest.

Through the windows she could see the reading area. Faulkner's cage still had the cover on, but she was certain the Amazon parrot was ready to be seen and fed. On the other side of the shop, the coffee bar waited for the doors to be opened and the customers to come in. Usually Chloe was bustling around getting things ready. But not today.

"Arlo."

"Huh?" She dragged her attention from the shop, only briefly aware that the men had switched places. Jason was now talking to Inna and Mads had somehow managed to turn Daisy away from the grisly scene.

"Are you just going to stand there?" Chloe asked. Her voice was only a stage whisper. As if she didn't want to be heard or noticed.

Was she just going to stand there?

Arlo gathered her thoughts and what she could of her composure, then headed into her store.

Chloe held one door open, then locked it as soon as it was closed again.

"Chloe?" Arlo whirled around to look at her best friend and business partner. Chloe's normally wild blond curls seemed even more riotous today. Or was that the light in her green eyes? She looked so completely un-Chloe-like that Arlo almost laughed. Maybe she would have if Wally Harrison wasn't lying dead on the sidewalk in front of her store.

"What's wrong? I mean besides…" She trailed off as she waved a hand in the general direction of the crime scene outside.

Chloe practically wrung her hands, then rushed over to the

sink. She pulled the two oversize coffee mugs from the drainer and started to wash them.

"Aren't those...clean?" Arlo asked. She barely got the words out before Chloe shook her head.

"No. I guess I forgot them last night."

Chloe never forgot anything. She was too laid-back and too utterly Zen to forget, unlike Arlo who needed a daily reminder to remember to put on her shoes. At least that's what Helen, Arlo's one-time guardian, said. Helen was the reason Arlo had been able to stay in Sugar Springs when her family was ready to move on.

"Courtney closed last night."

Chloe pushed her hair back from her face, but it sprang forward once again. "Did she?" She gave a nervous laugh.

Arlo narrowed her gaze and looked around the room. Something was up. But what? Dishes in the drainer, not actually forgotten, meant they had been used that morning. And that meant...

"He was here, wasn't he?"

Chloe laughed again, but the sound was choked. "He? Who he?"

Arlo propped one hip against the back of the couch that faced the reading area. Behind her she heard Faulkner flap his wings. The bird gave a small reminder squawk that no one had taken the cover off his cage. "You know who he."

"Why would who he, uh, he be here?" She grabbed a clean rag from the stack next to the sink and turned on the water.

"Maybe to relive old times?"

"What old times?"

"I don't know. How about that time up at Pickwick...?"

Chloe closed her eyes and held up her hand to stay that memory. "Please." Her fingers trembled.

"All right." Arlo straightened and grabbed Chloe by one string-bracelet-covered wrist. "Let's go." She herded her friend past the open-faced bookshelves with their sturdy oak ladders, then up the wide plank staircase to the loft above. There was more seating there, along with café-style tables and chairs, but more important, Arlo didn't have to see what was going on outside her store. Not for a while anyway. Hopefully long enough for Chloe to tell whatever story she was hiding.

She nudged Chloe into a deep armchair, then pulled her hair over her shoulder and sank down into the opposite one. "Wally was here. Don't try to deny that. What did he want?"

Chloe shrugged. "He said he wanted to talk," she sputtered. "Ten years later and *now* he wants to talk?"

"Why did you let him in?" Arlo asked. She waved a hand and shook her head, as if that would erase her words. "Never mind. Stupid question." She leaned forward and clasped Chloe's hands into her own. "Tell me what happened." She wasn't sure she wanted to know all of it. But Chloe was her best friend and she had to give her the chance to say her piece.

Chloe took a deep, shuddering breath. "He came by to talk." She snorted. "Talk. Imagine. And just like that, I got sucked up again." She sniffed and looked up at the ceiling, a ploy, Arlo was sure, to keep the tears from falling.

"And you thought 'what's the harm?'"

"Exactly."

"So you made the two of you a cup of coffee."

"I made him a coffee."

Of course. Chloe made the best coffee drinks this side of the Mississippi but only drank tea. "Was the shop open?"

"Not yet. It was barely six."

Arlo blinked. Had he been lying out there for hours? It was unthinkable.

Each morning Chloe came into the store at five. She baked for two hours, then opened the shop for the rest of the Main Street vendors to stop by for a pastry and a fresh cup of coffee.

"He said he wanted to see Jayden." The words fell between them like a wet bag of cement.

"He what?" Arlo had to whisper the words to keep from yelling them.

"Wally *is* his father."

Arlo *pfft*ed. "Who gave up his rights." Wally might be Jayden's father, but he had never been a father to the boy. It had always been only Chloe, right from the start.

Chloe shook her head sadly. "He's got attorneys working on the contract, trying to find loopholes. Good attorneys."

Better than she could afford. But Arlo hated to see Chloe give up without a fight.

Now Wally was dead. There would be no custody battle. A detail she felt sure she needed to keep to herself.

"How did he get onto the roof?" Arlo asked.

Chloe pulled her fingers from Arlo's grasp and stood. "How am I supposed to know? Through Phil's I guess." She propped her hands on the back of her hips and stretched, a gesture Arlo had seen her perform countless times over the years. Then Chloe shook out her short blond curls and sniffed once again. The action held a note of finality. "I guess there's no going back now."

"I suppose not." Death tended to do that to relationships. But Chloe and Wally's had been poison from the start. It needed ending. Maybe now Chloe could get on with her life, though Arlo knew if she said anything, Chloe would swear that she hadn't been waiting for Wally for the last ten years. Just as she had waited for him all prom night.

"Phil's, huh?" Arlo said after a few moments. Wally came by the bookstore, then left after…well, Arlo didn't want to speculate about that in too much detail. And he went to Phil's video store for… what?

Phil's was what a sane person would call a throwback sort of place. Yes, they rented a few DVDs and there were still a couple of VHSs hanging around on some of the back shelves. Mostly he rented video games to the younger teens while the rest of Main Street wondered how he stayed in business.

"I guess. How else would he have gotten up on the roof?"

How else? Their building only housed the two stores. The top two floors of Phil's were used for storage. She supposed Wally could have jumped over from another building, but why would he have done that?

"What did you say to him?" Arlo asked.

"Nothing. Why?" The frown puckering Chloe's brow was made of innocent confusion.

Arlo cleared her throat. She wasn't sure how to say the words without restarting Chloe's waterworks. "He left here, went next door, then jumped—"

"From the roof?" Chloe shook her head. "Wally's not the jumping kind. He was pushed."

2

"PUSHED?" THE WORD ESCAPED ARLO LIKE AIR FROM A POPPED balloon. It exploded, filling the space between them. *Pushed* had intent. *Pushed* meant murder and if he was murdered, Chloe might very well be the last person to have seen him alive.

"He had to have been." Chloe sniffed. "You know Wally."

That she did. And despite the fact that Chloe felt there was enough good in the man to pine for him for the last ten years, Arlo knew how he really was. He was too self-absorbed and arrogant to jump from the roof or to kill himself in any manner. Maybe that was what was so strange about the scene out front. Why it looked so wrong. So fabricated.

"What?" Chloe asked.

Arlo shook her head.

"You know it's true."

"Yes," Arlo whispered.

"You should tell Mads. He didn't really know Wally when he lived here. I'm sure to him it looks like a regular ol' jumping from the roof." She stopped, tilted her head to one side. "Is there such a thing?"

Arlo had the feeling her friend was slipping into shock. She was on her feet in an instant, guiding Chloe back to her seat. "I think you should sit down."

She went without protest.

Once again Arlo clasped her friend's hands in her own. Chloe's fingers were ice cold. "Let me make you some tea."

Chloe nodded obediently, another sign that something was wrong. Chloe had spent a year in Paris at a pastry school, though truth be known, Arlo suspected she had actually spent more time in England than France. There Chloe had learned the "proper way to make tea." She didn't miss an opportunity to remind Arlo of the fact. Until now.

Arlo released Chloe's hands and made her way back down the stairs to the main floor. She glanced up at the loft once more, then stuffed a tea bag into a mug, used the Keurig to heat water, and poured in the sugar and cream.

She stirred the brew and looked around for a moment. The bookstore had been a dream of hers for a while. Not just a bookstore, but her piece of Sugar Springs: roots, land, home. She had taken this desire and mixed it with her love of books. A few tweaks and a lot of paint later, Arlo and Chloe's Books & More was born.

"Arlo?" Chloe called.

"Coming." She tapped the spoon against the rim of the mug, then laid it on the counter. It wasn't like they would be opening today. She climbed the stairs to where Chloe waited.

Her friend smiled gratefully as she accepted the cup, then she took a tentative sip. No grimace followed, another sign that Chloe was more affected by Wally's death than she was letting on. Usually she couldn't stand the tea Arlo made. "Are you going to tell Mads?"

Go out there where the dead body still lay? No, thank you. She had seen the county coroner's car pull up while she was making Chloe's tea. Maybe after they...removed him.

Her mouth grew dry. She should have made herself a drink when she was downstairs, but she really wanted something a bit stronger than Earl Grey. About ninety proof stronger.

"Later," she finally said. Mads would be around awhile. And how long before he came in to talk to the one person who might have witnessed it all?

"Chloe," Arlo started, broaching the subject carefully, "did you happen to...what I mean is, did you watch..." Arlo shook her head. The words were tripping her up. They all sounded harsh. "Did you see Wally...fall?"

Chloe took another sip of tea, cradling the cup in her hands. She shook her head. "I had gone to the back to get more flour. I heard this noise—" She choked on the words. Arlo could only imagine what the sound was like. "And when I came back out here, he was dead. I called Mads, then I locked the door till you came."

She had called Mads, but she hadn't called Arlo. Dispatch had. Well, if you could call Frances Jacobs dispatch. She answered the phones at the police station, played right field on the county softball team, and kept the deputies in line. The woman was seventy-five if she was a day, but she could still hit a mean line drive.

"You locked the door?"

Chloe nodded. "The killer is still out there."

If there was a killer. The evidence pointed toward Wally Harrison taking his own life. But evidence could be deceiving. They both knew Wally wasn't the type. Could he have really been pushed?

"Do you think it was a mob hit?" Chloe asked, then took another drink of her tea. The sip was a big one, more like a gulp.

Arlo drew back. "A mob hit? What would make you think that?" Because there was so much organized crime in Sugar Springs. Not. The town was so quiet, if anything less happened, they would be in a coma. Before today anyway.

"I dunno. Wally has to do research for his books. Maybe he started talking to the wrong people. Then..." She made a squelching noise as she dragged a finger across her neck. She laughed, took another drink, then hiccupped loudly. If Arlo hadn't made the tea herself, she would have thought it had been spiked. As it was, she knew that Chloe was about to crack. Having your high school sweetheart and one-time lover fall to his death—by whatever means—was too much for one morning.

"I don't think it was a mob hit."

A knock sounded on the door downstairs.

Arlo stirred herself out of her chair and smoothed her hands down her sides. "That's probably Mads," she said. "I'll go down and talk to him."

Chloe shook her head. "I can't—"

"Shhh." Arlo patted her shoulder reassuringly. "I'll take care of it."

Sure enough, Mads was waiting outside the doors of Books and More. He waved Arlo over and she went reluctantly. She unlocked the door to let him in and tried not to look over to where Wally still lay on the sidewalk. By this time, he had been moved and was positioned in a more dignified pose for a dead person. Someone had taken the time and care to cover him with a sheet.

She *tried* not to look; not that she had succeeded.

"Could I trouble you for—"

She was not going to let him talk to Chloe. It was inevitable, but it wasn't going to happen this morning.

"—some coffee for the guys?"

Arlo glanced toward the stairs, back to the coffee bar, and once again to Mads. She was letting Chloe's imagination get way with her. Wally had jumped. It was that simple. "Yeah, uh, sure. How many?"

"Four," he said, showing her the number on his fingers as a physical backup.

"Coming up." Arlo moved behind the counter and got out four paper cups with sleeves, then started the Keurig once again.

Chloe hated the thing, preferring to make the coffee in the espresso machine or the French press. But it was easier for the customers who wanted a straight cup of coffee to use it as a self-serve.

"I'm going to need to talk to Chloe, you know," Mads said as she started to brew the first cup. He leaned one elbow against the dogleg bar and looked around as if he hadn't a care in the world.

"I know. Just not now, okay?" She didn't want to tell Mads how much Chloe still cared for Wally, or about all the promises he had made to her, then broken shortly after. If Wally had indeed been pushed, then that information would make Chloe look guilty as all get-out.

She resisted the urge to shake her head at herself and started the next cup of coffee instead.

Mads checked his watch and blew out a breath. "Once Bob gets his body out of here…"

Arlo added lids to the cups and nodded. "Okay." She didn't think Chloe would be better by then, but she would be better than she was now. Arlo hoped anyway. "It's just…"

"What?" Mads asked.

She shook her head. "You didn't hang around him."

"And when would that have been?"

"In high school." She dipped her chin toward the large sign hanging from the second-story railing. *Welcome Classmates All-School Reunion.* Unfortunately, Sugar Springs High School rarely had enough attendees for single-year reunions. Sometimes Arlo thought an all-school reunion was better since most kids were friends with others in different grades. This way everyone could get together and reminisce. "We were all in poetry club together. Me, Chloe, and Wally." Though, she had only joined because Chloe wanted to be close to Wally and she wanted Arlo there for moral support. "You were too busy with football."

Mads nodded and took a sip of his coffee. "What does this have to do with what has happened now?"

"Wally was always a bit…" *Arrogant? Full of himself? Haughty? How about all the above?* "Confident. Very, very, *very* confident." Even after the car wreck that nearly cost him his life. Most people would have been humble. Wally just grew more self-assured.

Mads turned as Faulkner rattled something inside his cage. The cover was still on, but Arlo had heard the noise before. The crazy bird was trying to open the cage himself.

"Faulkner," she said by way of explanation.

He squawked again, responding to his name.

Mads turned his attention back to her. "So he was a jerk."

"What?" Oh, Wally. "Something like that." But it was more. "He was always so damn sure of himself."

"And you think a guy like that wouldn't walk off a three-story building?"

"Yeah," she said, relieved that Mads had picked up on what she was trying to say.

"I worked homicide for five years. Those kinds of men? They are the worst offenders."

"But this isn't a homicide." Was it? *According to Chloe it is.*

"Murder is murder whether you kill someone else or yourself."

She hadn't thought about it that way. But still—

"Trust me on this one," Mads said with his own brand of blown-up confidence. Where did it all come from? Maybe there was a warehouse down in Jackson where men went to pick up the stuff by the truckload.

Mads picked up the paper carrier filled with the to-go cups that Arlo had prepared. "I've seen it all before."

....

It took the rest of the morning and the better part of the afternoon before Mads and Jason were finished out front. Arlo had uncovered Faulkner only to cover him again a couple of hours later. All the commotion outside agitated him and his squawks and cries of "He did it!" had started to put her on edge. The crime scene tape still partitioned off a strip of the sidewalk, though there was nothing to see. The men who normally ran the street cleaners had come out to work on the dark stain that Wally's fall had left behind. And even though the mess was gone, the too-clean spot on the pavement was something of a reminder. So there were still gawkers, edging by every so often to take it all in.

But that wasn't to say the investigation was over. It had only moved. Shortly after they had removed Wally's body and the street cleaners had gone as well, Mads had come in and told her that he needed the keys to her third floor. She only used it for storage, but

Mads explained he had reason to believe that Wally hadn't jumped from the roof, but from the third-story window.

She wondered why they could believe such a thing and wished she had looked up to see if the window was still open when she was out in front of the store.

She looked up at the ceiling now as if she could hear them moving around on the third floor. She couldn't, of course, but she was so aware of them being there, Jason and Mads poking around, doing heaven knew what. Finding clues against Chloe…?

She couldn't think about it that way. Chloe was innocent and she had to keep remembering that.

Arlo wiped down the bar, though she had only served drinks to the workers outside all morning. Wiping down the bar seemed to be the only activity that she could do with any precision today. No big surprise with everything that was going on. And yet…

She looked around the empty store, shoved the rag in its place under the counter, and headed out.

There were two ways to get to the third floor of her building. There was a staircase tucked in a closet near the back room, but it was kept locked at all times. In fact, she had even pushed a reading chair in front of it. If no one was using that entrance—and they weren't—then why should she leave empty space in the store? And there was the staircase at the side of the building. When Arlo had bought the store, she had wondered about the setup. She supposed sometime or another, the third floor had been rented out and the new tenants needed a measure of privacy. The door at the side of the building led to a covered staircase that only went to the third floor.

But the real rumor around town is that bootleggers used the space in the thirties to store moonshine. The legitimate business owner below, an insurance salesman, wanted no ties with his upstairs neighbor and made the landlord build the special staircase on the outside of the building to separate their businesses. It was an odd setup to be sure, and one that was working in her favor at the moment. Mads and Jason were upstairs investigating while Books

& More was still open down below. But she had to know what they were doing.

Around the building she went, through the door, up the stairs, and onto the third floor.

She had never seen a real police investigation before. She had seen plenty on TV, but this was completely different...and the same simultaneously.

Men were walking around with Tyvek suits shielding their clothes and covers on their shoes. Even their hair was hidden. But it was only the two of them, Mads and Jason.

"Bag it," she heard Mads say. She eased into the room as Jason picked up a piece of paper with his gloved hands and stored it in a plastic bag marked "evidence." Even from across the room she could see the word written there. Written was really too kind; scrawled was more like it: *I'm sorry*.

"Is that a suicide note?" she asked.

Mads's attention swung around, his eyes narrowing as he caught sight of her. "Not another step," he growled.

Arlo stopped, only then realizing that she had been steadily inching into the room.

"What are you doing in my crime scene?" He straightened from his task, which looked a lot like scouring the floor for a lost contact. He was down on his knees, a pair of tweezers in one hand.

"I just..." What was she doing? Just checking. Just trying to protect her friend. "I thought I would come up and see if you need anything."

"Like?" This from Jason.

"A cup of coffee? Maybe some water?" And this gave her the perfect opportunity to see what they had found. It didn't look like much: a paper coffee cup that she supposed had belonged to Wally, a wrapper that looked like the ones Chloe used when someone bought a muffin or a scone, and something else she couldn't see from where she stood. Or maybe the bag was empty.

"We're fine," Mads growled, but she didn't take offense. A little gruff and always to the point was merely his nature. Always had been.

Arlo nodded and started backing out of the room toward the staircase. The stairs that would take her back to the street. If the window had been open, it was shut now and she was certain it had been dusted for fingerprints. "Okay then. See ya." She turned and made her way down the steps, around the building, and back into her store.

And she had learned nothing. Except Mads thought Wally had been in her building on the third floor before he died. Could it be? How did he get up there? She and Chloe were the only ones with keys.

Arlo shuddered. She was tired of thinking about it, tired of the drama, tired of gritting her teeth and wondering if this was all. What was next? Somehow she knew there was more. She just *knew* it, and she could feel it in her bones.

She had learned long ago to trust her instincts. Or maybe it was throwback emotions from her hippie upbringing. But she remembered the nights long ago when she was a child. She would complain about not being able to sleep. Her parents would share a look, then pack them all up and move them to another campground, another field, another copse of trees where they could pitch their tent for the night. After a couple of times of Arlo not being able to sleep, an hour or so later, they would be chased off by the police or an angry farmer with a shotgun—sometimes loaded sometimes not. Mostly loaded. Of course that was after the commune days and long before she had insisted on putting down her own roots in Sugar Springs, regardless of her parents' reluctance to stay in one place for more than a couple of months. But that was long ago. And no matter where the feelings had stemmed from, Wally was still dead.

She had finally convinced Chloe to go home and get some rest, but it had taken two and a half hours to get her to leave. There was no sense in both of them being at the store. They might have been given the all clear to open from Mads, but there was nobody on Main Street today. Nobody shopping, that was. There were gawkers and police and a large roped-off section of sidewalk in front of her store, but not any customers.

But she had held on until closing time, having a couple of customers come in just after six. One was Travis Coleman. Arlo wasn't surprised to see him, for he came in from time to time and bought the latest bestseller in paperback. No, the big surprise was he brought a copy of *Missing Girl* to the counter.

"Will that be all today?" Arlo asked. She wanted to ask more. So much more. Like why Travis was supporting the man he thought was responsible for his twin brother's death.

"Yeah." Travis pulled out his credit card and handed it to Arlo.

She finished the transaction without bursting from the questions racing around in her mind. "How's business?" she asked.

"Good." He drummed his fingers impatiently on the counter.

She had known Travis since school but oddly enough rarely saw him outside Books & More, even in a town the size of Sugar Springs. Travis's family home was outside of town a little, just under halfway between Sugar Springs and neighboring Walnut. He had worked at his daddy's tire business since high school graduation and inherited it after his father died. Don Coleman passed away a couple of years ago. Travis's mother had died soon after his brother. From grief, if the rumors were true. Was that possible? she wondered. To actually die from grief?

She ran Travis's card and handed it back to him. He seemed to be in such a hurry.

"Thanks." Travis picked up his sack and receipt and headed for the door.

She watched him until the two girls behind him, both in their late teens, plopped a copy of Wally's book on the counter. The girls giggled as they waited for her to ring them up. Arlo wasn't sure what that was all about either, but she wasn't asking today. It was closing time and that was what she was going to do: close the store and head home.

Well, swing by Chloe's and check on her friend, *then* head home for a nice hot bath and a glass of wine or five—not necessarily in that order. Perhaps even simultaneously.

A knock sounded at the front door, even though Arlo had put up the *CLOSED* sign.

"We're clo—" she started as she turned, but the words dried up before she could finish.

Fern Conley stood on the other side of the double doors, peeking in the large glass window each boasted. Her picnic basket was hooked over one arm and the other hand was cupped around her eyes to help her see inside. Fern would be what some called the quintessential great-grandmother type. She wore floral-print dresses, had blue-rinsed curls that she set at home, preferring to get her gossip from Facebook rather than the beauty parlor like the rest of the over-seventy crowd in Sugar Springs. And she rocked her tan Nike running shoes and compression stockings with pride. "Arlo? Is that you?"

Arlo bit back a sigh and backtracked to the front of the store. She had been on her way to turn off the lights and start shutting everything down. So close to going home. But she had forgotten about one important event: book club.

She had started the book club a couple of months ago. Her plan had been to bring a bit of insight and culture into their sleepy little town. She had imagined all the twentysomethings in Sugar Springs meeting on Friday night to discuss the latest bestseller and drink Chloe's fabulous coffee concoctions. She had set the date for the first meeting, posted flyers all over town, and told everyone she knew. But when Friday night rolled around only three people showed up: Helen Johnson, Fern Conley, and Camille Kinney.

Arlo unlocked the door to let Fern in. "I really hadn't planned on meeting tonight," she said as she started to relock the door once again.

"You better keep that open," Fern said. She set her basket on a nearby table and untied the scarf from under her chin. She carefully removed it to protect her just-done hair. "Helen was right behind me and she has her Crock-Pot." Fern rolled her eyes. "You know how she likes to experiment."

"Yes, but—" Arlo got no further as a deep knock sounded behind her. She whirled around to find Helen Johnson, her surrogate grandmother, standing outside. Helen was about as opposite from Fern as she could be. Not only in stature—Helen was a tall woman, busty and solid, whereas Fern was what Arlo considered to be medium. Not too tall, not too skinny or heavy, not too... well, anything. Helen might be eighty years old, but she was fighting her age with all her might. She wore ripped jeans with bedazzled pockets, T-shirts with bedazzled emblems, and Nike running shoes with bedazzled hearts on the sides. Her hair was long, reaching halfway down her back. The top was a perfect more-salt-than-pepper gray, while the bottom was deep red, the color of a perfect Valentine. Most days she wore it in a braid. In her hands she carried her infamous Crock-Pot, the cord tossed over one shoulder to keep it out of the way. Her two-toned braid fell over the other one. From her stance, Arlo figured she had knocked on the door with her elbow.

Great, she thought, but she managed to keep the words in her head instead of letting them go to her mouth. She loved Helen and owed the woman so much. She wouldn't want to hurt Helen's feelings because she was having something of a bad day.

Arlo opened the door to let Helen in and left it unlocked, figuring Camille couldn't be far behind. The women were nothing if not punctual.

"Hello, sugar," Helen said, planting a quick peck on her cheek.

"Hey, Elly" was all Arlo could manage: her pet name for Helen. She was so important to Arlo that Arlo needed something special to call her. When Arlo had moved to Sugar Springs with her family, she had been a tender sixteen and desperate for roots. Her new age hippie parents thrived off new adventures, surroundings, and people. It seemed as if they never stayed in any one place longer than six months. Her brother, Woody, loved the free lifestyle, but Arlo had had enough. Thanks to her father's generous trust fund, she stayed on in Sugar Springs and took a room in Helen's Sugar Springs Inn. She had been there ever since.

"Why is Faulkner covered up?" Helen asked. "Where's Camille?" She looked around as if the other woman might be under some of the furniture, just out of sight.

"She said she was running late. Didn't you check your Facebook?" Fern asked.

Helen turned from pulling the cover from Faulkner's cage and shot Fern a withering look.

"I didn't—" Arlo started.

"No, I didn't check my Facebook."

"Facebook," Faulkner echoed.

"—want him uncovered," Arlo finished.

"Well, you should have, old woman." It was a continual discussion between the two of them. Fern was pretty tech savvy for a woman five years from ninety, and Helen felt social media was nothing more than a "time suck"—her words—and she had no use for it. Camille was on the fence.

"She sent a PM," Fern continued. "If you had a smartphone you would have gotten it there."

"I'm not getting anything that's so smart it's got the word in the name."

"Don't you own a Smart Car?" Fern asked.

And the argue-cussion was underway.

"Smart Car," Faulkner squawked. "He did it."

Arlo turned as Camille pushed her way into the shop. Born and raised in Australia, Camille had all the bearing of an English aristocrat. Her cap of small, snow-white curls looked as soft as cotton. She wore pastel pantsuits, cream-colored shells, and pearls—always. And she always matched her Nike running shoes with her outfit. Today's ensemble was lavender with shades of purple. Where she got purple and lavender Nikes in Sugar Springs, Arlo had no idea. Like the others, she carried goodies for their refreshments. Tonight's offering appeared to be pineapple upside-down cupcakes. Arlo's favorite, aside from Camille's strawberry scones with clotted cream. That was one thing the Brits had gotten right.

Camille tilted her head toward the pair of ladies. "Same ol', same ol'?"

Arlo nodded, then gestured for Camille to set the pan of cupcakes down on a side table in the reading nook.

"Reading nook" was a charming description for a very large part of her bookstore. Arlo had wanted a place where people could be comfortable, hang out if they wanted to read, chat about books, or simply get away from the real world through the pages of a book. The area had two couches that faced each other with a long rectangular coffee table in the middle. Behind one couch was a wall of used books, and perpendicular to that was Faulkner's cage. It gave him the chance to be part of the action as well as gaze out the window. People brought books in for trade, then visited with Faulkner and one another. It was an easy setup. Several chairs were peppered around the area along with an assortment of occasional tables for incidentals like coffee and pastries. All the furniture had been picked up at out-of-town garage sales and estate auctions. The mismatched, slightly worn look gave the place a homey, inviting feel. To Arlo it was perfect. She loved it, though she couldn't say it helped her sell any books. She and Chloe both knew the coffee shop profits kept the store in the black. Of course it would help a lot if she could get a renter for the third floor of the building. They only used it for storage. And having that extra income would surely help the shop. Maybe soon...

"I was thinking about canceling tonight." Arlo said the words to Camille, but the others stopped their friendly debate and turned toward them.

"No," Fern cried.

"Why would you do that?" Helen asked.

They didn't know? Wasn't Friday beauty parlor day? Arlo had assumed that they would have heard all about today's tragedy at Dye Me a River.

"Y-you didn't hear?" She wasn't sure how to start this revelation. The knowledge itself was hard enough to carry, but telling it all again...

"Of course we heard, dear," Fern said. "It was all over Facebook."

"Facebook," Faulkner echoed with a punctuating squawk.

Helen shrugged. "I heard about it when everyone returned to the inn."

Of course. As owner of the town's best place to stay, Helen was privy to anything and everything that happened to Sugar Springs' most prestigious visitors. When there were none, it was the unmarried male population that kept her informed. Many stopped by for a home-cooked meal in the evenings.

Arlo turned to Camille.

She smiled. "That's why I made your favorite cupcakes."

Arlo returned the smile, though it felt as brittle as autumn leaves after the first frost. "I guess I thought perhaps you would want to do something different tonight. Maybe go to the movies…or out on a date…" True, she suspected these women hadn't been out on dates in decades, but it was the only excuse she could think of now that she was on the spot.

"Nonsense." Fern scoffed. "I can't think of one place I'd rather be."

"That's true." Helen agreed. "The best thing to do after a tragedy such as this is to get your life right back on track."

"Back on track," Faulkner said.

That might be hard to do with the yellow police tape barricade still out front. It might not affect people coming and going into the store itself, but it was a little ominous. And the large patch of sidewalk that was cleaner than the rest…

"We've never had a suicide here before," Camille said in her soft, sweet voice. She had retained enough of her Aussie accent that everything she said sounded like the best thing in the world. "Not that I can remember."

"What about Heck Bascomb?" Fern asked.

As they talked, the women moved into their places in the reading nook.

"Give me a kiss," Faulkner called. "Give me a kiss."

"What was that, thirty years ago?" Helen leaned over and put her lips to the birdcage. Faulkner crab walked over and "gave her a kiss." Arlo kept telling Helen that one day he might decide he wanted a little more than to pretend to bite her lips, but Helen never listened. Affection given and received, she set her purse on the floor next to the armchair she preferred and eased down into it.

Fern frowned a bit but said nothing. That was another conten-
tion between the pair. Fern said Helen would never have any money
if she set her purse on the floor.

Helen would reply that she had never had any money, so changing her ways now was a "silly endeavor"—her words.

But it was Camille's purse Arlo was normally interested in. Miss
Camille sat with it in her lap the entire time they were at book
club…and church…and whenever the Kiwanis Club held a pan-
cake breakfast. In fact, every time Arlo had ever seen her sit down,
Camille's purse had been firmly in her lap. And it was always the
same purse. She might change her shoes but never her handbag—
large, white, nearly square with one short handle and a clasp that
audibly clicked when she closed it. When they got their plates of
refreshments, Camille hooked it on her arm. The blessed thing was
never unattended.

"Heck Bascomb didn't kill himself," Helen said.

"Heck. Heck. Heck. Heck," Faulkner chanted.

"That's right." Camille's voice was full of awed remembrance.
"His wife killed him."

"Wasn't he shot in the head?" Fern asked.

"That's right." Camille nodded.

"So, his wife shot him in the head and made it look like a suicide?" Fern asked.

"Yep," Helen said. "Right after she filled him with rat poison."

3

THE CONVERSATION CONTINUED AROUND HER, BUT ARLO HAD stopped listening. All she could think about was Chloe's theory that Wally had been pushed from the rooftop. Could it be?

"Rat poison," Faulkner repeated. The bird picked up the darnedest things. "He did it. He did it."

Then the terrible thought dropped into her head like a stink bomb. Did Chloe say that because she knew what had happened? She had been there, witnessed it? Was she the one who pushed Wally to his death?

The very idea sent Arlo's stomach plummeting. No. She couldn't believe that. Chloe was heartbroken, sure, but she still wasn't the kind to do away with ex-boyfriends. But if they had just had coffee... Wally left, then a bit later was lying on the sidewalk in front of the bookstore.

Arlo's heart gave a hard pound. It was completely possible that Chloe was the last person to see him alive.

Next to last person.

The killer would have been last. Chloe was not a killer.

"Arlo, dear?" Fern's voice brought her out of that unthinkable thought.

"Yes?"

"Are you coming to sit down?"

Did she have a choice?

She moved around the chair and fairly collapsed onto it.

"Sit down. Sit down."

Fern shot Helen a look. For once their expressions matched, and Arlo knew they had been talking about her. She mentally pulled herself together. She sat up a little straighter in her seat and smiled at the ladies she had grown to love. Not only Helen for the nurturing she gave Arlo as a teen, but all of them.

"It's just been an eventful day."

Nods went around their little circle.

"Is everyone ready to discuss the next chapters of *To Kill a Mockingbird*?"

For their first month, they had decided to reread a classic novel and discuss how it affected them differently as they had gotten older. So far it had taken them ten weeks to get a little over halfway through.

"Actually, we were thinking about putting a pin in this discussion and reading *Missing Girl* instead." Helen smiled at her expectantly.

Camille nodded, a serene smile on her face. "Yes, yes. We should read *Missing Girl*. After all, Wally wrote it."

"We all know Wally wrote the book." Fern frowned a bit, then smoothed out imaginary wrinkles in her skirt.

Arlo figured that while she had been lost in her own reverie, Helen had been elected to broach the subject.

"I'm not sure about that…" She had read the reviews. Most all were glowing, but they led her to believe that among the brilliant words was a lot of deception, sex, and grisly murder.

"Well, I am." Fern folded her hands complacently in her lap.

Camille nodded in agreement.

She would have been the holdout, Arlo thought, but since they all wanted to…

"I've read that it has a great deal of…sex in it," she said as gently as she could.

"Good, since you won't let us read *Fifty Shades of Grey*." Helen's mouth twisted into a chastising frown.

"*Fifty Shades. Fifty Shades.* Any copies of *Fifty Shades*?" Faulkner asked.

Arlo shook her head. Their talk about whether or not to read the hot book had been a lively discussion. "But what about—"

"No buts," Helen decided. "We're reading poor Wally's book."

"Fine," Arlo said on a sigh. There were times when trying to fight simply used up too much energy.

"Yay!" The ladies clapped their hands.

"Yay!" Faulkner mimicked.

"And that's why I left him covered."

Sometimes when they met, Faulkner was as quiet as a mouse. Other times, when he'd had a particularly stressful day, he talked and squawked nonstop.

"Go ahead." Helen waved a hand in the direction of the cage.

Arlo shook her head and retrieved the cover. She draped it around Faulkner's cage as he said, "Noooooooooo." He would only stop when he couldn't see any more of the outside world.

"Now." She sat back down with a sigh and picked up her copy of *To Kill a Mockingbird*. "Let's talk about Scout and Jem. Does anyone remember where we were?" She opened her book to the exact page but wanted someone to say it out loud.

"Dill had just run away and come up from Mobile," Fern said.

"Meridian," Helen corrected.

"That's right. He was in Mississippi while Scout and Jem were in Alabama."

"Why do you suppose a young man with his entire life ahead of him would do something like that?" Camille mused.

"I believe he was feeling left out at home and felt more comfortable with Scout and Jem," Arlo explained.

"Not Dill. Mr. Harrison," Camille said.

"Wally?"

"That's the only Mr. Harrison I know since his father died." Camille gave her a look as if to say *is there another that I don't know about?*

"I can't even pretend to know the answer to that, but as far as Dill…" Arlo tried to steer the conversation back to the book.

"Do you suppose Wally was depressed?" Camille asked.

"What did he have to be depressed about?" Fern countered.

"You don't need a reason to have depression. It just is." Camille's tone was softened with patience.

"I saw him yesterday when he first got into town," Helen said. "He was at the gas station. Imagine a famous writer like that pumping his own gas. Anyway, he didn't seem depressed to me. A little stuck up maybe, but not depressed."

"Helen," Fern exclaimed. "You shouldn't speak ill of the dead."

Helen shrugged. "I call 'em like I see 'em."

"Still." Fern shot her a disapproving look.

Stuck up. That was the perfect way to describe Wallace J. Harrison. But stuck up wasn't a trait that would turn a successful author into a dead jumper.

"Let's get back to Dill coming up from Mobile," Arlo said.

"Meridian," Camille corrected.

"Right." She bit back a sigh. After today she didn't know whether she was coming or going. "When Dill arrives in Maycomb, Atticus doesn't immediately call his mother and stepfather, or even his aunt across the street. This shows how compassionate he is and how loving toward all people, don't you think?"

"Maybe he was on the drugs," Fern mused.

"Atticus Finch was not taking drugs." Arlo's own patience was beginning to slip.

"Not Atticus. Mr. Harrison." This from Camille.

"Drugs do terrible things." Helen shook her head.

She would know, but Arlo wasn't going to remind her of the fact. Helen had been her own sort of hippie once upon a time, but she had put those days behind her. Helen wanted to run her inn and live out her days in quiet Sugar Springs.

"Can we get back to the book?" Arlo snapped. She closed her eyes and tried to calm herself. She wasn't normally this edgy. Then again it was hardly normal for former classmates to jump from her third story window.

Camille, looking utterly chastised, opened her book. "I think

Dill wanted what Scout and Jem had even though they didn't have a mother. Envy drove him up from Meridian. Pure envy and the worry that he was missing out."

What if it was no random roof Wally had flung himself off but one with a purpose? Had he been trying to get back at one of them? Maybe. If he had really jumped.

He was pushed. Chloe's words came back to Arlo. It certainly fit what they knew about him. But who pushed him? That was the question. And how long was it going to be before all fingers were pointed toward Chloe?

"That's a thing now, isn't it?" Helen asked. "People being anxious because they think they're missing something."

"They call it FOMO—fear of missing out," Fern explained.

Camille shook her head. "That's the craziest bloody thing I have ever heard." The more passionate Camille grew over something, the more her Australian background came forward.

"You were the one who brought it up," Fern pointed out.

"I didn't know it was a syndrome." Helen shook her head.

"It's not a syndrome," Fern explained. "It's a thing."

"What's the difference?" Camille asked.

Fern gave a dainty shrug. "I have no idea."

"You don't suppose he was pushed?" Arlo asked.

Three sets of eyes swung in her direction. The ladies were so accustomed to having her pull them back to task that they were all shocked at her deviation from the topic that had been a deviation from the topic they were supposed to be talking about.

Fern and Camille looked from Arlo to Helen.

"What do you mean?" Helen asked.

"Pushed. You know. He went off the building at someone else's insistence."

"I suppose anything is possible at this point," Helen said.

"Travis Coleman came in today," she mused.

"Coleman…Coleman…why does that name seem so familiar?"

"His brother had a wreck during his senior year and died," Arlo reminded them.

"That's right," Fern said. "I remember now."

Everyone in town knew about the accident that cost Toby Coleman his life and put Wally J. Harrison in the hospital for two solid weeks.

"Travis accused Wally of switching places with his brother in order to keep himself out of trouble," Helen said.

"Yes," Fern replied, her voice filled with remembrance. "Travis claimed that Wally was driving and his brother was a passenger."

Arlo nodded. "And Wally stood firm that Toby was the driver."

"I remember that big write-up in the paper," Helen continued. "Travis even wrote a letter to the editor."

"What became of all that?" Camille asked, her brow knit as she tried to remember.

"Nothing," Arlo said. "Travis couldn't prove anything since no one else was in the car."

"And Wally got out of the hospital and went about the rest of his life," Fern said.

"Yeah, but..." Arlo started.

If they were looking for someone who wanted Wally dead, Travis should be at the top of the list. But as far as she knew, he hadn't been anywhere near Main Street that morning. She was on her feet in an instant. "I've got to go," she said in a rush. She looked around at the floor, trying to figure out her next move. Her brain was whirring like a pinwheel in a hurricane. So much that she momentarily couldn't remember what to do next. "Purse," she said and headed toward the back of the store, where their office was located.

It was really nothing more than an oversized broom closet with a table set up as a desk that could be used from both sides. Oftentimes she and Chloe worked face-to-face on their business projects.

Arlo eased under the open staircase that led to the loft and into the part of the store where the new books were stocked. She stumbled a bit when she saw the enormous display she had designed for Wally's new book—a huge poster with the cover of the book and the tagline *Who will be next?*

At the time she had made the poster, she had thought herself to be so clever. Now the words seemed a bit threatening. She shivered.

She tried to ignore the stacks of books turned so shoppers could see the back of the dust jacket and Wally's mysterious look. If she squinted—a lot—she could make out the scar on his left cheek, a souvenir from the car accident so long ago. His arms were folded, the earpiece of the glasses he held in his right hand lightly touching his lips. And the turtleneck. The suave, *I'm so New York* turtleneck.

Arlo wasn't exactly sure that people in New York wore turtle-necks, but that's what everyone in Sugar Springs thought. There weren't many turtleneck wearers in town. At least not male ones.

But something about the picture... Her feet stilled as she looked at it. It wasn't a picture of the Wally she knew. Nor was her last view of him an image from the past. Wally had changed in his years away. Yet wasn't that why people left their sleepy town? To become the person they wanted to be? It seemed that Wally had succeeded.

Or maybe not, if he felt the need to fling himself out a third story window.

She continued to stare at the photo, somehow feeling the answer was there. Did she really want to know? "Arlo?" Helen touched her elbow as she said her name. Arlo had been so deep in her thoughts that she jumped as if she had been shocked by a cattle prod. "Sorry."

Arlo tried to smile. "It's okay, Elly."

"But are you okay?" Helen gently asked.

"Just a goose walking over my grave." It was something she had said all her Mississippi life and yet now it had a warning ring to it.

"Where are you going in such a hurry?"

"I need to check on Chloe. Can you lock up?"

Helen frowned. "You're leaving?"

She nodded. "It's important, Elly."

"Okay." Helen sighed.

Arlo could see the worry on her face. This...upheaval with Wally had everyone a little out of sorts. "Thank you." She kissed the old woman's cheek, then ducked into her office to get her handbag. "I'll see you later."

....

Chloe rented the former servants' quarters behind one of the largest houses in the area. An antebellum mansion of epic proportions, Lillyfield was more than a house. It was on the historical registry and had once belonged to General Eustace Lilly.

Lilly had never been an actual general, but the title was a courtesy given to him by the people of Sugar Springs and somehow it stuck. Rumor had it that good old Eustace was a gun runner during The War—the only one that mattered around there, the one of Northern Aggression—but wasn't so choosey about which side he sold to. Of course, this was explicitly denied by any of his descendants, no matter how far removed.

Still, there was a lot of money involved and the four-story sprawling structure with colonial columns and a ballroom on the third floor was as impressive today as it had been then. The servants' quarters were a little less spacious, but it was enough for Chloe and Auggie, her ginger striped cat.

"Chloe." Arlo knocked on the door and impatiently waited. "Chloe. I know you're in there. I want to make sure you're okay." She knocked again. "Chlo—"

The door was suddenly wrenched open.

"Thank heaven," Arlo said. She gave her friend a quick hug, then pushed past her into the cozy house.

"I'm okay," Chloe said, but it was an obvious lie. Her eyes were puffy from crying, her nose red and swollen. She was wearing that sweater Arlo hated, the one that Wally had left behind ten years ago. If Arlo ever caught that sweater out alone, it was history. But its presence tonight revealed how upset Chloe was.

"Who would want to kill him?" Chloe moaned as she sank into one corner of the couch.

Arlo figured there might be a list somewhere starting with Wally's wife, Daisy, and possibly ending with Chloe herself. And then there was Travis Coleman. But Arlo decided not to say that out loud. "I'm not worried about that," she said instead. "I'm worried about you."

She believed with all her heart that her best friend and business partner was innocent, but the evidence was working against her. And there was the fact that Wally had been mean, cruel even, to Chloe when she told him she was pregnant. Because of her decision to keep the baby and Wally's decision to leave, Chloe's life had been forever altered. She hadn't gone to college or business school. The lessons she had learned had been from hard knocks. She had been left to raise the child on her own, and she had turned to the only people she knew she could trust to help her—her parents. And that help had led to Jayden living with his grandparents and Chloe getting a cat so her own place didn't seem so lonely.

Anything Chloe had dished out to Wally had been well deserved, but Arlo knew it was only a blistering tirade about how he had no rights to Jayden and had signed them away years ago, instead of a short trip back to street level.

She sat down next to Chloe. Auggie jumped onto the back of the couch, kneading his paws into the worn quilt lying there. Then he stretched his back legs and moved close enough for Arlo to pet him. It was his standard, *I guess you can touch me, peasant* move that she knew so well.

"I'm fine." Chloe stood and crossed the room, staring into the empty fireplace.

"You don't seem fine. In fact, I'd say you are the opposite of fine."

"I thought I could handle it, you know, him coming to town. But…" Chloe shook her head. "I wasn't expecting to talk to him. We settled all that a long time ago."

"Then why did you let him into the shop?"

Phil's wasn't the only store with access to the roof. Chloe had invited Wally in and given him coffee. It was only two flights of stairs to the roof from there. The thought made Arlo's stomach pitch.

Chloe took a shuddering breath and pressed the wadded tissue she held to her mouth. "I don't know."

Arlo waited. She had never seen her friend like this.

"He said he wanted to talk about Jayden. That he wanted to see him."

"What did you say?"

"I told him no. He made his decision a long time ago."

"Good for you." Arlo was genuinely proud of her friend.

"But Wally said he would find a way. That I owed him that much."

"Skunk," Arlo hissed. "That man is nothing but a skunk."

"Was," Chloe corrected.

"Was." The word sobered her anger. "Then?"

"I told him good luck and pushed him out the door."

"I wish you wouldn't use words like that," Arlo said.

"Oh my gosh, you're right." Chloe sniffed. "This makes me look that much guiltier." Her tears started again. "I guess it's a good thing Jayden lives with Mama and Daddy. His father is dead, and now his mother is about to be accused of murdering him."

"Don't say that."

Wally jumped. Wally jumped. Maybe if she said it enough times, she would believe it were true.

Chloe had discovered that she was pregnant two days after their high school graduation. She immediately told Wally, but he told her that he didn't want anything to do with her or the baby. He was getting out of town as soon as possible, and they weren't going to hold him back. He was probably packing his bags when she told him the news. He left the very next day.

Chloe's father hired a PI to find him and an attorney to draw up the papers, and had Wally make it official. He gave up all rights to his son. Now, ten years later, he was back in town and wanted to see the boy? Impossible.

Chloe had worked hard to support herself and Jayden, but when it became apparent that she couldn't do it alone, she moved back in with her parents. Five years later, she wanted some independence and moved out again. Knowing Jayden needed the stability of her childhood home, she allowed him to stay with his grandparents. It was a magnificent and dreadful sacrifice, but one that was necessary. And to have Wally threatening any of that...

Arlo shook her head. She didn't want to think about it. It gave

Chloe way too much motive. Mads probably didn't know that Wally was Jayden's father. But once he found out…

There was no doubt: Chloe would be his number one suspect.

4

EMOTIONALLY AND PHYSICALLY DRAINED. THE PHRASE WAS trite but true to how Arlo felt when she pulled into her own driveway. She turned off her car and sat there for a moment, just…waiting…on nothing…something…anything…

That's how the day had been. Hurry up, wait. Wait some more. Book club, Chloe, and now. Here she sat, strangely unsatisfied. Completely unsettled. She should be doing something. Helping Chloe. Straightening up the store. She shouldn't have left the book club early. She should have talked to Mads more. She needed to do something to help Chloe.

And yet there was nothing to be done.

She sighed, palmed her keys, and headed for the door. The small house with yellow siding might be sitting on its own parcel of land in Sugar Springs, but it wasn't much larger than Chloe's. Arlo didn't mind. Any bigger and she would have knocked around a little too much in a space too large for one person. And she loved the house. It was the one place that had ever been all hers. Her parents had never stayed in one place long. Then she had moved in with Elly. Off to college and she'd had a roommate. But this house—412 Wisteria Drive—was all hers, complete with a creaky wooden porch with a swing on one end, box planters under the windows, and a front door painted a cheery cherry red.

"Yoo-hoo."

The voice stopped her in her tracks.

And nosy neighbors.

Arlo pulled in a fortifying breath and turned to face her very own Mrs. Kravitz: Cindy Jo Houston. Cindy Jo wasn't much older than Arlo herself, but a tragic car accident on the highway turnoff leading into Sugar Springs had given her a permanent limp and a brain injury that left her unable to fulfill her teaching duties at the high school. The entire time Arlo had known Cindy Jo, she had wanted nothing more than to marry her high school sweetheart, teach at Sugar Springs High, and live in the tiny Mississippi town forever.

One out of three ain't bad.

She pasted on the best smile she could muster and turned to face her neighbor. "Hi, Cindy Jo."

Cindy Jo returned her greeting, then sadly shook her head. "I suppose you heard what happened."

Arlo resisted the urge to tell Cindy Jo that Wally Harrison had fallen to his death right outside her store. If she gave away that detail and Cindy Jo didn't already have it, then she would spend the next forty-five minutes recounting everything she knew about the crime scene and having to speculate at her neighbor's insistence about what "Sheriff Mads" was going to do about it. "Yes," she said simply.

"What are we going to do?"

Arlo shot her a sympathetic smile. What were they going to do? Pray that Mads found no reason to charge Chloe, that the real murderer would step forward, or both.

What was she saying? She had gotten too caught up in Chloe's theories. They didn't know if there was a real murderer. It could simply be a matter of too much fame getting to a narcissistic jerk— not that she would ever say those words aloud—and maybe, just maybe, Mads was right. Maybe Wally really did willingly jump to his death.

"Let the chief handle it as best he can, I suppose."

For a moment Cindy Jo's expression froze in shock, then it puckered to a frown. "Sheriff Mads?" She said his name as if it was ludicrous that anyone would expect him to do anything concerning the matter.

"That's right," Arlo replied, not bothering to correct Cindy Jo over Mads's official title. It would do no good to remind her neighbor that Tom Watson was the sheriff of Alcorn County.

Cindy Jo's face immediately brightened. "Is he on the board now? What a blessing! It's kind of late in the game, but better now than never, eh?" She winked at Arlo, then shoved her hands into the front pockets of her floral housedress. She frowned again. "You don't suppose that he'll get some of those frozen things from Sam's, do you? I mean, they're good and all, but not the thing for such an important reunion."

"Of course." Arlo nodded, then turned to go into her house. Then Cindy Jo's words hit home. She swung back around and eyed her neighbor. "Reunion?" They were talking about two entirely different things.

"Uh-huh," Cindy Jo said. "Mary Beth told me today when I was down at the Piggly Wiggly that something had happened to the order of food that was supposed to be for the reunion. Something about the shrimp truck breaking down, and the driver wasn't able to keep everything at a low enough temperature." She wrinkled her nose, the movement making her dimples deepen. "But that's good of Sheriff Mads to take over like that. I hope he doesn't take the easy way out, Sam's and all that."

Arlo shook her head. "Cindy Jo, I—" She stopped. There was no sense going into it now. Cindy wasn't on the committee and Mads wouldn't be responsible for the replacement food order. It was a misunderstanding, but Cindy Jo didn't need to know all that. It would only confuse her more and cause Arlo another forty-five minutes trying to sort it out with her. "That's right," she said again. For once she wished for a pet she could claim she needed to feed so she would have an easy excuse to escape into her own house, but there was no fuzzy creature waiting for her. Just a lonely supper and a bottle of wine. On second thought, she might skip the food altogether. Less calories that way. "I've got to…go," she finally said.

Cindy Jo smiled. "Sure thing. See ya tomorrow."

"Tomorrow?" Arlo asked before she could stop herself.

"At the reunion," Cindy Jo patiently explained.

"Right." Arlo jangled her keys against her palm. "Tomorrow."

Arlo made her escape to her front door and let herself into her house trying hard not to rush. She didn't want Cindy Jo to think there was anything wrong when there was. Several things were wrong. Starting with but not limited to the fact that she may have volunteered Mads to supply some kind of appetizer at the high school reunion tomorrow.

She had barely changed out of her work clothes and into her pajamas when her phone started to ring. With a wince, she checked the caller ID. Mads.

"Hey, Chief," she said brightly.

"Why is it that Lorie Blake just called and asked me what I was planning on bringing to the reunion mixer tomorrow?"

"I—uh…" Arlo searched her brain for a logical answer. Finding none, she said in an apologetic voice, "Because I might have told Cindy Jo that you had it."

"It?" His voice was flat across the phone line.

"Not it." She tried to explain. "Had it. You know, under control." She bit her lip. "Okay, I'm not explaining this very well and I suppose it doesn't matter. I mean, are we really going to have the reunion mixer after what happed today?"

"I wish I had a nickel for every time someone asked me that since breakfast."

"You wouldn't be able to retire," she joked. "There's not that many people in Sugar Springs."

"No, but I'd be able to buy the appetizers I'm told I'm bringing."

Arlo flopped down on the sofa and stacked her feet onto the steamer trunk she used as a coffee table. "Sorry about that. Really. I thought Cindy Jo was talking about Wally's…accident." Why couldn't she bring herself to say the word? Death. Wally's death. "She asked what we should do about the problem."

"And you told her I had it."

"Yeah, something like that."

"Thanks for the vote of confidence, but I think the shrimp rolls I'm supposed to bring tomorrow will be more challenging than figuring out what happened to Wally Harrison."

Arlo almost imparted Cindy Jo's wish that he not bring anything from the freezer section at Sam's, but she had to keep things in perspective and the part concerning Wally was much more important. "Why do you say that?"

On the other end of the line, something rattled, and a dog let out a deep bark. "Hush, Dew," Mads chastised. "I'm feeding you as fast as I can."

Mads's overgrown Airedale terrier barked again.

Arlo sucked in a breath and told herself to be patient. "Mads," she said, trying to get him back on the subject she wanted to talk about.

"Yeah?"

"What about Wally?"

"We're waiting on the coroner's report since it is classified as a suspicious death, but I think it's pretty obvious. Wally Harrison killed himself."

Arlo allowed the air to seep slowly from her lungs. Mads and his crew looking at Wally's death as a suicide meant no one would be asking too many questions of Chloe. She knew it! And once again she had let herself get caught up in Chloe's drama. In her love and passion for Wally. In her hopes that he wouldn't do something so terrible as take his own life. But as awful as it sounded, it was better this way. "And the reunion mixer is still on?"

"I think so, don't you? We should keep things as normal as possible."

But normalcy meant going on as if Wally's death never happened. Obviously Sunday's book signing would have to be canceled. Arlo winced at the thought of all the expensive books she had ordered for the event. Her mind spun faster. Should they invite Daisy and Inna to the mixer? What was the etiquette? She wasn't sure even Emily Post could sort through this one.

"Yeah. I suppose." But even to her own ears, her voice didn't sound convincing. There were too many thoughts running through her brain at once and, try as she might, she couldn't get ahold of one long enough to filter through it. It was like trying to hang on to a greased pig at the county fair.

"What?" he asked. His tone had changed from casual friend to chief of police just that fast.

"It's not normal. None of this is normal."

"And canceling everything and hosting some type of memorial service is?"

"It's what people normally do when someone dies."

Across the line, Mads sighed. He hadn't been back in Sugar Springs long, only a couple of months. Long enough to clean off his desk and order his uniforms. And in all the time he had been gone, he had forgotten what living in a small town meant. "Okay." His voice sounded tired, as if the day had pushed him over whatever ledge he had been standing on. "I'll talk to Mary Jo tomorrow and see what she has to say about it."

"Mary Beth," Arlo corrected. "It's Mary Beth and Cindy Jo. You went to school with both of them." The school wasn't that big. Everyone knew everyone, just the way it was in small towns. "I swear, Mads." It was like he had forgotten more than he remembered about life in Sugar Springs. If he hated it so much, why had he returned?

"Right. Mary Beth. I remember."

"And you better call her tonight. She'll have a cow when she finds out you want to change something."

"Do people still have cows these days?"

Arlo chuckled. Across town, she heard Dewey bark through the phone line. "You tell Mary Beth there's an addition to the program tomorrow and watch what happens."

Mads sighed again. "So she has a cow. With any luck she can enter it in the county fair this year."

5

ARLO SLIPPED OUT OF HER SHOES AND WIGGLED HER BANDAGED toes. The one good thing about hosting the mixer in the high school gymnasium was that no one was allowed to wear dress shoes on the polished wood floor. After yesterday's long and trying day in a new pair of heels, she was more than grateful to the overzealous janitor, Leonard Moore, for his diligence in keeping the floor unscuffed.

She smoothed her hands down her dress and tried not to appear nervous. But she was. She was always nervous around so many of the indigenous residents of Sugar Springs. No matter how long she had lived here, she knew she would never completely fit in. She wasn't a Yankee. No, it wasn't that bad, but when everyone gathered around like this, it became apparent that she wasn't southern. It didn't matter that she had spent most of her formative years in Mexico or farther south in Central America, she was still an outsider. Around here "South" was more than a direction; it was an attitude. A way of life. And she was not southern enough for anyone in the room. Except for maybe Chloe.

Arlo waved to her friend and made her way over to where she stood next to the refreshments table.

"The planning committee really outdid themselves," Arlo remarked. Or rather, the high school art department did. Blue and silver streamers draped down from the center of the gym, giving the place a carnival-tent effect. Matching balloons were tied to every available surface, bobbing on the gusts of air coming in from the vents. Crepe paper flowers of blue and white were clustered together, filling the basketball goal nets and otherwise tricking a person into not immediately realizing they were in a gym. Only the royal-blue-painted bleachers and the grinning face of the Blue Devils mascot in the center of the court gave it away. And the scoreboard, of course, but the overall effect was nice. Even the tablecloths, cups, plates, and plasticware matched to the school's colors. On the table next to them sat two large bowls of punch: one lime green, the other sweet pink. Some trickster had placed a card in front of each. The card in front of the green punch had the word "virgin" written on it; the pink punch's card said "experienced." She could only hope that no one brought cocktail wieners.

"You're late." Chloe hissed.

"I got caught up with Cindy Jo," Arlo explained.

Chloe nodded to the far corner of the room where Cindy Jo stood by herself, nursing a blue plastic cup of punch. The virgin version if Arlo was guessing right. "She made it on time."

"She was already dressed when she stopped me from going into the house and getting ready," Arlo returned.

"I needed you here." Chloe's voice held a panicked edge.

"I'm here now. What's been going on?"

"Same ol', same ol." Chloe took a long draw on her punch—definitely the spiked version.

"Better slow down on that." Arlo reached to take the glass from her.

Chloe held it out of her reach. "Get your own."

Arlo poured herself a cup of the pink punch, vowing it would be her one and only. After this drink, she would switch to the virgin punch. If she was guessing right, she was going to have to take Chloe home at the end of the evening.

Chloe raised a hand to her riotous blond curls, pulling on one behind her ear. Her fingers were shaking as she unwound it and let it spring back into place.

"Why are you so nervous?" Arlo took a sip of the sherbet-based concoction. It was actually pretty good. A little strong, she thought as the liquor hit the back of her throat, but good. Yes, definitely only one of these would do the trick. She glanced at Chloe. *Wonder how many she's had.*

"Are they coming here?"

"Who is *they*?"

Chloe tugged on a curl, then wrapped it around her finger. She pulled her finger free and the curl bounced back into place. "They. Daisy. Or Inna. Scratch that. Just Daisy."

"I don't know. Does it matter?" Chloe's fidgeting was starting to put Arlo on edge. Despite all her theories about Wally's death, Mads was ruling it a suicide and that was good enough for her. Never mind that it would keep her friend out of a lineup.

"Of course it matters." Another curl popped back into place.

Arlo grabbed Chloe's fingers, stopping her mid-fidget. "You don't have anything to worry about." And how she hoped that remained true.

"Oh, yeah? I'll have two very pissed-off women coming after me if they find out I was the last one to see Wally alive."

"And how are they going to know that?"

"It's in Mads's report. I gave a witness statement. You think Andie Donald is going to let something like that escape the front page?"

"I suppose not." Arlo took a large drink of her punch and tried not to wince as it went down. Super reporter Andie Donald was worse than a nosy neighbor. She lurked all over the place, instead of just next door. Arlo had never had a problem with her before, but that was…before.

"The second glass is better," Chloe remarked and lifted her blue plastic cup in salute.

Arlo could only hope that Chloe was still on her second serving of punch, but she doubted it. "Just tell the truth. There's nothing wrong with that."

Chloe rolled her eyes. "You're beginning to sound like my

mother." She reached for the punch ladle, but Arlo stopped her from pouring.

"Girl, it's three o'clock in the afternoon."

"Yes." Chloe eyed her coolly and started in for the punch once again.

"Don't you think it would be better to face off with Daisy sober?"

That brought her up short. "I suppose you're right."

"Not counting all the grams of sugar in this stuff."

Chloe looked into her empty cup with wistful eyes. "Nice knowing you." She tossed her cup into the trash and dusted her hands off.

"Other than Daisy, what's got you in such a state?" Arlo could probably guess, but she thought it best for Chloe to say it all out loud. Maybe then it would put things in context. Problems were rarely as large as they seemed in a person's head.

"Look at everybody." Chloe gestured toward the clusters of people milling about the gym floor. Someone was playing an odd mix of music that Arlo assumed was from the individual years that the guests had graduated. There was Prince, Nirvana, Pink Floyd, even Buddy Holly. Except for the music, the gym was as hushed as a funeral.

"I thought we had more RSVPs than this," she commented.

"We did. But with Wally…" Chloe's eyes filled with tears and she reached into the bodice of her dress and pulled out a tissue. She daintily dabbed her eyes as Arlo stared.

"Did you stuff your bra out of nostalgia or are you on the prowl?" She was hoping to get a laugh out of her friend, or at the very least a punch on the arm, but Chloe shook her head. "My dress doesn't have any pockets."

"Ones like that never do."

Chloe had chosen a dress Arlo knew was to show Wally exactly what he had been missing the last couple of years. Short, tight, black—it was a little much for an afternoon cocktail mixer, but Arlo understood Chloe's need for ammunition, even with Wally gone. And honestly, she looked as good as Daisy and Inna even on their best days. But to Wally, Chloe and a baby were too much a part of the Sugar Springs he wanted to escape. Arlo wondered if he would have gotten the message Chloe was sending.

So why now, after all these years, did he want to see Jayden? It didn't make sense. It wasn't like Jayden was a secret. Wally had known all along. Heck, everyone in Sugar Springs knew that Jayden was Wally's son, though most people were careful not to mention it. At least not where Chloe's mother could hear. But if someone did mention it, since Wally was back in town and all, it was very possible that word had gotten 'round to Daisy, or even Inna.

Chloe elbowed Arlo hard in the ribs, startling her out of her thoughts. "She's here. I mean, they're here."

Arlo swung her gaze around toward the gymnasium door in time to see Janitor Moore block Daisy and Inna's way into the gym. He gestured toward their feet and then to the line of shoes belonging to the guests. For a moment she wondered if they would refuse and have to leave, but finally they slipped out of their shoes and headed toward the refreshment table.

"Oh, shoot." Chloe ducked behind Arlo as if that would block her from the women's line of vision. "They're headed this way."

"Because we're standing right by the food." She gestured toward the table, laden with all sorts of appetizers, half of which looked as if they had indeed come from the freezer section at Sam's Club, the fancy "thaw and eat" kind.

"I'm going to stay like this," Chloe said from her crouched position bent nearly in half. "You walk toward the bathrooms and I'll—"

"Stand up," Arlo said in a stage whisper. "Face the music and get it over with."

"Right. Fine." She straightened. "How do I look?"

Arlo fixed the curl that Chloe had tugged particularly hard on and smiled. "Like a million bucks."

Chloe sucked in her stomach and held her breath as Inna and Daisy came closer. She practically vibrated with nervousness as they approached. The smile on her lips was forced, brittle, her eyes a little too bright from all the punch.

Daisy and Inna came closer, closer until they were right in front of Arlo and Chloe. Then without a backward glance, they walked right past.

Chloe looked almost disappointed as she glanced toward Arlo.

Arlo shrugged.

Together they watched the two most important women in Wallace J. Harrison's life fill little blue plates with half-frozen hors d'oeuvres.

Chloe looked to Arlo. She stared back. "What do I make of that?" she asked Arlo.

"No idea." Arlo shrugged. "They might not believe that you had anything to do with Wally's uh...fall. Or they could be biding their time until they can get you alone."

Chloe swatted Arlo's arm with the back of one of hers. "Stop it. Now I'm not going to be able to go to the bathroom all night."

"Not without a chaperone."

Chloe chuckled, and Arlo was glad to hear the sound. It seemed like forever since she had heard her laugh, when in fact it had only been two very long days.

"Seriously though," Arlo said. "Do they even know that you and Wally, once upon a time...?"

Chloe shrugged. "Probably not. At least not unless Wally or someone in town said something."

Arlo cast a sideways glance at the two women. They seemed totally unconcerned with both Arlo and Chloe. "They don't know."

"If you say so," Chloe said, but her eyes were still clouded with worry.

Thankfully, Daisy and Inna moved away from where they were standing. Chloe visibly relaxed.

Arlo allowed her gaze to float around the room once more. People she hadn't seen in years milled around drinking green or pink punch, talking in subdued tones as they flitted about. So many people had RSVPed for the event, but not nearly as many as expected had made a special trip back to Sugar Springs for the reunion once word of Wally's death had gotten around.

It took Arlo a minute to notice that Chloe was wandering away. "What are you doing?" she whispered loudly.

Chloe cocked her head to some point behind her. Arlo realized her friend was indicating Inna and Daisy. Chloe waved to Arlo with the flap of one hand. "Come here," she whispered in return.

"Are you eavesdropping?" she asked as she scooted closer.

Chloe lifted one finger to her lips and cocked her head to the side.

"Stuffed mushrooms." Inna held the hors d'oeuvre in front of her, turning it this way and that as if inspecting it from each angle. "Do you love them, Daisy?"

"They're okay, I guess."

"But I thought your family owned a mushroom farm."

Daisy James-Harrison came from a farm?

Arlo did her best not to whirl around in surprise, but she had to see the woman's face. Daisy was about as far from a farm girl as Arlo herself.

Daisy's beautiful face flushed a perfect pink as she murmured something incoherent. So it was true. And for some reason, she didn't want anyone to know. A rural snob.

"Well, I for one thank your family for their endeavors. A mushroom farm is not exactly a clean place. And the smell." Inna shuddered. "Even worse, how do you tell the difference between ones that are poison and ones that aren't?"

A war of *to answer or not to answer* waged on Daisy's face. *To answer* won the first round in three short seconds. "It's not like you have to go out into the forest and forage for them. They're grown there for a purpose."

"And you only grow the ones that aren't poisonous?"

Not to answer won round two. "I need to powder my nose." She brushed past Inna and walked over to the door that led to the locker rooms.

Inna caught Arlo watching and a ghost of a smirk crossed her lips. She shrugged. "Some people are so sensitive, yes?"

"I suppose so," Arlo murmured and turned back to Chloe.

"What was that all about?" she whispered.

Arlo waited for Inna to move away before she answered. "I have no idea. But it seems weird, don't you think?"

"Not any weirder than the widow and the mistress arriving at the party together."

"Touché," Arlo said. But something about the entire exchange seemed off. And she couldn't figure out if that feeling came from Daisy or Inna.

....

Despite the hors d'oeuvres coming from a discount box store, Arlo started to enjoy herself at the reunion. She hadn't realized how tense she had been over Wally's death until she started to relax. The pink punch was a big help. The food might have been a little pedestrian, but the drinks were first-class.

"There you are."

Arlo turned as the man came near. It took only a heartbeat for her to recognize him. "Sammie Tucker?"

"You know it." He scooped her into his arms as if they had been separated for a long time and he couldn't get enough of her. Well, they had been separated, but the thing between them had been over a long, long time.

He set her back on the floor and kissed her soundly. More than friendly but not too familiar. A tease from the past, improved by time.

She and Sam had chemistry way back when, both in their class schedule and in their relationship. She had broken up with Mads knowing that he was destined for the NFL. In senior year, he had already secured a scholarship with the Crimson Tide. One more year and he was out of the town he seemed to hate. Away from his drunkard of a father, his runaway mother, and every bad thing he knew. Arlo had loved him the way only a teenage girl can love the boy of her dreams. But she knew he wanted out of Sugar Springs and all she wanted to do was stay. Enter Sam Tucker, who wasn't on the football team, wasn't a track star, didn't play baseball. How was she supposed to know that he would leave too? On an academic scholarship all the way to Northwestern in Illinois. She wouldn't say either of them were the reason she hadn't gotten married yet. When you lived in a town the size of Sugar Springs, your choices were limited.

"Man, it's good to see you." He held her at arm's length and smiled.

Behind him she could see Mads. But the look on his face was unreadable. It was prom all over again and despite the years that had passed since that fateful night, Arlo felt herself blush. She pulled her gaze from Mads and centered her attention on Sam.

Living up north hadn't changed him at all and yet he was completely different. Same sandy-brown hair, same electric smile. The creases fanning out from his green eyes only served to add a maturity to his boyish charm. He had grown up, but not too much.

"How've you been?" he asked, still holding her hands in his.

She wanted to pull away, and yet she didn't. It felt good, that gentle touch. "I've been…fine," she said. "Real good." And she had been. "You?"

"Can't complain. I saw your store on Main Street. It's nice."

"Thanks."

And just like that, the conversation dwindled. The boy she couldn't stop talking to had turned into the man she had nothing to say to.

"Let me get you a drink."

She nodded. "Green." She had had enough of the pretty pink punch.

Arlo could feel Mads's gaze on her as she waited for Sam to return. That was the thing about reunions: they dredged up old memories. Good and bad. Like prom night so long ago when a girl threw over one boy for another only to have both of them head out of the town that she had adopted as her own.

It seemed to take forever before Sam returned, but she refused to move out of Mads's line of vision. And she definitely refused to look at him and acknowledge his stare. With Sam gone from Sugar

Springs, she could pretend that prom night had been nothing but a dream. Now that he was back in town, for however long, pretending was out of the question.

Maybe she was being hypersensitive. Maybe Mads had looked away long ago and his hard gaze was a figment of her imagination.

Only one way to find out.

"Here ya go." Sam sidled up to her, effectively stopping her from checking to see if Mads was still staring.

"Thanks," she murmured and cast him a forced smile.

"So a bookstore, huh?" He took a sip of his punch, then stared into the pink depths of his cup. "Wow."

"That's why I'm drinking this." She lifted her cup.

"Maybe if we mixed it together?"

Arlo shook her head. "Chloe and I already tried that. It makes this brown sludge. We thought it might be like drinking a chocolate milkshake, but since it's fruit flavored it sort of ruined the fantasy."

"Huh." He looked into his drink once again.

"My suggestion is switch off. One pink, then a green, and so forth."

"Good plan," Sam said with a grin and drained his cup. He winced. "Not so bad once you know what to expect. But that pink…"

"Throws a person off."

"Completely." He looked to her and their gazes locked. Time seemed to stand still for a moment, then Sam grinned, and those lines creased out from his eyes and brought her back to the present.

She pulled her gaze from his and allowed it to wander around what remained of the mixer. A few people still milled about. Chloe had gone over to talk to Charla Sampson, cheer captain circa 1990. Mads was deep in conversation with Dan Bachman, the school's football coach. But for the most part, the people she wanted to see, and some of those she didn't, including Inna and Daisy, had all gone to wherever they were staying—with family, the motel, or Helen's B&B.

There would be a banquet that evening. Wally was to receive an award for his contributions to society. It was sort of a Sugar Springs High School Hall of Fame, though the only people Arlo knew to be in it with him were Mads for his football career and General Lilly, who put the town on the map back before the Civil War. Of course he didn't graduate from SSHS, but no one complained about that oversight. Arlo supposed now Daisy would accept the award for Wally.

"So that third floor of yours," Sam said. "What are you doing with it?"

"What?" His question took her off guard. She whipped her attention back to him. "Why?" The third floor was taped off as part of the crime scene, since Wally had stopped there and had a pastry before doing himself in.

The weirdest thing among all the weirdness was that Wally was in her third-story storage floor without her knowing about it. What was up with that?

"I'm looking for some office space, and I heard you were wanting to lease your third floor."

"Office space?" Why did she suddenly feel as if she had lost thirty IQ points?

"Yeah, I'm thinking about hanging around for a while."

"And doing what?" Why did the thought of having Mads and Sam in the same town again send shivers of dread down her spine?

"I'm a private investigator."

6

"REALLY?" AND WHAT WOULD A TOWN LIKE SUGAR SPRINGS have to offer that would need to be privately investigated? Maybe the fact that Imogene Sanders liked to steal her neighbor's tomatoes? But everyone knew that. Even the neighbor. As far as Arlo could see, said neighbor planted too many tomatoes to begin with. On purpose? Who knew?

On second thought, maybe having a private investigator around might not be so bad. But did it have to be Sam?

"I'm just ready to come back home, you know."

Arlo nodded. Home was the most important thing to her. Staying in one place. Having roots. It was all she had ever wanted from life. "I heard about your mom."

A dimness washed over his features, but in an instant it was gone. "Yeah. Cancer sucks."

She clinked her cup to his. "Amen."

"She's a fighter though." And Sam would be there to support her. Even if it meant moving back to Podunk, Mississippi, and investigating missing cats and cheating spouses. That was just the way he was.

He cleared his throat. "About that third floor...can I take a look at it? That is if you're willing to rent out the space."

"It's a crime scene." The words slipped out before Arlo could stop them.

"A crime scene?" Sam's eyebrows almost disappeared under the fringe of hair covering his forehead.

"That's where Wally…" She didn't say the words, but Sam understood.

"What was he doing up there?"

"Apparently he decided that was the best place to end it all."

"So it was a suicide? I heard rumors, but you know how that can be."

She did. Gossip was one of the drawbacks of living in such a small town, but it was one worth living with. "Yeah. It appears that way."

"And he jumped from your third floor?"

"It would seem so."

"Why?"

That was the question everyone was asking, but no one had an answer to. "Who knows? Mads and Jason have searched it for clues. They didn't find much."

"Did he leave a note?"

"Just a scrawled message on a piece of printer paper saying *I'm sorry*. He didn't even sign it."

"Hmmm…"

"What?"

"Nothing."

That wasn't a *nothing* sort of noise, but Arlo didn't question him. There was too much about the situation that didn't click and if Wally hadn't killed himself, she was afraid all fingers would end up pointing at Chloe.

"Monday night we're having a book club meeting at the store if you're interested in stopping by."

"Book club?"

She nodded. "We're reading Wally's book. Normally we meet on Friday, but since all this, the ladies wanted to meet again."

"I wouldn't want to come in during the middle."

"We just started. It would be the perfect time to join."

"Ladies, huh?"

She laughed. "Slow down, stud. It's Helen, Camille, and Fern."

"Johnson, Kinney, and Conley?"

"You got it."

"I see."

With that lineup, she was sure she would get a definite no. But she wasn't giving up on getting a younger crowd to read, then meet to talk about it.

"I don't know," he said, absently stroking his chin as if deep in thought. "I'll consider it."

....

Arlo pulled on the hem of her dress and sighed. She wished it had a couple more inches on the bottom. When she went home after the mixer to change, she had almost put on her standard black dress to come to the banquet, minus the sweater she wore over it to funerals, but she knew Chloe would have a fit. So here she stood in a dress that made her feel a little exposed and a lot uncomfortable.

"Would you stop that?" Chloe hissed. "You're going to ruin it."

Like she was ever going to wear the dress again. When the class reunion date had been announced and Wally had RSVPed, she knew it was her chance to promote her store. All eyes would be on her—at times anyway—and she wanted to look her best. One special shopping trip to Memphis later and she was the proud owner of a designer dress that "showed off the length of her legs and rounded out the rest of her tall frame." At least that's what the salesperson had said. Chloe had agreed, and the short dress with a heart-shaped bodice and small pieces of chiffon that passed for sleeves went home with Arlo.

Note to self: never buy a dress while high on advertising opportunities. A person's self-confidence is fickle, and you never know when it will slip.

Like now.

"If we were in school, they would not let me stay because I can't pass the fingertip test." She stood straight and pressed her arms to her sides. Her fingers touched the skin of her thighs. All of her fingers. Even the pinkie, though just barely. But still.

"Good thing we're not in school then."

Arlo sighed again, or maybe it was closer to a groan. At least they would be sitting soon at the various tables the reunion committee had set up for the evening. The white tablecloths draped over each one would hide her legs from view. One positive note for certain. Now if they would call for everyone to sit down, she would be all right.

She glanced at her wrist to check the time, then groaned again. She wasn't wearing her watch. And she always wore a watch. She wanted to know what time it was without messing with her phone, but tonight Chloe had made her leave it in the car, saying it ruined the look she was going for. Arlo hadn't realized she was going for any look in particular, but there you had it.

"Hey."

She turned at the sound of that deep familiar voice. "Mads." She had been kind of hoping that he wouldn't show tonight. That maybe the SSHS baseball team would pick tonight for their annual initiation ritual. They made the incoming freshmen take a dunk in Marty Harper's cow pond. Disgusting, yes. Dangerous, not really. So everyone turned a blind eye. But sometimes it got out of hand. Why couldn't tonight be that time?

Or maybe she should ask herself why she didn't want to face both Mads and Sam in the same room? What was in the past was in the past. And it had been a long time ago. And a stupid mistake on her part. Years had gone by since then. Everything was different now.

"I wasn't sure you'd be here," Arlo said.

"I'm gone." Chloe waggled her fingers in a quick farewell, then disappeared in the milling crowd of partygoers.

"I almost wasn't." He chuckled. "Jason graduated from here too, so we drew lots to decide who would come."

"And you won?"

"No," he said, the one word clipped and uncomfortable. "I lost."

Arlo almost laughed. Almost.

Mads shoved his hands into his pockets and surveyed the room, his gaze sharp and attentive. And she was glad she hadn't actually laughed at his joke. He wasn't there for pleasure; he was working a case!

"You don't think Wally killed himself, do you?"

Mads settled his attention on her, and once again she was reminded of how handsome he was and what a mistake she had made all those years ago. "Let's say the crime scene isn't as cut-and-dried as I wish it was."

"Really?" That perked her interest. Simply because she was worried about Chloe. "How so?"

He shook his head. "I am not going to discuss an ongoing investigation with you."

"Right." She switched tactics. "When do you suppose you'll release my third floor?"

"Do you have stuff up there you need?"

"Sam wants to look at it for office space." And Arlo and Chloe's Books & More could use the extra income for sure. All she had stored up there were some boxes of used romance novels and a case of coffee filters she should have thrown out weeks ago. They didn't use them these days, what with the espresso machine and the Keurig. Maybe she should make a wreath out of them. The coffee filters; not the books.

"Sam?"

She nodded. "He's staying in town to be with his mother. He's a private eye now, did you know?"

Mads's jaw tightened and took on a this-town-ain't-big-enough-for-the-two-of-us slant. "I knew."

"I think it will be good to have him home," she lied.

"Can I have your attention please?" The request was followed by an earsplitting squawk of microphone feedback. "I need everyone to take their seats. Your name will be on the place card on the table. Seating arrangements were done by random drawing. So please, no swapping. Get to know your SSHS alum neighbor. Bon appétit." Another ripping blare of feedback, then everyone was in motion.

"I don't care where he is, he better stay out of my investigations."

And that was when she knew. Some hurts never went away. Like being left at the prom when your date went home with someone else.

....

Sunday dawned with bright sunshine and a pink punch hangover. Arlo pulled herself out of bed and managed a couple of Tylenols and a cup of strong coffee. She scraped her hair into a ponytail, pulled on some yoga pants and a T-shirt that said *I read. What's your superpower?* and headed out the door.

She needed a superpower today. She needed the superpower of patience. Waiting for the reports from the coroner was about to do her in. She needed the superpower of friendship. She had to do something to keep Chloe on the ledge instead of jumping— figuratively speaking. Maybe that wasn't the best analogy, but her brain was still sloshing around in a sea of ruinous pink punch. Which brought her to the third superpower she wished for: the ability to fight hangovers in a single bound. Or something like that.

"You look awful." Chloe stepped back from the door and allowed Arlo entrance.

"Thanks," Arlo drily replied. She knew she looked like death warmed over. She didn't need her bestie reminding her. "You're not so bad yourself."

Chloe closed the door behind them, then pushed a curled lock of hair from in front of her face. "What was in that pink stuff?"

Arlo chuckled, then groaned as the sound echoed in her teeth. "I don't think we want to know."

"Breakfast at The Diner?" Chloe asked.

"I thought you would never ask."

They turned back toward the door.

"It's on me," Chloe said.

"But there's a catch?" It wasn't exactly a question.

"You have to drive. I'm still seeing double."

....

Once upon a time The Diner had had a real name—Ford's or some such—but over the years it had become known as "The Diner." It had been called that for as long as Arlo had lived in the town and she suspected the shift had occurred way before that. Tyrone and Neddie Porter had owned it for as long as she could remember, and the change had happened before them.

The Diner was quiet at this time on a Sunday morning, mostly because the majority of the good citizens of Sugar Springs were in church. There were ten churches in town. Yes, that was a lot for a town their size, but five of them were Baptist churches that had split over some disagreement or another. If nothing else, it made for an interesting parochial softball season but was a little confusing to any newcomers. When a new Baptist family moved into town, the race would be on to capture them as part of the church membership. It was the Freewill Baptist versus the First Baptist versus the Southern Baptist versus the Fourth Street Baptist versus the Missionary Baptist. And all around like that.

Chloe usually attended the nondenominational church but had fallen victim to the class reunion the night before. Or maybe it was the combination of lethal punch and Wally's death.

As it was, the two of them had The Diner to themselves, save for Joey from the dry cleaners and Cable from the menswear store. The men had straightened when she and Chloe walked in the door. It was obvious that they were a couple, but they kept it hidden as much as possible. No PDA or wedding rings. Same-sex marriage might be legal, but there were some towns still where a person or persons needed to keep something like that to themselves. Sugar Springs was one of those places. The town could abide as long as it wasn't flaunted. Maybe that should have been the town motto: *If you don't acknowledge it, it ain't happening.*

"Sit anywhere," a voice called from somewhere in the back. The Diner was set up in the traditional way with a small but long window where the diners could see into the kitchen. There was a bar for eating with stools that swiveled and stacks of gum and chips behind the cash register.

Chloe and Arlo chose a table on the opposite side from Cable and Joey. It wasn't much, but at least it was a little bit of privacy for the pair.

Ashley Porter appeared from the back. Ashley was good friends with Courtney, who worked part-time at the Books & More. They were on the cheer squad together and could often be seen walking down Main Street arm in arm. They were an unexpected pair— Ashley with her dark skin and long weave of braids and Courtney with her blond hair and perpetual tan. They were always smiling and made everyone around them smile as well.

Ashley's folks owned The Diner and took turns as to who cooked on Sunday and who got to go to church. They were Freewill Baptist. Not that it made any difference to Arlo. Except for what she would order. Neddie, Ashley's mother, made the best biscuits and gravy, while Tyrone, her father, could make an omelet that would melt in your mouth.

"Who's behind the grill today?" Chloe asked as Ashley approached their table. She had already grabbed the coffeepot and two mugs from the stacks behind the counter, next to the gum and chips.

"Mama." Ashley plunked the cups down onto the table and filled one of them with coffee. "Two biscuits and gravy?" she asked without taking out her notepad. They had done this many times before.

Chloe and Arlo nodded.

"One side of bacon. One side of sausage. I'll be back with your hot water in a sec." She didn't wait for them to answer but turned on her toes and sauntered back toward the kitchen. She called out their order and finally wrote it down on the ticket book she usually carried in her pocket.

"So how does it feel to have Mads and Sam back in the same town again?" Chloe raised an eyebrow at Arlo.

Arlo gave her a look, then reached for the creamer. "With everything else going on in the world, this is what you want to talk about this morning?"

"Yep." Chloe tore the end off of three packets of sugar at the same time and dumped them into her cup. She swore that was the only way she could stand the tea in The Diner, but the same trick didn't work for the coffee.

"O-okay." Arlo stirred her coffee, added a little more cream, then tentatively took a sip. "It's weird."

Chloe sat back in her chair as Ashley approached with the coffee urn filled with hot water. "And?" she prompted.

Arlo waited until Ashley had retreated back to her perch behind the cash register before continuing. "It's weird."

"It's more than weird." Chloe dunked her tea bag into the water and pinned Arlo with her toughest stare. Not that it had any effect on her. They had been down that road too many times.

"It's just weird."

"Please…" Chloe's eyes clouded over and Arlo knew what her friend needed from her: a diversion. Something else to think about other than her own problems.

"I guess I never thought I'd see Sam again." Most everyone who left the small town found reasons to never come back. Like that took much effort. Unless a person had family or good friends in the town, there wasn't much call to return. Or stay. Arlo was the exception. She needed someplace to belong. Sugar Springs had become that place for her.

"He's come back before," Chloe pointed out. "To visit his mama."

"Yes." But more often she had heard of Sam sending for his mother to come visit him. "When he left, I figured he'd be like all the others, and once they saw how the town looked behind them, they never wanted it in front again." And then there was Mads…

"What about Mads?"

Was Chloe reading Arlo's mind?

"That was so ten years ago."

Chloe spooned up a small taste of her tea, tried it, and added some cream. "I've seen how he looks at you."

The words sent a pang through her heart that extended down to her stomach. "He doesn't look at me any differently than he looks at Frances from dispatch." But there were times when she wished he might. But she had been young and stupid all those years ago. She'd broken Mads's heart and Sam had broken hers. She supposed that was poetic justice.

Chloe opened her mouth to respond but stopped as Ashley slid a full plate in front of her.

Two plates of biscuits and gravy with hash browns on the side, a shared plate with sausage and bacon, and two bowls of grits. A carb lover's dream. Though after last night, Arlo should have ordered the steak and eggs to soak up all the alcohol.

"Can I get you anything else?" Ashley asked. "Ketchup? Hot sauce?"

"No," Chloe replied, as Arlo said, "Yes. Both."

Ashley pulled them from the table behind them. "Don't know why I didn't bring them out before." She smiled and went to check on the other table. They only had about an hour before the church crowd would be released, but Arlo knew Cable and Joey would be gone long before that. She and Chloe would most likely be gone as well.

"Don't you want to know how he looks at you?" Chloe asked.

Arlo did her best to give one hundred and ten percent of her attention to getting the ketchup out of the glass bottle. Who had ketchup in glass bottles these days? Didn't they all come with squeeze tops now?

"Arlo?"

"Just a minute." She stuck a knife into the bottle.

"You're dodging this," Chloe accused.

"I'm trying to get ketchup." Because she didn't want to hear how Mads looked at her. It might get her hopes up.

Wait…it wasn't like she was still in love with him or anything, but he was a good man. That was all.

"And so is Sam," Chloe said.

Had Arlo said those last words out loud? She really had to be more careful with her runaway mouth.

"Yes, they are both good men."

She could admit that without divulging her little secret: that she had wondered what her life would have been like if she hadn't thrown over Mads for Sam. But to keep things equal, she also mulled over how her life might have been if Sam hadn't had his own plans that were bigger than Sugar Springs, Mississippi. What if, what if, what if… That kind of thinking got a person nowhere. But it lingered there in the back of her mind, and she didn't need Chloe fueling it with proclamations of Mads looking at her one way or another.

"Wally…" Chloe said the one word with such reverence that Arlo abandoned her attempts at ketchup for her hash browns and instead turned her attention to her friend.

"Chloe?"

Her eyes filled with tears. "He wasn't a good man," she said, "but I loved him."

Arlo clasped Chloe's hand where it lay on the tabletop and gently squeezed. "Everyone deserves love, even if they don't appreciate it."

Chloe sniffed and gave a small nod. "I keep telling myself that, but the doubts are still piling up."

Arlo understood. As much as she daydreamed about Mads and Sam, she was certain Chloe wondered about Wally even more. How could she not? At night when she was alone, at all the places where they had shared memories, maybe even when she looked at Jayden.

"He was coming around though," Arlo said. She released Chloe's fingers and picked up her fork, hoping her friend would do the same. No sense wasting good biscuits and gravy on even more what-ifs.

"You think so?" Chloe asked.

Arlo cut off a piece of gravy-covered biscuit with the side of her fork. "I do." She ate the bite and thankfully Chloe did the same. She might be upset, but she was eating. "I know you didn't like it," Arlo continued, "but to me, Wally asking to see Jayden meant he regretted his decision to pretend like his son didn't exist."

"Maybe he changed his mind."

Arlo shrugged. "Does it matter?"

Chloe forked up another bite and chewed slowly before answering. "I guess not. Not now for sure." Thankfully, she kept herself together and no more tears rose in her eyes.

"If he wanted to see Jayden, he wanted things to be different."

"And how much would they have changed if he hadn't...died?"

Arlo shook her head. "I guess now we'll never know."

7

THEY FINISHED THEIR BREAKFAST WITHOUT ANY MORE TEARS. Despite Chloe's agreement to pay the bill if Arlo drove, Arlo picked up the check. After the week Chloe had had, it was the least she could do.

"Let's go to the park." Chloe's suggestion took Arlo by surprise. "Maybe go by and get Jayden for a bit. That would be fun, don't you think?"

Anything to keep her friend on this side of the ledge. Chloe still seemed a little fragile and unsure. She needed time with her son, fun time without having to worry about family, or the bills, or that the only man she had ever loved had fallen three stories to his death.

"That's a great idea."

They drove Arlo's car back to the bungalow and got Chloe's Range Rover out for the trip. Jayden would be much more comfortable in Chloe's SUV than Arlo's vintage VW.

"Come in, come in." Liz Carter stepped to one side as Chloe and Arlo entered the large brick house that sat on five beautiful acres of manicured lawn. Daniel Carter, Chloe's father, owned a small chain of sporting goods stores with five locations in northeast Mississippi. It was amazing to Arlo how different she and Chloe had been raised, and yet they were such good friends.

"Mommy!" Jayden came running from the living room and

threw himself at Chloe, automatically expecting her to catch him. Arlo knew Chloe would always try, but there was going to come a time when he would get too big to jump into her arms for hello hugs. "What are you doing here? You don't have to work?"

Chloe's smile was sweet if not a bit sad. "The Books & More is closed on Sunday." She ruffled his blond curls with affectionate fingers.

Typical of the male species, he pulled away. "That's right. We went to church today. I forgot."

Because that was so half an hour ago.

"You want to go to the park?" Chloe asked. Arlo could almost see her fight to run her fingers through his hair. She knew it was hard on her friend to leave him with her parents, but everyone agreed it was best for all involved. Chloe needed her own space, but Jayden needed the stability of staying in the home he had always known.

"Can I bring He-Man?"

"Of course."

"Yay!" He skipped off to find the leash for his dog, a four-year old bichon frise named He-Man. And that was exactly what happened when a person let a five-year-old name a puppy. At least the pooch had been dubbed "Manny" by everyone but Jayden. Though lately Arlo had caught him using the moniker as well.

"Manny," he called.

Arlo had heard him barking when they had first arrived at the house. Manny was a tough little white poof ball…until the door was opened. That was when he ran for cover.

"You don't mind, do you?" Chloe asked her mom. "I should have asked first."

Liz shook her head. "He's your son. You can come get him whenever you want."

But Arlo knew that Chloe didn't want to upset Jayden's schedule.

"Get your shoes on," Liz called.

Chloe looked down at the shiny parquet floor beneath their feet. They hadn't even gone into the house, only into the foyer. That wasn't the problem. Arlo knew that Chloe felt like she should be the one to tell Jayden to put his shoes on. And he should live in a house with a mother and father who loved each other. Maybe that's why she had held on to the idea of Wally for all these years. It was part of her fantasy of how life should be for her son. But now Wally was dead. There was no hope of those dreams becoming a reality. Arlo was certain that had affected her more than Wally's actual death. After all, Chloe hadn't even seen him in ten years or more.

"Yes, Honey," Jayden called back. Honey was the name Liz had chosen for herself as a grandmother. No Nana or Grammy for her. At first Arlo had found it a little pretentious, but over the years it had grown on her. Now she couldn't image the cultured Liz Carter being called anything else.

"Are you all right?" Liz asked. She didn't have to ask for the particulars. She didn't have to say the words: *How are you holding up since Wally is gone?*

"I'm fine," Chloe said. There was a slight edge to her voice, like she wanted to add, *I wish everyone would stop asking me that.* "Where's Dad?"

Liz cocked her head to one side, indicating the living room behind her. "Watching the game." But Arlo had been over enough times to know that was code for "sleeping in the recliner while the game plays on the television set."

In the small space of silence that separated them, Arlo could hear the tick of the large grandfather clock on the opposite wall and the faint noise of the baseball game. Then Jayden started back up again and everything was drowned out in his nine-year-old chatter. He was talking to the dog, apparently trying to get his leash attached to the pup's collar without getting licked in the face.

Good luck with that, buddy.

"Are you getting enough sleep, sweetie?" Liz reached a hand toward her daughter.

Chloe took a small step back. "I'm fine."

A quick flash of hurt flared in Liz's eyes, then it was gone. "How's the store, Arlo?"

"Doing good." She nodded. If she said anything else, Wally, the elephant in the room, would wake and once again stomp through the conversation. After all, the book signing was supposed to bring people in from all over. Maybe even from Memphis and Tupelo. Wally didn't do a lot of signings and Arlo had been hoping that some of the big-city dwellers would come to her indie bookstore in small-town Sugar Springs. She had needed the opportunity, but she supposed she couldn't really complain. Wally had taken the brunt of that accident. At least Arlo was still "on this side of the dirt" as old man Gilbert would say.

"I'm ready." Thankfully, Jayden picked that moment to allow Manny to drag him in the middle of the three of them, effectively splitting them apart—Chloe and Arlo on one side, Liz on the other. Behind him, Jayden dragged a duffel bag that was almost as big as he was.

"Whatcha got there, sport?" Arlo asked.

Jayden gave a negligent shrug. "A couple of things to play with."

Liz shot him an indulgent smile while Arlo tried not to laugh. He had enough toys packed for a lifetime of trips to the park. But he missed his mother as much as she missed him, and when they were together, he seemed to cram as much into each minute as possible.

"I'll have him back for supper," Chloe promised.

Liz nodded. "And please don't give him ice cream after three. It makes him too hyper and he doesn't want to eat his food."

"Aw, Honey." Jayden made a face at his grandmother and grimaced as she kissed him on the cheek.

"And mind your mother," Liz warned.

Arlo wasn't sure she would ever get used to that—Liz telling Jayden to mind his mother. It was backward for sure.

She didn't say anything. They all knew it.

....

"She means well," Arlo said once everyone—including He-Man—was settled in the Range Rover and moving down the road.

"I know. But every time I turn around..."

"Every time you turn around what?" Arlo asked.

"I'm reminded of..." Chloe checked the rearview mirror, most probably to see how much Jayden was paying attention to the conversation. "...him." Little big ears must have been listening.

"It's only natural," Arlo said gently. "It is a small town."

Chloe shook her head. "I've lived here for the last ten years without hardly hearing his name. Now he's everywhere."

And dead.

"Can we play ball when we get to the park?" Jayden asked. He was staring out the window as if somehow the view from the Range Rover had changed from the last time he had seen it.

"Did you pack a ball and gloves in your bag?" Chloe asked. Arlo could tell by the look on her face that she was hoping he would say no. Chloe wasn't the most sports-minded person. Never had been.

"Of course."

Chloe sighed. "Then we'll play ball."

Arlo choked back a laugh.

Chloe elbowed her.

"Aren't you glad you had a boy?" Arlo asked.

Chloe looked at her son in the rearview mirror, love shining in her eyes. "Yeah."

....

"Like this." Jayden once again demonstrated the proper way to throw a baseball, but Chloe was hopelessly uncoordinated.

No, that wasn't true. She used to do gymnastics and had been on the cheer squad a year or two. She was even voted best dancer senior year. But if there was a ball involved, all her rhythm went out the window.

Chloe tried to throw it, but the ball veered to the left. It wasn't a bad throw as far as distance, but direction left something to be desired.

Jayden shook his head and started toward the ball. But he was too slow. From out of nowhere, a large Airedale terrier bounded after the baseball, snatching it up in his mouth and running away as fast as those long legs of his could carry him.

"Hey," Jayden hollered and started after the dog.

"Jayden." Chloe chased behind them.

Arlo stood in the middle of the field, glove on one hand and the other shielding her eyes as she watched the three of them run—dog, mom, and child.

The park in the middle of Sugar Springs took up a four-block section. A row of trees split the space down the middle. On one side was a field for playing sports. At one end a couple of kids kicked around a soccer ball and at the other was a small patch of concrete with a basketball hoop and a large net to keep the ball from rolling into the street. The other side of the park boasted a huge jungle gym, a sandbox, a swing set, and several slides.

The dog ran along the tree line, happy to be chased by not one but two people. Arlo could see the joy on his face.

Manny, ever vigilant, took up a defensive stance on the blanket they had laid out and was running from corner to corner, adding his sharp barks to the cacophony of human shouts.

"Get back here," Jayden called.

But Arlo knew the dog and she knew how to handle it.

"Don't run," she called. "He wants you to chase him." Her words were echoed back to her in a smooth baritone. She knew that dog and she knew that voice.

"Mads." She breathed and tried not to seem happy to see him—but she was.

"Stop," he called to Jayden. Then he whistled and motioned the boy to come back.

Jayden cast one last look at the black-and-tan dog, then turned and jogged over to where they stood. The look on his face said he was certain that he would never see the ball again.

Chloe followed her son. She stopped next to them, greeting Mads with a breathless hi and a small wave. She no sooner got the salutation out than Dewey, the dog, stopped and looked back toward the people who had been chasing him. Once they stopped, he dropped the ball, tilting his head to one side and giving them a curious and sad look. This wasn't going at all like he planned.

"Now," Mads said. "Go back over to your stuff and sit down like you haven't got a care in the world."

Chloe shot him a look but didn't say anything. The four of them trudged back over to the blanket that Chloe had spread out for them to sit on. Manny was guarding the space, running across the fabric to bark at anyone who came too close to the corners. Everyone was at the other end of the park, but as far as he was concerned, that was too close. Arlo knew that if anyone actually got near him, he would sit on his haunches and growl. Close enough to touch and he would run for cover. He was that kind of dog.

Manny barked until they sat down, then he climbed into Jayden's lap and tried to lick his face with great success.

"Jayden," Chloe started, but caught herself. She was like Lucy van Pelt when it came to dog germs.

Arlo smiled as Chloe tried to relax and not scold Jayden or the dog for all the "kisses."

They had barely sat down on the blanket when Dewey took the ball into his mouth and tossed it in the air, playing some sort of minigame of fetch with himself. Or maybe he was trying to tease them into coming after him. When it finally became apparent that he wasn't going to regain their attention, he picked up the ball and trotted over to where they sat.

He wagged his stump of a tail and dropped the ball in Jayden's lap.

Manny yelped and scampered out of the way, behind his young master. He peeked out to see if the monster had gone, but Dewey stayed, tail wagging, awaiting their approval and praise.

"There," Mads said triumphantly. "You can play ball again."

Jayden picked up the slobber-covered ball, barely holding it with two fingers. His mouth was curled into a grimace of disgust. "I'm not sure I want to."

"I don't blame you," Chloe said. "Sorry, buddy."

Mads looked from Chloe to Jayden, then back again. "Seriously? You're going to let a little dog spit keep you from playing baseball?"

Jayden looked to his mother, then over to Mads. It was clear he had no idea how to answer that. "I—"

"The answer is no." Mads took the ball from Jayden and wiped it on the grass, anything left after that was cleared away by his shirttail.

"Come on." Mads stood and waved for Jayden to get up too.

Dewey, who clearly thought his game was about to begin again, bounded ahead, spun around, and waited for them to catch up. His stumpy tail was still wagging ninety to nothing.

"Me?" Jayden clearly wasn't sure this big burly man was talking to him.

"Yes, you. You think I want to play with these girls?"

"Hey now," Arlo protested. "I'll have you know I was considered the number one pitcher in our softball division."

Mads scoffed. "Softball. And slow pitch at that, I bet."

"Come on, Chloe." Arlo pushed to her feet before she realized that was all part of Mads's evil plan. Lure them into playing ball so he could show them up in front of Jayden. Or maybe he was trying to be nice to a young boy whose dad had been recently killed—no matter that he didn't know the man was his father—and whose grandfather and caregiver worked way too much.

"I'm not much good—"

Arlo shook her head. "Nope. If I'm playing, you're playing too."

Chloe sighed. "I was afraid you were going to say that."

....

One thing became entirely evident as they tossed around the mostly dry baseball: Jayden needed a man in his life. A young man who could do all the things with him that his father had done with his grandfather...but Arlo knew that wasn't true either. Wally's dad and Wally himself were about as different as two people could be—related or not. But the sentiment was the same. Jayden was missing out and Arlo could see it. Even more heartbreaking was that Chloe could see it too.

"You didn't happen to see Wally's widow at the inn, did you?"

Mads asked the question nonchalantly as he pitched the ball Arlo's way.

Arlo caught it, then threw it to Chloe. They were all four standing in the shape of a square throwing the ball, one to the other. Manny continued to guard his blanket, while Dewey bounded after the "toy." He was excited, but well-behaved enough that he didn't jump on any of them to get the ball, only followed behind it. "No. I didn't go out there this morning."

"A little too much punch at the party?" Mads asked.

"Come on, Mommy," Jayden coached. "Just like I showed you."

Arlo ignored Mads and instead turned her attention to her best friend. "You can do it, Cee."

Maybe in another lifetime. Chloe did her best to throw it overhand, but she released it too late and it hit the ground and bounced. Jayden blocked his nose with his glove and caught the ball. "Better," he said.

Arlo smiled. Nothing like pint-sized encouragement.

"She's staying at the inn still, right?" Mads asked.

"Yeah. I mean, I guess."

Jayden threw the ball to Mads.

Mads threw it to Arlo. Was he closer to her than he had been before? It sure seemed like it.

"Just wondering," Mads said.

Arlo tossed the ball to Chloe. "Why?" She turned her attention to Mads, not taking time to monitor Chloe's toss to her son.

Mads was closer. This time she knew for certain.

"Get back over there where you belong, Sheriff."

He rolled his eyes. "I see you've been talking to Cindy Jo again." He caught the ball with an athletic ease that made a mockery of the lazy act he put on most of the time.

"Not since I volunteered you to bring the appetizers." She smiled at him sweetly. But once again he was even closer to her.

"I don't want Chloe to overhear," Mads said. He was close enough now that he could walk the ball to her. Instead, he tossed it to Chloe.

"Overhear what?"

"I think Wally might have been pushed."

Chloe had been saying that all along.

Arlo opened her mouth to tell him that but closed it instead.

"What?" Mads asked.

Realizing that he had lost two playmates, Jayden started giving his mother a one-on-one lesson in throwing the ball, which left Mads plenty of time to question Arlo. Or stare at her with those incredible eyes that seemed to see more than what was on the surface.

"Nothing."

Mads shook his head. "I know 'nothing,' and that wasn't it."

"Wrong again, Sheriff."

He ignored the gibe. "If you hear of anything, you'll let me know immediately, right?"

It was as if he knew she was protecting Chloe.

Arlo smiled, even as her mouth went dry. "Of course."

....

The rest of the weekend went by without a hitch, unless you counted Cindy Jo backing her car into the garage door while it was still closed. The good news was Cindy Jo wasn't hurt, but the injuries to the door were fatal.

Arlo's phone dinged, and she pulled it from her back pocket. A text from Helen.

Making this for tonight's meeting! Yum!

The picture attached was of some sort of baked Mexican dip with olives, cheese, and a whole lot of refried beans.

Arlo had to admit that it looked good, but she got hung up on the fact the book club was meeting tonight. She had forgotten all about it. In fact, she hadn't thought about the meeting again since Saturday night when she invited Sam.

"Ugh," she groaned, and typed an appropriate response.

Double yum. Can't wait.

"What's wrong?" Chloe asked. As usual, she was wiping every-thing down between customers, though Arlo felt she was more thorough today than usual. She was a little on edge waiting to get the coroner to confirm Wally's death was a suicide.

Mads said it would probably be Tuesday or Wednesday, but Arlo knew Chloe was hoping for something quicker. It was obvious to Arlo that Chloe believed if anything was off about the report, she would be the one blamed. Her DNA and fingerprints were all over the cup Wally had been drinking from. The whole thing was making her nervous.

"I told the book club they could have a meeting tonight."

"On a Monday?"

"They want to read Wally's book and couldn't wait to get started."

Chloe nodded sagely. "I guess there's not many other places for them to meet."

"I suppose not." There was The Diner, the drugstore that still sported an old-fashioned soda fountain, and Mac's, the unpolished little honky-tonk that sat on the edge of town. But Arlo couldn't see the three ladies there. "Maybe the library." But even as she said the words, she knew Miss Goldie, the librarian, wouldn't abide the noise the ladies would bring with them.

"Uh, yeah." Chloe switched her attention from the espresso machine to the sink. "That wouldn't go over well."

"You're going to rub a hole straight through the stainless steel if you don't ease up."

Chloe stopped scrubbing but didn't answer as the bell over the door chimed.

Arlo turned to find Sam standing just inside the store. He looked as handsome as ever in jeans perfectly molded to his body, denim shirt, and ostrich cowboy boots. But he also looked a little unsure of himself. Not like Sam at all.

"Come in! Come in!" Faulkner squawked.

"Oh my," Chloe breathed under her breath.

Arlo spun around to shush her, then turned back to Sam. "Hey. What are you doing here?"

"You invited me to the book club thing tonight."

"Of course." She tried to smile. She hadn't expected him to show up at all, much less be the first one there. "You're a little early."

"I thought I might look around. You know, at Wally's books."

"Sure." She indicated the table on the other side of the floating staircase. "He only has one. Published, I mean. Getting a book ready for publication takes a while. His publisher might have another in the works. Though I haven't heard one way or another."

Sam made his way to the display table and picked up a copy of *Missing Girl*. He lifted it as if weighing the sheer volume of the book, then flipped it over to look at the back of the jacket cover. "Huh."

"What?"

He put that book down, then picked up another.

"What is it?" Arlo asked.

Even Chloe had stopped scrubbing to watch.

"The back." He turned the book around so she could see it. A big red *X* had been drawn through Wally's author photo.

"I don't understand." Arlo frowned and coolly made her way over to the table. She had done that very thing a few days before—picked up the book, checked the back. None of them had had big red *X*s on them then. At least not the one she had looked it.

She went to the other side of the table opposite Sam and snatched up a copy from the top. No *X*. But the one on the stack next to it had one. But any more than two down and they were untouched.

"Should we call Mads?" Sam asked.

"And what? Have him dust the books for prints to find out that half the people in Sugar Springs have touched them at one time or another?"

"Who would do this?" Sam mused.

"Someone who has read the book," Chloe joked.

"Is it that bad?" Sam thumbed through the pages as if that would tell him.

"It spent weeks at the top of the bestseller list," Arlo replied.

"So it's a good book."

"It's clever, but the writing…" Arlo trailed off.

Chloe rolled her eyes. She had dropped her polishing rag and joined them at the display. "Pay no attention to the bookseller. They can be a little biased when it comes to modern fiction."

"I resent that," Arlo shot back.

Sam chuckled. He sat the book down but continued to finger the dust jacket as if he were reluctant to walk away and leave it behind. "So it's a clever book, and it's sold well, but the writing leaves something to be desired."

She lifted one shoulder. Maybe she was a little tough on books. One day she might just write one herself, but until then, she read everything she could get her hands on, Wally's book included. "He has a very different voice."

"Voice?"

"Way of telling the story. Words that he uses, phrases. Have you ever read any Faulkner?"

"William Faulkner, Aisle 2B. Or not to be," Faulkner chanted from his cage.

"Don't mind him," Arlo said. "He does that anytime someone says his name but isn't talking to him." And what else was a bookstore bird to do but quote Shakespeare?

"Got it. And no. Not since tenth grade."

Arlo gave him a pained smile. "We had American Lit in the eleventh grade."

"Right." Sam's grin was sheepish but showed his dimples to their maximum charm level.

"Anyway, *Missing Girl* is written in stream of consciousness much like William Faulkner's *As I Lay Dying*. It can be hard to read at times. But the critics claim that Wally's—"

"'Overall style trumps the written word, leaving the reader gasping for breath with each passage reread, each word redefined.'" Sam tapped the back cover of one of the books. One without the added adornment.

"Something like that," Arlo agreed.

"It's a train wreck," Chloe interjected.

"Come on, Chloe, don't hold back. Tell us what you really think."

"Just saying." She tossed the bar rag over one shoulder and made the trip back to her coffee nook without a backward glance.

"Did the two of them ever…?" Sam asked.

Arlo shook her head.

"Wait…wasn't she—"

"Yep."

"And the baby?"

"He's nine now." Arlo lowered her voice so Chloe couldn't hear. "He lives with Chloe's parents. Long story."

"I know you're talking about me. Whispering doesn't make it any better."

Arlo didn't answer as the door to the bookstore swung open and Helen made her way inside carrying her large Crock-Pot.

"Mexican casserole," she said in a singsong voice. "Plenty for everyone." She set the pot down on the side table, then looked to where Arlo was standing. "What?" Then her eyes lit up like a child's at Christmas. "Sam Tucker. Look at you!" She opened her arms and descended upon him, wrapping him in a hug ten years in the making. "My goodness, you're a sight for sore eyes."

"Hi, Helen. It's good to see you too."

"I was just telling Arlo last week that she should have never let you go. And here you stand, proof positive of that fact."

Wait…what? There had been no such conversation, at least not in the last five years. At the very least not one that Arlo had been a part of. But she would never call Helen out on it. And Helen knew it.

"What are you doing here this afternoon?" Helen rubbed his arm as she spoke. She was like that, touchy-feely. It had taken Arlo a while to get used to having someone show their love by little touches. A tuck of hair behind the ear. Back of the fingers down the side of her face. Even a kiss on the top of her head for no reason at all. But that was her Elly.

"I've been trying to convince Arlo to lease me the top floor for my business."

"You're moving back to Sugar Springs?" Helen asked. "I heard about our mama. Sad state."

"Thank you." He cleared his throat. "I want to stay and help her."

Helen effectively turned him around and headed for the sitting area, one arm looped through his as she dragged him along. "What business are you in these days?" Helen asked. "When I knew you, your primary business was girls."

"I'm a private investigator."

"Well, kiss a pig. The wonders of this world will never cease."

Sam chuckled, but Arlo was too busy putting one and one together to join in.

"Sam," she said. "Can I talk to you a second?"

"Sure." He left Helen by her beloved Crock-Pot and made his way back over to Arlo.

Just then Camille knocked on the door. She carried a covered tray almost as big as she was.

"I'll get it." Chloe moved from behind the coffee bar to open the door.

"What is it?" Sam asked.

"Are you here to lease the third floor or investigate Wally's death?"

8

"WHY WOULD I WANT TO INVESTIGATE WALLY'S DEATH?"

"You tell me."

Sam shook his head. "There's nothing to tell. I'm interested because the whole thing is interesting." He gave a negligent shrug. "Job hazard. What can I say? I'm nosy. Though I have to admit it's an interesting tale."

"How so?" Arlo asked.

"So many problems with the crime scene."

"How would you know?" Arlo's eyes narrowed.

"Yes, love, and speak up. We're having trouble hearing you from way over there."

Sam flashed Camille a smile, then moved toward the sitting area. Charming rat.

"Hold on a minute though," Camille instructed. "Fern was right behind me, and I'm sure she'll want to hear this."

It took another ten minutes to get Fern in the door, food down, and sitting in the armchair so Sam could tell what he knew.

"What's wrong with the crime scene?" Helen asked.

"I haven't actually examined it," Sam started.

Arlo cleared her throat.

Sam ignored her. "But there seem to be several inconsistencies with the evidence."

"Bad evidence," Faulkner squawked. "Bad evidence."

"Like?" Camille prompted, ignoring the bird. It was usually the best plan of action. Once he realized he wasn't garnering all the attention in the room, he'd settle down and leave the conversation to the humans.

"Why would Wally hastily write a suicide note if he was going to jump out of a building?"

All five of them looked at Sam as if trying to decipher what he was saying.

"Oh, I get it," Fern said. "He wouldn't hastily write a note if he climbed three flights of stairs in order to kill himself. That's planned. Not spur of the moment."

"Suicide note, suicide note, suicide note," Faulkner chanted. "I love you. I always have."

"Ignore him," Arlo told Sam once again.

"Yes, Fern. I think so too," Sam agreed. "Wally would have most likely written his note before climbing up to the third floor. And what was he doing up there anyway?"

Chloe chose that moment to return to her spot behind the coffee bar and resume her cleaning.

"Maybe he was looking to rent that space. You know, for an office or something." This from Fern.

"Good point." Sam swung back to Arlo. "Has anyone contacted you about renting that space?"

She shook her head. "People don't call me. They call the Realtor."

Sam squinted toward the window where the *Space for Rent* sign was propped up next to the one that declared, *Come on in! We're Open.* "Who has your listing?"

"Sandy Green."

"She didn't graduate with us, did she?"

Arlo shook her head. "She was a few of years ahead. Five, I think."

"But she could have had a problem with Wally." Sam thoughtfully tugged on one ear.

"Sam, there are less than a thousand people in our town. Most everyone has had a problem with everyone else at one time or another. That doesn't mean you go around murdering people."

"So true," Camille said. "Why just the other day, Dan at the Piggly Wiggly was arguing with Stan from the Sac and Save about milk prices. I guess Dan had enough and punched Stan right in the face. Who would have thought the price of milk would be worth fighting over?"

Secretly Arlo had a feeling that Stan and Dan were fighting over the fact that Dan's wife had been seen sneaking around with Stan. But who was she to say?

"So you don't know if Wally was here to meet Sandy or someone else."

They whirled around as the sound of breaking crockery filled the air.

"Sorry," Chloe mumbled, then headed for the stock room to retrieve her broom.

"I have no idea why Wally was on the third floor." And that statement was completely and one hundred percent true. She knew why he had been in her building. But that was another question, wasn't it?

Silence filled the space around them. Even Faulkner had ceased his constant chatter for once. Chloe came out of the stockroom and stopped, the quiet that greeted her like a barrier. She visibly shook it off and continued on her way to behind the coffee bar to sweep up whatever she had dropped.

"I guess we'll know more when the coroner's report is released," Helen finally said.

"I thought you guys were meeting to talk about his book." Chloe blew a strand of her curly blond hair out of her face and eyed the book club members. Book club plus one, anyhow.

"Yes. Of course you're right, dear." Camille looked at the others. "*Missing Girl*, right?"

Mumbles that sounded a lot like agreement went up all around as the ladies pulled their copies of *Missing Girl* from their respective bags. Each one had place markers of some sort sticking out here and there to remind them of something interesting they found in the book.

"So what did you think?" Arlo asked, looking at the three wrinkled faces.

"I'm more interested in what Sam thinks." Camille swung her attention to the only man in the room.

"Yes. Yes," Fern and Helen agreed. First time for everything.

Sam looked at the book in his hands as if he had no idea how it had gotten there. The brief glance had Arlo once again wondering what Sam's fascination with Wally might be.

"You ladies have an advantage over me. I haven't read it yet." Classic Sam.

"It's hard to read." Helen said what everyone else was thinking.

"And I thought you said there was a lot of sex in it. I read three chapters and didn't find one paragraph of sex." Fern looked from Helen to Camille for backup.

Out of the corner of her eye, Arlo could see Sam's lips twitching as he fought back a smile. "That doesn't come in until later."

Fern's frown deepened. "I knew we should have read *Fifty Shades*."

Sam dropped his head and pressed his fingers to the bridge of his nose. He was fighting back laughter and Arlo knew one look from him would take her back ten years. But there was no profit in strolling down memory lane. She and Mads managed to avoid doing it on a daily basis. So why was she having trouble keeping her feet out of the past when Sam was around?

"Be that as it may," she started, "lack of sex aside, how was the book for you?"

"Hard to read," Fern admitted.

All eyes turned to Camille. The tiny woman reminded Arlo of a small bird—delicate, light—her hands flitting about the snap of her large white purse. It would be nothing to simply snatch the purse from her and look inside. That was all Arlo wanted, just a look. But she managed to control herself as they waited for Miss Camille to add her opinion to the conversation. "You know I've read Mr. Faulkner's work."

"William Faulkner," the bird chimed in. "Aisle 2B. Or not to be. Wrong William. Give me some Shakespeare, honey."

"Honestly." Fern shot Faulkner a disapproving look. "Where does he learn such things?"

"He just picks it up." Arlo had thought having a bird around the shop would be an interesting addition. Birds weren't as needy as a dog or as allergy provoking as a cat. She had found him by chance on Craigslist, and when she heard the creature's name, she knew it was fate. But whoever had Faulkner before her had definitely been a colorful character. It had taken months, but Arlo had managed to tone down the bird's salty vocabulary, but she couldn't do anything about the quick way he learned.

Camille cleared her throat and all attention swung back to her. "I've read this other author's work and found the unusual method of writing to enhance the overall story, not detract from it."

"Are you saying the method of writing takes away from the over-all story in Wally's novel?"

"I don't know, love," Camille said. "I almost feel like Wally didn't edit himself very well and his editors took it as stream of conscious-ness and ran with it."

Helen had moved around the back of the couch and lifted the lid from her Crock-Pot. The smell of garlic and spices filled the room. Arlo's stomach rumbled, and she realized that she had missed lunch. How many days in a row now had she done that? Too many, she was certain, and she made a vow to start taking a half hour during the day to sit and eat.

"So his writing style was unintentional?" Helen asked as she started filling plates.

"I didn't say that, just that it seemed that way. Stream of conscious-ness is about interior thought. Our brains tend to jump from one sub-ject to the next. But the sections where Mr. Harrison uses this method and his lack of punctuation aren't always in a character's thoughts."

"That's right," Fern chimed in.

"I feel certain that's the way Mr. Harrison intended for it to be perceived, but to me it seemed like he sort of threw it together."

"So we have to chalk that up as experimentation with voice," Camille mused.

Only a former English teacher would make an observation that concise. Maybe their book club would be all right after all.

....

Experimentation with voice. The words knocked around inside Arlo's head for the remainder of their meeting. The ladies seemed to enjoy having Sam infiltrate their hen party, but Arlo still wasn't entirely convinced he was only there because he was interested in a third-floor lease. It wasn't like he could even walk the space. All he could do was stand at the doorway and stare over the yellow crime scene tape to the spot where Wally had spent some of the last moments of his life.

The bell over the door rang. Arlo looked up from restacking the copies of Wally's book to find Mads coming through the door.

"Hey, Chief." She straightened the last book, stood, and dusted herself off.

"Got rid of your display?" He gave a quick nod to the empty table where all Wally's books had been the day before.

"Yeah, I thought it best." Her first plan had been to take down the unintentionally prophetic sign. She had debated on whether to leave up the display. Was it tacky? She couldn't be sure. Her decision was made for her when she removed the sign. Without it, the table looked bare. Even more so when she removed the vandalized copies of *Missing Girl*. Ten in all. At almost thirty dollars a pop, it was a lot of inventory to write off. But what choice did she have really? There were no security cameras, and she couldn't say that the marks hadn't been there when she built the display and she simply hadn't noticed. So she would smile, hide her aggravation, and take the loss. But she had to wonder if the marks were there when Travis Coleman was making his selection.

Mads walked over to where she stood, his keys jingling with every step he took. Every law officer she had ever known had carried around a ton of keys. What were they all for? One day she might ask, but today was not that day. Mads was normally a contemplative sort of fellow, but today he looked almost morose.

"Want a coffee?" she asked. "Chloe's straightening up the storage area, but she'll come make you one."

He shook his head. "I need to go upstairs."

She nodded, a quick smile flashing across her lips. "Are you going to take down the police tape?" It would be great to have the third floor back again. She was anxious to get it leased. When that happened, a huge financial weight would be lifted from her shoulders.

"I'm afraid not," he said. "The coroner's report is in."

Arlo waited as he cleared his throat. Chloe picked that time to come out of the storeroom with two stacks of to-go cups and lids balanced in her arms.

"Wally's death was no suicide. He was murdered."

Arlo felt as if all the air had been sucked from the room. Chloe trembled in place, not moving an inch despite the awkward load she carried.

Wally had been murdered. Pushed from the window of their third floor. "So he didn't jump? How can you be sure?"

Mads shook his head. "The fall killed Wally. But there was foul play involved."

Chloe was speechless.

Arlo gasped. "What do you mean?"

"Poison," Mads said. "Wally was poisoned."

9

"POISONED?" THE WORD THAT ESCAPED CHLOE WAS MORE OF A hushed squeak than anything. Arlo was amazed she even heard it over the clatter of the boxes. Everything Chloe had been carrying hit the floor with a crash. "How could he have been poisoned?" she muttered as she stood there among the to-go cups, paper sleeves, and plastic lids. She wrung her hands, making Arlo think of Radonna Caldwell as Lady Macbeth in their junior year drama project.

Arlo moved toward her friend. Lady Macbeth hadn't killed the father of her children. And neither had Chloe. And that's all Arlo would allow herself to think of the situation.

She clasped Chloe's cold fingers between her own hands and gently squeezed. "Come sit down." She tugged her friend toward the reading nook. Thankfully Chloe was too shocked to do anything other than obey.

"Who poisoned him?" Arlo asked. She needed to get her friend some tea and allow its healing properties to soothe away her stress, but that could wait a minute or two.

"I don't know yet."

"But you're going to find out," Arlo said, pressing him.

What remained of Chloe's color drained from her face. Arlo hoped Mads hadn't noticed. Chloe had all but sworn that she hadn't hurt Wally, but there was a wild look about her now that Arlo didn't know how to assuage. Chloe looked frazzled and forlorn all at the same time.

Mads didn't bother answering. He turned to Arlo. "I need to go up to the third floor again."

"Sure thing." She gave a quick look around. A couple of kids, no more than twelve years old, were thumbing through the books at the beginning of the Home and Garden section. They had come in after Mads, and Arlo was fairly certain they weren't interested in *Grilling Solutions for Small Spaces*, the book they were currently using to block her view of their faces. Other than them and Sally Dell, a new mom who came in every day with her cherub of a baby to browse through picture books, the store was empty. Arlo had determined weeks ago that Sally needed an excuse to get out of the house and a place to go once she managed her escape. Chloe could handle these customers in her sleep. She just wished her business partner was napping instead of staring at the magazines and obviously seeing nothing. "Let me get my keys."

"I'll be right back," she told Chloe.

Chloe nodded in return.

Together Arlo and Mads went out the front and around the side of the building.

"Is there a door from the inside that leads to the third floor?" he asked.

"Of course, but I thought this would be easier. The store access is blocked." And going outside gave her the excuse to get out into the sunshine, if only for a couple of minutes.

"Where is that door?"

Arlo jerked a thumb over one shoulder as if that in any way indicated the direction. It did not. "Back in the store. Opposite the bathrooms. It stays locked most of the time. Especially now that we're offering the third floor for lease." She used her key to open the separate door on the side of the building. The space was barely the size of a bathroom stall, but it held the staircase that led to the third floor.

Mads stepped in behind her and tilted his head back, looking around as if he had never seen it before.

Arlo flipped on the switch and light trickled down from the bulb three stories above. By the time it got to them, it was not much more than a promising shadow. Mads unhooked his flashlight from his belt, switched it on, and shone it in front of him as he climbed the stairs. Arlo followed behind.

"What are you looking for?" she asked.

"I can't discuss the case," he said shortly. He trained the beam of his flashlight on one side of the staircase, then the other. She was fairly certain that Jason Rogers had done that same thing after Wally had taken his nosedive, but she wasn't about to point that out to Mads. If Wally had indeed been poisoned, then a killer was still out there on the loose.

The thought almost buckled her knees. She missed a step and nearly face-planted on the stairs. Only Mads's quick reflexes kept her from tumbling all the way back down to the bottom. And she thought he had forgotten she was there.

"Careful."

She nodded.

They continued up to the third floor. Mads was still examining the walls and stairs as he climbed the steps. Arlo concentrated on putting one foot in front of the other to keep from having another slip. Almost falling at her ex-boyfriend's feet once a day was more than enough.

They reached the third-floor landing and Arlo used another key to open the final door.

"Was this locked the day Wally died?"

She shook her head. Mads had asked her before, and she had given the same answer then as she did now. "The door from the street was locked, but I left this one unlocked so the Realtor would have an easier time showing the space."

"And once you lease the space, the tenant will want his own keys."

"Of course."

Mads nodded, then flipped on the light switch just inside the room.

A series of lights came on, lighting the space with a soft yellow glow that added to the rays of bright southern sunlight that managed to filter through the dirty windows.

Two wooden crates left by the previous owner sat facing each other near the window. The window where Wally had been pushed to his death.

Goose bumps skittered across her arms. She wasn't going to think about that. The wide inside ledge on the window gave the room a charming look. Like a person could sit there and gaze down at all the people on Main Street. Was that what Wally had been doing? Come to think of it, she didn't remember seeing the crates in front of the window the last time she had been on the third floor. They must have been pushed over next to the stack of boxes stored there. Or had they? She wished she knew for certain.

Aside from the couch Arlo had picked up for the second-floor reading nook that she never ended up creating and the half-dozen cases of paper supplies that Chloe had squirreled away over time, the space was empty.

"Chief? You up here?"

And speak of the devil.

Jason Rogers rounded the corner, pulling Mads from whatever thought he was processing.

"Yep." He waited until Jason crossed the room to stand next to them before he continued. "Show me where the cup was again."

Jason pointed to one of the crates. "Next to the wooden box."

"On the floor," Mads said. It wasn't really a question.

"On the floor," Jason said by way of confirmation.

"And there was only one." Mads again.

"Yes."

Which meant whoever pushed Wally had taken their own cup. If they had had one. Which could go either way really. But if it had been Chloe, then the tea would have given her away as surely as her DNA.

"What's wrong?" Arlo asked.

Jason jerked a thumb toward Mads. "Chief is upset. I know I put the cup in an evidence bag, and now we can't find it."

Mads shot him a look. Arlo had seen it before. Some things didn't need to be shared, and his chief officer's incompetence was at the top of the list. But Jason was a hometown boy who hadn't gone away to find a better life and then come back when it all fell through. He had been in Sugar Springs since birth, taking the occasional trip to Memphis and Tupelo to break the monotony. He was Sugar Springs through and through and the people there liked him. Even if he occasionally messed up.

"I kept the earring," Jason boasted, receiving another look from Mads.

"What earring?" Arlo asked.

Mads started to say something, but Jason plowed ahead. "I found a diamond earring. Right over there by the window." He puffed out his chest.

"I see."

"Big sucker too. Maybe even three carats. Biggest diamond I ever seen."

"Jason." Mads's tone was low in warning.

"Sorry, Chief."

A moment of silence fell among the three of them before Mads spoke again. "There was only one," he mused.

One cup and one earring. One *diamond* earring. Couldn't be too many pairs of three-carat diamond earrings out there. Only a handful of people in Sugar Springs could afford such an extravagance.

Mads turned and pinned Arlo with a sharp look. He was in full-out professional cop mode now. "Can you come down to the station this afternoon?"

"The station?" It was perhaps the last thing she expected him to ask. "I-I guess. I mean…why?"

"I want to go over your statement with you again."

"Yeah. Okay. Sure." Though she couldn't help wondering the reason.

"Good. See you then."

....

Soon after one o'clock, Arlo excused herself from the bookstore and took a walk down the street to the police station. She hadn't wanted to tell Chloe where she was going, so she mumbled something about the bank and made her escape.

She had been to the police station her fair share of times during her life in Sugar Springs. There had been the time that someone had let all the air out of the school bus tires and the principal had filed a police report over the matter, claiming he knew one of the members of the senior class had committed the act. They never did find out who was responsible. And then there was the time that Joe Campbell had thrown a tailgate party, not bothering to tell everyone that they weren't on his daddy's land when they parked. Instead, they had been in old man Gilbert's pasture, and old man Gilbert did not take kindly to trespassers. Those were probably the worst two times, but the atmosphere today was different than it had been then. The air almost crackled, as if the murder were zapping people like a jolt of static electricity. And everyone was working. Even Frances Jacobs, who answered the phone, was busy. Normally she was seated at her desk, today's *Commercial Appeal* open to the crossword and sudoku. She claimed it kept her mind sharp. Today, on her desk was a thick book like the old dictionary the school library had had when Arlo was a child. Well, one of the schools anyway. Her parents had moved her around so much she couldn't remember which. Only that the book had sat on a pedestal and was usually open to the page displaying unmentionable body parts.

"Did you find anything?" Mads came out of his office to peer over Frances's shoulder.

She sighed. "Not yet, and I wish you wouldn't do that. I'm trying to read."

He took a couple of steps back and held his hands up in surrender. "Okay, okay. But I still think it would be easier if you looked it up on the internet."

"Uh-huh." Frances dragged out the word to show her disbelief. "You have your way and I have mine."

Mads looked up and snagged Arlo's gaze as if he had only then realized that she was standing there. "Hey. I've got somebody in my office right now. Can you wait a few minutes?"

"Sure." She didn't want to wait a few minutes, but she didn't want to have to come back either.

"Good." Mads flashed her a quick smile, then ducked back into his office.

"Honestly, I adore that man, but his obsession with the internet." Frances shook her head.

Arlo bit back a laugh. "Most people are obsessed with the internet," she replied as gently as possible.

"I don't understand why." The chain that held her glasses around her neck swayed as Frances bobbed her head from side to side, her attention still trained on the enormous book in front of her.

"Maybe I can help you understand how the internet works."

"Mads and Jason have already tried."

And neither one of them would have the patience to teach a seventy-something-year-old woman who had never owned a computer how to use the internet.

"It's up to you," Arlo offered once again.

Frances cast a quick look to the door behind her, Mads's door, then motioned her over. "Come show me. He needs this information and I'm apparently the only one who can get it for him."

"Where's Jason?"

Frances waved a flighty hand in the air, her gaze once more on the tome open in front of her. "Somebody painted the school mascot on four of Johnny Ray's cows."

"Sounds like a senior prank."

"Probably, but he's upset since he was fixing to take them to the auction. Now he can't sell them until the paint wears off."

Arlo nodded. Johnny Ray Horton, part-time rancher, part-time preacher, was a stickler when it came to his cows. He was also adamantly opposed to the school mascot—the Blue Devils. Inevitably, at some time during the school year, someone from the senior class painted at least one of his cows with the mascot. Even with only a couple of weeks left in school, it seemed the pranks were still in full swing.

"We didn't need this with everything else going on." She motioned Arlo to come behind the desk. "Pull up a chair. This might take a while."

Arlo grabbed one of the padded desk chairs from the waiting area and hoisted it behind Frances's desk. "What are you needing to find?"

Frances glanced back at Mads's door once again and chewed on her lip, obviously trying to decide how much she could tell Arlo and still keep things confidential. "The coroner's report came back, and there was a strange poison in poor Mr. Harrison's blood. I'm trying to find it to see if we might be able to trace the source."

"That's easy enough. What's the name of the poison?"

Frances handed her a piece of paper.

Amanita phalloides.

"Okay," Arlo said, tucking a wayward strand of her hair behind her ear before bending close to Frances. "Type this into your search bar and hit the magnifying glass."

"Then what happens?"

Arlo straightened. "The internet gives you a list of possible sites to read about the subject you typed in."

Frances eyed her skeptically, then turned back to her computer. If she didn't use the internet, what did she do with the thing? "What's a search bar?"

Arlo bit back a sigh. This might not be as easy as she thought. She moved the mouse to wake up the black computer screen. A picture of Frances's three great-grandchildren popped into view.

"See this icon here?" She moved the cursor to the browser. "Click it. Viola. Search bar."

"And all I have to do is type this in and I'll get that list?"

"Yep." Arlo waited patiently for Frances to type in the unfamiliar words. It was as if the woman thought she was going to break the computer. Or the internet.

After a tentative click, a list of search results lined up like neat little soldiers, with image results in a sidebar on the right.

"Mushrooms?" Arlo asked.

"They can be deadly," Frances assured her. "I watched a documentary on it the other day."

"But people don't just go out and pick mushrooms, do they?"

"Of course they do."

After saying the words, Arlo remembered a trip into the forest in Oregon, she thought it was. It had simply been too long ago, and the memory wasn't anything incredibly special. Just a day she, Woody, and her parents went exploring. At the time she had thought they were doing something fun as a family, but now she knew better. Her parents had been out foraging for mushrooms. Probably the hallucinogenic kind. It was a wonder they all hadn't been poisoned.

"Is it a certain kind or something?" It had to be. Not all mushrooms were poisonous.

"Right here." Frances tapped the screen. Arlo simply stared at the mushroom pictured there.

It was white with a flat top and for the most part seemed perfectly harmless.

Frances peered closely at the screen and started to read. "'Amanita phalloides, commonly known as the *death cap*, is a poisonous basidiomycete fungus. Amanita phalloides forms ectomycorrhizas with various broad-leaved trees. It is one of many deadly fungi in the Amanita genus.'"

Death cap. Wally had eaten a death cap? The name alone was enough to turn anybody off. But the fact only solidified Mads's earlier words. The fall killed him, but he had been poisoned as well. Had the same person who poisoned Wally pushed him to his death?

10

"WHY WOULD ANYONE EAT SOMETHING LIKE THAT?" FRANCES asked.

"Arlo?"

She startled as Mads spoke her name. She was still sitting behind Frances, still staring at the sweet-looking little mushroom that, according to Wikipedia, had killed thousands in the Unites States alone. She straightened and smoothed her hands down the front of her slacks. She had given up skirts when she opened the bookstore. So many trips up the ladder would do nothing more than show everyone her underwear. "Yes?"

"Are you ready?" He frowned at her as if just then realizing that she was behind Frances's desk and was staring at the woman's computer screen.

"I should go."

Another man spoke, and Arlo watched as Sam stepped out from behind Mads.

What was he doing there?

"What are you doing here?" She blurted out the words.

Sam and Mads shared a look. Surely it had nothing to do with prom night. Surely...

Mads extended a hand toward the other man. "Good talking to you."

"You too." Sam clasped the chief's hand in his own and gave it what looked like a firm shake. Nothing out of the ordinary. Just a handshake between two friends.

As if.

But that had been years ago, and it looked as if Sam and Mads had buried the hatchet, so to speak. Or maybe they were plotting against her.

She almost laughed at the thought. All this murder business was starting to get to her.

"Arlo." Sam moved toward the front door, brushing past Arlo as he went, almost but not quite touching her as he moved away. She could smell the warmth of his body and his aftershave. It wasn't the same as way back when, but it smelled familiar all the same. As if something in Sam was a part of her, and now that he was back in town, that little part had suddenly woken up.

Ridiculous.

"You'll call me when everything's set?" Sam asked. He had stopped at the door.

"Of course."

That seemed to satisfy him. He nodded to Arlo and Frances, then pushed his way through the door and out of the building.

"Ready?" Mads gestured toward his office and Arlo breathed a sigh of relief that her thoughts were her own. And that she hadn't appeared to be staring off into nothing land as she dreamed about days long gone.

She was ushered into his office, then offered a chair and a drink before Mads moved behind his desk and pulled a piece of paper out of the side drawer. She couldn't read what was written across the top, but her gut told her that it had to do with Wally's death.

"So the morning that Wally was murdered. Where were you?"

Hadn't she already answered that? Twice even. Once for her official police report and the other to Mads himself just this morning.

"I was at home."

"You were at home until Frances called and told you to come down to the bookstore?"

"That's right."

"And that was around 9:00 a.m.?"

"Yes."

"Then what did you do?"

"I came down to the bookstore." She shot Mads a frown. Maybe Jason was right and being so long on a big police force like Memphis had turned him from hometown boy to super cop. "What is this about, Mads?"

"Answer the question, please."

"I already did." She frowned again.

"Did you go to the bookstore between the time you left Thursday evening until Friday morning when Frances called?"

"No."

"Did anyone else go into the bookstore then?"

"No. I mean, no one but Chloe."

He knew how it worked. In fact, he was one of the regular customers, coming in and getting a coffee long before the 9:00 a.m. mark when Arlo came in and officially opened the store.

"Could anyone else have come into the store without your knowledge?"

Did he know about Wally's visit with Chloe? She couldn't say anything in fear that it made Chloe look guilty as hell. No one had such a strong reason for wanting Wally dead as Chloe had.

But there was one thing that she was sure of and that was her friend's innocence.

"No. I mean, I suppose if they had a key. Look, do I need to get an attorney?"

It was Mads's turn to frown. "Of course not. I'm merely trying to determine who might have had access to the third floor at the time Wally was pushed out the window."

"Me, Chloe, and Sandy Green."

Mads wrote her name down. "And she's your Realtor?"

"That's right." In fact, she was the only one in town. There wasn't much competition on the real estate front in Sugar Springs.

"Are you aware of Sandy giving someone the key to the third floor that Thursday evening or early Friday morning?"

"No, but I suppose she could have given it to someone to check out the space for themselves." It wasn't like a big city where people didn't care, wouldn't lock up behind themselves, or would even need to lock up for that matter.

"Thanks, Arlo."

She blinked at him stupidly. "That's it?"

He nodded, then turned his attention to the notebook in front of him, the one he had been writing on the entire time she had been in his office.

She stood, unsure of what had transpired between them. "O-kay." She tugged on the tails of her button-down shirt and tucked that same strand of waist-length hair back behind her ear. She gave him another heartbeat to say something else. When he continued to make notes on the tablet in front of him, Arlo headed for the door.

"Arlo."

She stopped, one hand on the knob, ready to turn it and make her escape.

"When you get back to the store, send Chloe down. I need to talk to her next."

....

Every footstep grew heavier as she neared Books & More. Her shoes felt like they were made of marble. Or concrete. Wasn't that what the mob was famous for using when they tossed people into the river? Arlo's thoughts circled back around to the morning Wally was found in a broken heap on the sidewalk. Hadn't Chloe said something about a mob hit? Surely she had been joking...

Arlo shook her head, her imagination once again getting away from her.

The bell over the door was a welcoming sound as she returned to the sanctuary of her store. Was it bad to feel that this little piece of Sugar Springs was her safe place? Not even her home felt as homey as the bookstore.

"Welcome back," Faulkner squawked. "Come on in. Rest yourself."

Arlo smiled at the crazy bird. Maybe she did need a pet for her home. Or maybe she should try taking Faulkner home with her again. The last time she had done so, he had pulled out his tailfeathers, a sure sign of stress, so she had stopped. The tailfeathers had grown back and Arlo left Faulkner in the store overnight. It seemed to be the perfect arrangement. Faulkner had found a safe haven in Books & More.

"There you are." Fern rushed toward her, white handbag bumping her hip as Fern clasped her hands and pulled Arlo close. "Be careful," she whispered. "Camille is on the warpath."

Uh-oh. What was this about?

"We were about to send out a search party." This was from Helen.

Arlo smiled at her godmother, then turned her attention to the other member of their little group. Camille was frowning, but she didn't seem to be overly upset.

"What brings y'all out today?"

"We thought we'd meet again today to talk about the book."

"It's something else," Camille muttered.

"Now?" Arlo asked. "In the middle of the day?" There were customers milling around and a few gawkers that she had never seen before. Since Wally's death, the town seemed to be overrun with people out to see where he had died. *Takes all kinds.*

"Hey." A familiar male voice sounded behind her.

She had forgotten that they had added a member to their number. "Hi, Sam."

"I told them you were in talking to Mads so they wouldn't worry."

"Thanks." She wasn't sure she wanted the three overprotective ladies to know that Mads was still questioning people in Wally's case. Or that it had turned into a murder investigation. They would all find out soon enough. But it wouldn't be from her telling. "Speaking of…" She eased over to the coffee bar where Chloe was still over-polishing every piece of stainless-steel equipment they had. "Mads wants to talk to you." Arlo lowered her voice so only the two of them could hear. She knew all four of them—the three ladies and Sam—were watching, but that didn't mean they needed to know what she was saying.

Chloe stopped polishing, placed her hands on the counter, and lowered her head. "All right." She heaved in a big breath and started to move away.

Arlo stopped her with one hand on her arm. "Is there something you want to tell me?"

Chloe shook her head.

"You know you can tell me anything right?"

She nodded.

"We're best friends and I love you."

"I didn't kill him," she whispered. Not vehemently, as one might expect, but resigned. As if she knew she would be called to repeat the words over and over whether anyone believed her or not.

"I know." Arlo squeezed her arm reassuringly, then let her go.

"I'll be back when I can."

Arlo smiled and watched her friend walk out the door without removing her apron.

"Is she okay?" Sam asked.

Arlo brightened her smile, deepened it until it hurt her cheeks. "Of course. I think her allergies are bothering her."

Helen *tsk*ed. "Summer allergies are the worst." But Arlo had a feeling, no matter the truth in her words, Helen only said them to back up Arlo's excuse. The woman might be a little eccentric, but she was one smart cookie.

"Why are you all here again?" Arlo asked.

"We've decided to meet every day for lunch to read our chapters. Isn't that a great idea?" Fern gushed.

"It was Helen's idea," Camille added a little less enthusiastically than Fern.

She probably wanted to get away from the inn for a couple of hours and this was a sure way to do it.

Arlo turned to Sam. "You're still going along with this new schedule?"

He smiled that smile she remembered so well. The smile that had broken her teenage heart into a billion pieces. "Sure," he said. "Why not? It'll be a fun way to reacquaint myself with Sugar Springs."

"Why not?" Arlo mumbled. *Because you have a job*, she wanted to yell. *And because the last thing I want to see is your handsome face every day!* Or really the truth was the last thing she wanted to want was seeing his handsome face every day, but the thought made her a little light-headed, so she pushed it aside.

"When Sam gets the third floor, all he'll have to do is come down for the meeting and then go right back to work when it's over."

If he gets the third floor, you mean. It wasn't his yet. But if he wanted to lease it, there was no way she could justify not letting him. Books & More needed the extra money it would bring in. It was a hard business, living in a small town. A successful person had to be clever.

She looked back to him. He was still smiling, the skunk.

"Isn't that a wonderful idea?" Fern put in.

"Wonderful." Arlo agreed.

An everyday book club that met to read the book together? It was a little off the charts, but there it was.

....

The book club sans Sam—thank God he had a previous engage-ment and only stopped in to let the ladies know—settled down in the seating area, and Arlo tried to ignore both them and the fact that Chloe was gone. She had gotten so used to her friend sitting behind the angled counter of the coffee nook that not having her there left a feeling of emptiness. Not to mention there was no one to make any coffee drinks until three thirty when Courtney Adams, the high school senior Chloe had hired as part-time help in the afternoons, came in. The mornings weren't so busy that she couldn't handle it by herself, but Arlo knew that after such a long shift, it was good for Chloe to get out from behind her counter and breathe in some fresh air. Or even just air that wasn't urban roast scented.

"Sorry," Arlo called from the top of the ladder in general fic-tion. A customer was standing at the coffee bar. That was one good thing about having to climb the ladders in the store: she could see the most of it in one sweeping look. "We won't have a barista for another thirty minutes. If you care to wait, your drink will be half off."

The woman turned and Arlo saw it was Daisy James-Harrison, Wally's wife. "I'm—" The woman's voice was high pitched enough to bring the dogs in. She cleared her throat and started over. "I'm here to see Chloe."

Interesting.

Arlo eased down the ladder, then set the stack of books she had been shelving on a nearby display table. She resisted the urge to smooth her hair and check her clothing before making her way over to the woman. Daisy James-Harrison really was a stunning creature. She was the kind of person who had such a natural beauty it was hard to imagine them in any sort of nonbeautiful situation, like going to the bathroom or having hat hair. And though Arlo had never been considered beautiful or even cute—she had always been pretty, but in a soft tone, as if to say *she's not ugly so what else can you call it?*—next to Daisy James-Harrison, she felt a little like a homeless person at the Miss America Pageant.

Ridiculous.

She pulled on her shirttails and raised herself to her full height. Daisy was small even in her high heels but instead of feeling powerful, Arlo felt like a lumbering giant. "What do you need to see Chloe about?"

Arlo was all too aware of the book club members watching her every move.

"It's of a personal nature." Her accent wasn't Deep South and not even close to Midwestern. Arlo remembered she was from Missouri, born and raised in the Show Me State. It was part of the "greater south," as Helen liked to call it. The greater south was the Deep South along with two states on any side: Mississippi, Georgia, Alabama, Tennessee, Virginia, Oklahoma, Arkansas, Missouri, and of course Texas.

"She'll be back in a few minutes." At least Arlo hoped she would. Chloe had been gone for almost two hours.

Daisy glanced one way and then the other. The book club ladies watched her every move. When Arlo looked at them, they all went back to reading. Or pretending to.

"It's about Wally's will," Daisy admitted.

"What about it?"

Arlo could almost see the wheels in her mind turning as Daisy decided what to say out loud. "Chloe may have been mentioned in the will, and the attorney wants her there for the reading."

"Bill Lansing?" He was the only attorney Sugar Springs had.

Daisy shook her head. "Joseph A. Cartwright. He's coming in from New York. Wally always said he wanted his will read before the funeral, and since we aren't allowed to leave town yet…"

Arlo hadn't thought about that. Of course Daisy and Inna would both be suspects in the murder investigation and unable to leave until Mads released them. "I'll let Chloe know," Arlo said. "When's the reading?"

"Tomorrow afternoon at three. The attorney has rented a room at the inn."

Perfect. Now Helen was involved, and if she knew Wally's attorney was in town, it was a sure bet the others knew as well. Arlo could only imagine. The ladies would probably move their book club meeting to the inn so they could eavesdrop on the reading. She wouldn't put it past any of them, not even Helen.

"Thanks," Arlo said.

Daisy gave her a hesitant smile, then left the bookstore.

"I knew it," Helen said. "I told you a fancy New York lawyer could only be here for Wally's death."

"Pay up." Fern held out one hand to Camille, who frowned but fished into that huge white bag of hers and pulled out a dollar bill.

"How did you know he was an attorney?" Arlo asked. It wasn't like that was necessary information for renting a room.

Fern looked up, her eyes as innocent as a small child's caught with his hand in the cookie jar. "Google."

"I guess if Chloe's going to the will reading, then Wally's leaving her something for Jayden," Helen said.

Camille gasped. "I forgot all about that boy. Well, not forgot him, but that his father was Wally Harrison."

"Wally gave up all legal rights to Jayden a long time ago," Arlo commented. "He doesn't owe them anything."

"Legal rights be damned," Fern said vehemently. "When a man fathers a child, he should take care of it."

Arlo agreed one hundred percent but had been around enough to know that it wasn't always the case. Jayden wasn't the only child forgotten by a parent. Some were forgotten by both. It was one of the things in the world that saddened her most. That and those SPCA commercials that came on late at night.

She checked the large library clock hanging above the upstairs bookcases. What was taking Chloe so long?

The door opened and Courtney walked in. A chorus of greetings came from all around as she made her way to the office to store her tiny handbag. It was almost as much of a mystery as Camille's, except Arlo wanted to know if Courtney could actually fit anything into the tiny pouch.

Arlo checked the clock once more as Courtney came out, tying her apron behind her back.

How many times had she looked at the clock? Too many to count. But now that Courtney was there, she wasn't tied to the bookstore. And now that she wasn't tied to the bookstore…

"Arlo?" Helen's voice floated around her like a warm hug.

"I'm going to check on Chloe." How long did things like this take anyway? "Courtney?"

The young girl nodded. "I got this."

"I'll go with you." Helen placed her bookmark between the pages to save her place, then set it aside and stood.

"Brilliant idea." Camille beamed. She followed Helen's lead, saved her place, and adjusted her purse for the short walk to the police station.

Not to be outdone, Fern dropped her copy of *Missing Girl* and was on her feet in a heartbeat. "Let's go."

"Ladies…" She didn't want them to cause any more problems

for Chloe—and it seemed inevitable now that she was definitely having a problem or two—but she also wasn't looking forward to walking into the police station alone to whatever news awaited her. She sighed. "Come on." She waved one arm over her shoulder and smiled her thanks to Courtney.

The ladies chatted about Jayden, Wally, and Chloe all the way to the station, but Arlo was too nervous to pay much attention.

She stopped at the double glass doors that led inside and took a deep breath. Sugar Springs Police Station twice in one day. That had to be a record.

Frances looked up from her place behind the desk as Arlo came in, relief flooding her features as she hung up the phone. "Thank heavens you're here."

"What's wrong?" Arlo had a terrible feeling she knew exactly what was wrong.

"It's Chloe. Mads arrested her for Wally's murder."

11

THAT LOUD BUZZING STARTED IN HER EARS AGAIN.

Chloe can't be a murderer! Have you lost your marbles?

What in heaven's name possessed him to do something so stupid?

This is ridiculous! I demand you release her immediately.

But Arlo knew the truth of the matter: Chloe looked guilty, even if she wasn't.

And by now she had surely told Mads about Wally's early morning visit. How she had given him the coffee that had been the last thing he had ingested. And by now Mads had remembered all the stories he had heard about Chloe, Wally, and Jayden. It didn't matter what he knew and what he had been told. There was a big enough grapevine that repeated and re-repeated the stories that a person had trouble remembering what they knew firsthand and what they had heard at the barber shop.

But what about the earring? That was the one piece of evidence that didn't fit.

Arlo marched around Frances's desk to the closed door of Mads's office. She wrenched it open without knocking, somewhat surprised to find him alone.

"Arlo." He didn't seem surprised to see her. It was almost as if he had been sitting there waiting for her to storm into his office. He was seated behind his desk, one booted foot crossed over his other knee. He loosely held a pencil in one hand as he lightly bounced it against the wood of his desk, eraser end down.

"You have made a big mistake," she said on one long rush of air.

"I have?" More pencil drumming.

"Huge," she said. "And now you have to let Chloe go."

"I wish I could." His words sounded sincere enough, but they weren't at all what Arlo wanted to hear.

"She's innocent. She doesn't even own diamond earrings, much less ones that are three carats."

He frowned and his pencil tempo increased. "I have a lot more evidence that fits. The earring…we don't even know if it was left there by a previous tenant—"

"In Sugar Springs? Please. Only Judith Whitney has that kind of money here and we all know she would die before she would surrender a diamond that big."

A deep crease marred Mads's forehead. The pencil bouncing stopped.

Poor choice of words on her part.

"Mads," Arlo tried again. "You and I both know that Chloe isn't capable of murder."

He shook his head sadly. "Everyone is capable of murder."

What a cynical way to look at life.

"You know what I mean."

He sighed, tossed the pencil onto his desktop, and stood. The yellow no. 2 rolled to a stop before toppling over the far edge. "I do, and I'll tell you what else I know. Ground up death cap mushrooms were found in the coffee cup Chloe gave Wally that morning. The morning he told her he wanted to forget the legal document he had signed ten years ago and visit with his son. We know that Chloe has been having a little bit of financial trouble—"

"Who hasn't?" Arlo was barely aware of the book club ladies and Frances clustering around the office door. Mads had to have seen them. He saw everything. But he ignored them and continued. "Her father is about to lose his business."

"Why didn't she tell me?" Arlo whispered.

Mads shrugged. "Maybe she didn't want to worry you."

It wasn't like Arlo had any funds to help. Her entire life savings, along with a hefty loan, were all wrapped up in Books & More.

"Money troubles don't make her a murderer," Arlo said.

Mads tipped his head to one side. "Did you know she was part of Wally's will?"

Arlo nodded slowly.

"With a number-one bestseller under his belt, Wally has the kind of money that can make a difference in her parents' situation. And since Jayden lives with them…"

"Can I see her?"

Behind her, a chorus of pleas to do the same rose from the book club ladies.

Mads held up both hands. "Okay. Okay. One at a time. But you only have about five minutes. The transport vehicle to Corinth will be here soon."

A round of protests went up from the book club.

Arlo pinned Mads with her hardest buy-the-book-or-get-out look. He didn't seem fazed. But she plowed ahead anyway. "Why would you take her all the way to the county jail?"

"She has been charged with murder." It wasn't much of an explanation.

"You and I both know she's not guilty. I don't even know why you arrested her," Arlo said. Maybe if she continued to say those words, they would sink into his thick skull.

"Evidence." The word was clipped, hard and cold, like shards chipped from an iceberg.

"Evidence my—"

"Arlo!" Helen, the ever-diligent godmother, interrupted from behind.

Arlo turned back to Mads. "Fine. Arrest her. But don't send her to the county jail. She doesn't belong there."

She could almost see his resolve cracking. "What am I supposed to do with her?"

"Release her on her own recognizance?"

"It's not up to me." Mads crossed his arms and puffed out his chest. He seemed to grow two feet across. It was an intimidating pose and he knew it.

"Then keep her in a cell here so she can be close to her family."

He opened his mouth to protest, so she continued. "She's not stupid. She's not going to try to escape. Let her stay in the holding cells."

"I can't keep her there indefinitely."

"A week or two then." Just long enough for Arlo to figure out who really killed Wally.

She wasn't sure where the idea came from, but there it was.

She had read plenty of mystery novels in her lifetime, from Encyclopedia Brown to Sherlock Holmes. She might not have police skills, but she was smart. Mads had all this training and still didn't know Chloe was innocent. How much good could all those police schools be anyway, if someone like Mads couldn't figure out that Chloe wasn't capable of murdering Wally Harrison? She simply wasn't strong enough to topple him out the window.

Another thought popped into Arlo's head. Chloe wasn't strong enough to kill Wally...unless he was already weak and dying. Then she would only have to push him forward and use his own weight to do the rest.

But had he been sick? How long did *Amanita* poisoning take? She had no idea. There was another project for Camille and her beloved Google.

"Ten days," he finally said. "But you'll have to feed her."

"What?"

"We aren't set up to have long-term detainees. She'll need three meals a day, and I can't provide them. So if you want her to stay, the five of you"—he pointed a sweeping finger at them—"will have to make sure she eats."

"Deal," Frances said immediately.

"I'll do supper," Helen said. "I'll already be cooking for the inn, so it's no bother to make a little bit more."

"Good. Good," Frances said. "And I'll be here for lunch so I'll bring in some for her."

"Arlo." They all turned to look at her. "Can you do breakfast?" Camille asked.

Was this really happening? Were they really discussing who would bring Chloe her meals *in jail*?

"Arlo?" Helen nudged her arm.

Arlo pulled herself from her stupor. "Yeah. Breakfast. Got it."

"Good," Mads said. "Now that it's all settled, get out of my office."

"After we see Chloe." Arlo gave him a bitter smile.

She hadn't managed to free her friend, but perhaps this was a start.

....

The holding cells at the Sugar Springs Police Station were small but clean. There were two of them side by side in a far room of the building. The bars were painted black and chipped in a few spots, the walls a pukey green. A few people had left their mark behind, scratched into the walls. *Freddie was here. This sucks.* And a few other things Arlo wouldn't repeat. It was ugly and sad, and for a moment Arlo wondered if there was a failed designer out there somewhere who had come up with the color scheme. Hopefully they had another job now.

"Arlo." Chloe rushed to the bars of her cell, her face lighting up with joy.

"Hey, girl."

"I didn't do it." Her eyes filled with tears. "I know it looks like I did, but I swear I didn't. I swear."

"Shhh…" Arlo did her best to hug her friend through the bars.

Chloe pressed her face into Arlo's shoulder and started to cry.

"Come on, now," Arlo said gently. "Mads only gave me five minutes. I don't want to spend all of that with you crying."

Chloe pulled away, sniffed, and wiped her tears with the back of one hand. "Sorry."

"It's okay." Arlo smiled gently at her friend. "And it's going to be okay. We convinced Mads to let you stay here for a while." She didn't bother to tell Chloe how long. Ten days was an eternity and a drop in the bucket when looking at life without parole for murder.

"We?"

"The book club ladies came with me. And Frances."

"Frances from the front desk?"

Arlo nodded. "Mads said you can stay here, and we'll bring you food every day."

"Why?" Chloe shook her head. Arlo knew she didn't want to get her hopes up. "It'd be easier if they took me to the county jail."

"We don't care about *easier*, and I won't be able to focus on finding the real murderer if I have to worry about you all the way over there."

"Find the real murderer?" Chloe repeated.

"That's right. We're going to bring you food, figure out who killed Wally, and get you out of jail." All in ten glorious days.

"And feed my cat."

Arlo smiled. "Of course."

A knock sounded on the open door.

"Time to go." Mads stood just this side of the doorway.

Arlo smiled at Chloe. "Be patient," she said, then lowered her voice so Mads couldn't hear her next words. "I'm going to get you out of here."

....

"How?" Helen asked as they all settled back into the reading area at Books & More. Arlo had expected them to disperse, go back to their homes and lives, but there they sat, drinking coffee from the Keurig and discussing ways to get Chloe out of jail instead of reading or talking about *Missing Girl*. You know, like a book club should be doing. A normal one anyway.

"We need to find out who the real killer is," Camille said in that soft, lilting accent of hers.

Fern shook her head, obviously annoyed. "Really? We hadn't thought of that."

"I mean to say that's the only way we're going to get poor Chloe out of jail. Mads isn't going to let her go for anything less," Camille returned.

"She's right," Helen said.

Those words stilled the air around them as each of the women let them sink in. Fern finally broke the silence.

"I don't know how to find a killer."

"Follow the clues," Helen said simply. The words held everything and nothing, the secret to the universe and the most useless advice ever muttered.

"What clues?" Fern was losing her patience. She, of all of them, favored Chloe above everything else. Arlo wasn't sure why.

Helen snapped her fingers, then swung her two-toned braid onto her other shoulder. "What was it Sam was saying?"

"He was talking about the suicide note," Camille said. "But we know now that it's a fake."

"The killer must have written the note while on the third floor with Wally," Fern added.

Which could mean the murderer hadn't meant to kill him then and pushing him out the window was a secondary plan to poison.

That was assuming that one person poisoned him, then pushed him to his death. But who would want Wally dead that badly?

Or perhaps they were dealing with two killers...

"Arlo."

The sound of her name brought Arlo out of her stupor, and she turned to face Helen. "Yes?"

"Do you have Sam's phone number?"

That really brought her back to the here and now. "What? Why would I have his number?"

"You two were a thing back in the day. So I thought he might have given it to you since he's been home."

"I had a thing with Mads too and I—" Bad argument. "No," Arlo said as calmly as possible. "I don't have his number. Why do you need it?"

"We were thinking about hiring him to find out who really killed Wally."

She really needed to pay more attention to the book club ladies if they were going to go off on missions like this. "No. Absolutely not."

Fern nodded, as if she had expected as much. "Then it'll be up to us."

"Wait. What?"

If Arlo had hoped to stop them, she was too late. The ideas flew fast and furious.

"We need to find our number-one suspect first, then stake out his house." Helen clapped her hands together.

"Or *her* house," Camille corrected. "The killer could be a woman."

"Right." Helen nodded.

"Oh, a stakeout." Pure joy lit Fern's features. "What will we wear?"

"Do you think the hardware store will have one of those black knit caps?" Camille asked. "You know like the kids wear in the wintertime. Well, and sometimes in the summer. You know, right?"

Yes, Arlo knew exactly. And she had seen these women at work together at school auctions, bake sales, and other fund-raisers. When they set their minds to something, there was no way of stopping them.

Ground rules. That's what they needed.

Arlo came around the side of the couch and sat down near Camille and her purse. "Listen," she started gently. "I know this is a big happening in Sugar Springs. And I know that you ladies care about Chloe and want to see her out of jail. But you have to be careful about what you do and say."

Sugar Springs might be the kind of town where a person could leave their door unlocked and not worry, but there was a murderer among them now.

Chances were the killer had a direct problem with Wally and most likely wouldn't kill again—unless their life felt threatened. Like with twenty to life for first-degree murder because some little old meddling grannies decided to play *Law & Order*. If the ladies were going to poke around, they needed to be careful.

"Of course, dear." Helen smiled.

"I don't want any of you going around questioning people or—" She had been about to say *going on stakeouts,* but she didn't want them to get excited again. "Poking into things you shouldn't. I know Chloe appreciates your love and concern, but you have to keep yourselves safe."

"But, love—" Camille started in protest.

Arlo shook her head. "Safety is key."

"And what will happen to Chloe if we don't find the killer?" It was the one thing on everyone's mind, but only Fern was willing to say it out loud.

"I'll talk to Mads," Arlo promised. She wasn't sure what good it would do, but she would talk to him.

"Didn't you already do that?" Fern asked.

"I'll do it again." And again and again, until she was blue in the face. Maybe that would convince him to release Chloe and drop these ridiculous charges.

Helen pursed her lips and nodded. "I understand. You're concerned for us."

"That's right. And you can talk about what's happening, but you shouldn't start running around looking for clues that may or may not be there. It's simply too dangerous." *Especially if the killer is desperate.*

"I suppose you're right," Camille said, sounding resigned.

"Good." Arlo smiled at the little group. "So you'll meet here and talk about the case here, and then once you leave, it's like a book. You put it down and walk away until you can pick it up again." She was entirely too proud of the analogy.

The ladies nodded.

"Then we're definitely meeting every day," Camille said.

"Absolutely." Fern nodded.

"I'll have news from the inn," Helen said. "Hopefully. Single men do like to talk."

Arlo sighed. "We can't have book club every day."

The ladies turned to look at her as if she had lost her cotton-pickin' mind.

"What?" she asked.

"Dear," Fern started in that not-so-gentle voice of hers. Arlo had heard her use it many times before with her pre-teen Sunday School class. "Of course we're not having book club every day. The book-store store isn't open on Sunday."

"We can meet at the inn on Sunday," Helen added.

Fern turned back to Arlo. "See? We *can* meet every day."

"And we should," Camille said emphatically. "Until we get this killer behind bars."

....

I'm not going to worry. I'm not going to worry. Arlo chanted the mantra silently over and over, hoping that she would actually stop worrying. But the words just made her remember all the crazy ideas the book club ladies had about the case and ways for them to get information—everything from prank- calling anyone involved in hopes that they would slip and reveal something to petitioning Mads for a police report.

Thankfully, the rest of that meeting happened without any major incidents. They simply talked about people who were involved and made a list of everyone suspicious. Maybe by tomorrow they would grow bored with the whole idea and give it up permanently, but Arlo was not holding her breath.

She parked her car in Chloe's drive, grabbed the spare key from the birdfeeder that hung by the front door, then made her way inside.

And then there was Auggie and his feeding. Not that Arlo minded, but she didn't think the cat liked her all that much. He might let her pet him from time to time, but there were definitely some trust issues.

As Arlo stepped over the threshold, her first thought was that someone had broken into Chloe's tiny house. The freestanding lamp had been knocked over, the shade torn. The quilt Chloe kept on the back of the sofa had been dragged onto the floor and...was that a hole in it? It was. Yet Chloe's laptop was still sitting on the coffee table. Arlo glanced around; other items that were considered valuable remained untouched.

The one plant Chloe kept on the small kitchen bar had been knocked over and dirt was scattered across the floor. But it was the marks in the dirt that exposed the culprit.

"Auggie," she called. Of course he ignored her. What else were cats good for? "You dang cat."

Auggie meowed at her from the bedroom door, then sauntered down the hall toward the kitchen. His tail twitched as he slunk along. He stopped halfway and cast an amber glance over one ginger-striped shoulder, seeing if she had obeyed and was following him.

"I know you want to be fed, but this mess needs to be cleaned up first. See, if you hadn't made the mess, then you would be eating right now."

Auggie meowed again, then ignored her as she set about to straighten up.

In under fifteen minutes, she had almost everything back in order.

"How did the quilt get a hole in it?" she wondered.

Auggie blinked his golden eyes at her, but he didn't have a comeback. He was standing next to his dry-food bowl, as if that alone would show her that it needed to be filled. Not that it was empty. It never was, but Auggie liked fresh food every day. She supposed she couldn't blame him for that.

"Just a little longer," she told him, then she went to the hall closet to get out the vacuum cleaner.

Auggie saw what she intended to do and bolted under the couch.

"Dumb cat," she muttered, although deep down she liked the orange beast. Tuna breath, moody temperament, and all.

The vacuum cleaner whooshed to life. Auggie's tail stuck out from under the couch, swishing rapidly back and forth. Arlo wondered what would happen if she touched it. That cat would probably jump through the roof.

She turned off the vacuum and shooed Auggie down the hallway and back into Chloe's bedroom. He would be happier there while she cleaned. The dirt from the plant had managed to get under the sofa. Arlo unhooked the hose and added the attachment to clean under the edge of the couch.

The nozzle hit something, maybe a cat toy, and the suction attached whatever it was to the end of her hose.

She pulled it out from under the couch.

It was a small velvet box, deep purple in color and made of velour. It was the kind of box that jewelry came in. Expensive jewelry.

Arlo opened the box and gasped. It contained an earring—not two, but one—one earring. One earring just like the one Jason found at the crime scene.

She snapped the box closed, then opened it again to be sure. Yep, one three-carat diamond earring. Only one.

"Meow." Auggie wound himself between her legs, looking for attention and food. Mostly food.

"Fine," she muttered, then closed the box once again. She didn't want to look at it. It sent too many questions flying through her brain. Like where Chloe had gotten such an earring. Why wasn't there a pair of them? And what was this earring doing underneath the couch?

Arlo filled Auggie's dry-food bowl, gave him fresh water, and gave him the can of special food that Chloe provided each night. Arlo suspected the choice treatment made the cat a bit spoiled, but she could find no fault with it. Especially not tonight.

She picked up the little velvet box from where she had placed it on the table and opened it once again. Nope, while she had been feeding and caring for Auggie, the second diamond hadn't magically appeared. She snapped the box closed and put it back on the counter. She shouldn't have moved it. She shouldn't have messed with it at all. What if that was the other earring to match the one Jason had?

What was she saying? She knew it was. The question was what was it doing in Chloe's house?

12

ARLO WAS PRETTY SURE SHE LOOKED LIKE DEATH WARMED OVER when she walked into the police station the next morning. She had spent a near-sleepless night trying to figure out how the earring got into Chloe's house, where it had come from, and if her best friend was capable of murder.

The first two questions had no answers but the last one was an emphatic no. Chloe was not capable of killing Wally. Unfortunately, she still loved him very much—a fact she brought up every time she'd had too many piña coladas at the Round Up, the local watering hole just outside of Sugar Springs.

Chloe had loved Wally since they started high school and she loved him still. He was the father of her child and despite all the controversy and adversity they had suffered through the years, Chloe could never have killed him.

"Good morning," Arlo said as she neared the front desk.

Frances looked up with a smile. "Here for Chloe's breakfast?"

Arlo held up a paper sack containing two bagels and a container of strawberry cream cheese. The small purple jewelry box was tucked into the front of her bra, and she was careful how she moved her arms for risk of exposing it.

"Go on back." Frances went back to the crossword in the morning *Commercial Appeal* as Arlo slipped past.

She was nervous, as if she were sneaking in a file or a gun. The earring was nothing so useful or lethal as the two, but she had a feeling it held a power all its own.

"Morning, Dan." She waggled her fingers in an almost-wave at the other full-time officer in Sugar Springs. Dan Hayden had been on the force as long as Arlo could remember. He was as big as a mountain and as sweet as pie. A gentle giant. Over the years his hair had turned gray and his demeanor had further mellowed, but no one had the heart to tell him it was time to retire. Not much happened in Sugar Springs anyway. So what did it matter if one of the officers was a little slow on the draw?

"Morning, Arlo." Dan nodded his head in time with his deep voice as Arlo walked past.

It took everything that she had to walk slowly down the hall to the room where Chloe was being held. She was sure she looked suspicious, guilty even, as she smuggled in the small velvet box, but no one stopped her as she entered the room that contained the cells.

"Hey." Chloe's voice was as tired as she looked. As tired as Arlo felt.

Arlo pasted on a bright smile and held out the sack. "I have breakfast."

"Is there fruit?"

"There is if you consider strawberry cream cheese a fruit."

Chloe sighed. "I guess it'll have to do."

"I'll have one of the ladies bring you some watermelon later, okay?"

Chloe nodded. "I don't mean to sound ungrateful."

"I know." Arlo took the bagels from the sack and handed one to Chloe.

It was an old argument between the two of them. Arlo had grown up eating quinoa before it was cool, kale and bran and wheat germ and all the other disgusting things that were considered healthy. If she never saw another kale leaf in her entire life, it would be too soon.

Chloe, on the other hand, loved to eat anything green and everything healthy. It was the one big thing that separated them.

They spread the cream cheese on their bagels, then started to eat.

"Anything interesting happening?"

Arlo nodded. "There was one thing I wanted to talk to you about."

Two really.

"Yeah?"

"Auggie is acting out. He trashed the living room last night."

Chloe closed her eyes and leaned her head back against the cinder block wall. "I was afraid of that."

"What?" Arlo took another bite of bagel and waited for her to answer.

"Remember Cancún?"

Arlo smiled. Did she ever! Cancún was among her all-time favorite memories. They'd had such a good time. Danced, drank, flirted with men, and walked on the beach—alone and with said men. But… "What does that have to do with Auggie?"

"He did the same thing while I was there. I think it's separation anxiety."

"Separation anxiety? In your cat?"

Chloe nodded miserably.

"But he's…a cat."

"I know."

"That's ridiculous," Arlo said.

"What can I say? He loves me. Plus, he was a shelter cat, so I'm sure he's been abandoned before. He's afraid it will happen again."

"What do I do?"

"Take him home with you?" Chloe suggested, but it was almost a question.

"So he can trash my house? I won't be there during the day either."

"To work then."

"Faulkner—"

Chloe shook her head. "Please. Faulkner can hold his own. He's almost as big as Auggie is anyway. And if he's in his cage, Auggie won't be able to get to him. Perfect."

It was far from perfect, but what else could Arlo do?

"Fine." She sighed and dumped her trash back into the paper sack, then held it open for Chloe. "Last night, when I was cleaning up the mess, I found something."

"What?"

Arlo looked to the security cameras they had on the front corner and turned her back to it. Anyone watching wouldn't be able to see what she was doing. She hoped anyway. "I found this." She fished out the velvet box and showed it to Chloe.

"What?" she asked. "You found that in my house?"

"Are you listening?"

"I've never seen that before. What is it?"

Arlo flipped open the box and showed Chloe what was inside. She recoiled like it was a snake.

"Wh-where did you get that?" she whispered.

"Under the couch."

"In my living room?"

"Do you have another couch I don't know about?"

Chloe shook her head. "But how did it get there?"

"That's what I was hoping you would tell me."

Chloe closed her eyes as if trying to put everything in focus. "This really messes me up."

It was the only piece of evidence that didn't fit.

"Have you told Mads?" Chloe asked.

"Are you crazy?" Arlo's words were an urgent, incredulous whisper.

"You have to." Chloe seemed resigned to the fate that would fall if Mads knew.

"I don't."

"You can't withhold evidence."

"Thank you, Judge Judy, but I know it doesn't belong to you. So whose is it and how did it get in your bungalow?"

....

"Only two people have earrings like that in this town and neither one of them live here, so I say it's a bust." Helen threw up her hands and let them fall back into her lap.

The book club meeting was not going as planned. There had been no breaks in the case other than the earring Arlo found in Chloe's house, and Arlo had not mentioned that to the ladies. That information would stay between her and Chloe.

After promising to take Chloe a fresh set of clothes appropriate for the reading of the will, Arlo went back to the bookstore and did her best to act like nothing important had happened. She had been holding the secret for an entire day and it was starting to wear on her.

"Help! Help!" A loud squawk came from Faulkner's cage.

"Bad kitty," Camille said, jumping to her feet. She tried to shoo him off the top of Faulkner's cage. Auggie wasn't budging.

The cat was barely balanced on the thin wires. Faulkner continued to holler *Help* though every time Auggie's foot slipped through the tiny bars he nipped at it.

It was clear the tabby had found himself in a situation that wasn't as he expected.

Arlo rushed over, jumped onto the couch, and pulled him from the top of the cage. "How did you get up there?" She hugged the cat close as she hopped to the ground. Auggie held on for dear life, digging his claws into her shoulder and stomach as she escorted him from the reading area.

"Go play upstairs," she said, releasing him onto the staircase.

Auggie hissed, like he was a mean cat, then scampered up the stairs and disappeared among the large bookshelves.

Arlo shook her head. Maybe bringing him to the store was a bad idea.

"Here, kitty, kitty, kitty," Faulkner called.

"Hush, Faulkner."

A deep masculine laugh sounded close to her and she turned to find Sam Tucker standing next to her.

How had he gotten in? Had she been so preoccupied with the bird and cat situation that she hadn't heard the bell?

"What are you doing here?"

"Hi to you too." He smiled. "I am part of the book club, and we're meeting every day to get Chloe out of jail. Aren't we?"

"That's right." Fern raised her arms above her head in triumph. So far there had been nothing to celebrate. At least her enthusiasm was encouraging.

"Plus, I'm your new neighbor." He pointed toward the third floor.

"Seriously?" She smiled at Sam but the motion felt a bit forced.

"I signed the lease this morning," he said. "I came by to tell you that the locksmith will be here first thing tomorrow morning to rekey the third-floor door."

Perfect. Now she would get to see both exes every morning. Life was good.

"Okay."

"You don't seem very enthusiastic," he commented.

She shook her head. "Chloe."

"I understand."

Arlo sighed. "I'm trying to take care of her cat—who by the way has separation anxiety—along with a bird that keeps calling him over, as if he wants to get eaten."

Sam chuckled. "Tell you what. Let me get my desk and files moved in, and I'll keep Chloe's cat."

"Really?" It was the best news she had heard all day. It might take a bit for Sam to get moved in, but surely she could stand a couple more days living with the orange beast.

"Sure."

Arlo eyed him suspiciously. "Why are you being so nice?"

"I wasn't nice before?"

"Well, yeah. But not now. I mean, is there an ulterior motive to your offer?"

He propped his hands on those slim, denim-clad hips and eyed her right back. "Way to put it all out there, Arlo."

"Are you going to answer?"

"Yes."

"Yes, you're going to answer—or yes, you have ulterior motives?"

"Both. Have dinner with me."

Arlo took a step back. He had broken her heart once. She wasn't going to let it happen again. "I can't."

"Can't or won't?"

"Both," she answered.

"Heavens to Betsy." It was Helen. "That girl."

"Go out with him," Fern hissed in a stage whisper, easily heard by anyone on the second floor.

"You know I'm going to keep asking," Sam said. "And they're all backing me up." He gestured to the ladies, who nodded happily.

Arlo rolled her eyes. "And I'm just going to keep saying no."

....

"You are the most stubborn child I have ever known," Helen said once Sam had left.

Arlo shrugged. *Do not engage.* It was the best way. How could she explain to her godmother that Sam asking her out would be like her asking Mads on a date? Those ships had sailed and sunk. There was no going back to that port. Or whatever sailing analogy was appropriate. It wasn't going to happen.

"Go away! Go away!" Faulkner screeched.

Arlo looked up from sorting through the box of second-hand romance novels that she'd had stored on the third floor. Anything she could do to help Sam get settled in and take Augie off her hands.

She had thought she would donate the lot to the nursing home but worried some might be a little racy for the residents. On further inspection she had been glad that she had made the choice to look them over. A few were a little questionable for the over-ninety crowd. But she was having a heck of a time finishing the chore. Auggie was in rare form this afternoon.

"Help," Faulkner continued. "Go away."

She jumped to her feet and raced over to his cage. Auggie let out a bloodcurdling "yeow" as he hung from the bottom two wires, his paws hooked in between. Faulkner alternately begged for assistance and pecked at the cat's toes.

Halfway to his cage, she felt something slither down her front. She didn't have time to register what it was before it fell to the ground with a small thud. Midstep toward yet another kitty rescue, Arlo kicked the object toward the bird's cage. Auggie, not one to miss a pouncing opportunity, released his hold on the cage and dove after the small, wayward thing. His efforts pushed it under the fabric cover that surrounded the stand where Faulkner's cage sat.

Arlo stopped.

"What was that?" Camille asked.

It could only be one thing. "Nothing," she lied.

"That was a big noise for nothing."

"I don't know what you're talking about. I didn't hear anything." Why hadn't she put the jewelry box in her purse when she'd had the chance? Because she hadn't had the chance with all the book club murder investigation that had been going on when she got back from the police station. And then she had simply forgotten to take it out of her shirt. Well, the truth was she *wanted* to forget about it, so she chose to ignore its existence.

"I heard it too," Helen said.

Arlo opened her mouth to deny the existence of the one clue that could surely put Chloe away for life when Auggie batted it out from under the table cover. The small velvet box slid to a stop next to Camille's rose-colored Nike running shoes.

Fern gasped.

"What is it?" Helen asked.

Camille retrieved the little purple box and held it up for the others to see, then snapped it open. One blaming, damning earring winked back at them.

"Is that what I think it is?" Fern breathed.

"If you think it's the mate to the earring that Jason found upstairs, then I would say yes," Helen said.

"Where did it come from?" Camille turned it from side to side to allow the light to catch the large diamond.

Arlo cleared her throat. "My shirt. I had it in my shirt." She plucked the box from Camille's fingers, then started to turn it in much the same way. Something about the diamond was mesmerizing.

"And you've had it all this time?" Helen asked.

"Couldn't you have found a better place to carry it?" Fern frowned.

"Where did you get that?" Camille demanded.

Arlo sighed. "I found it in Chloe's bungalow."

"What? Where?"

"That can't be hers."

"I know." Arlo snapped the box shut and tucked it back inside her shirt. She didn't want to chance it being in her purse and out of sight for most of the day even though the cat had been let out of the bag, so to speak.

She looked to Auggie, who sat on his haunches and started to groom himself as if his work there was done.

The shop doorbell rang and Arlo whirled around, a bit guiltily.

Once again Sam was invading her personal space. Or at least it seemed that way.

"What was that?" he asked.

"Wh-what?"

"You put something in your shirt after showing the book club. I'm a member of the book club. What was it?"

"What are you doing back here?" Arlo countered.

"I came to remind you that the locksmith will need the old keys in order to change the lock. Not sure why. Maybe to prove it's your place?"

"In Sugar Springs?" she asked.

"Right." He nodded. "So what is it?"

"Tell him, love."

No. And Way.

"I don't think—"

"It's the earring. The mate to the one the police found." Fern nodded with a satisfied smile.

"Hush, Fern. You have a big mouth," Helen admonished.

"I think he needs to know. He's right. He's part of the book club too." Fern crossed her arms, content with her position and not moving from it.

A wave of curiosity and something she couldn't name washed across his handsome features, but in a second it was gone, only to be replaced by a look of genuine interest and care. "Where'd you get it?"

Arlo shook her head. "I don't want to say."

"Chloe's?" he asked, though the one word was far from a question. It was as if he already knew.

Arlo gasped, then shook her head with more force. But it was too late to deny it now. "Lucky guess."

"I'm a private dick."

"I wouldn't go around telling just anyone that." She snorted.

He shot her a look.

"It's not Chloe's," Arlo said. "Obviously."

"Okay."

"That's why I can't take it to Mads."

"So you're withholding evidence?" he asked.

Arlo threw up her arms and stalked away. "Not you, too." For lack of anything else to do, she started herself a cup of coffee in the Keurig. She missed her partner, missed the laughs and the fancy coffee drinks.

"Everyone else thinks you should turn it in to Mads?" Sam asked.

"Just Chloe," Arlo sighed.

"We hadn't gotten there yet," Helen added.

Arlo whirled toward the reading area where they were all sitting. "You guys too?"

They nodded in unison.

"Fine. I'll take it to Mads. But it makes Chloe look guilty."

"But she's not, love," Camille said. "And we are going to prove it."

Helen nodded. "Now get your butt down to the police station before Mads comes up here and arrests you too."

....

Arlo stepped into the well-lit lobby at the police station and blinked to allow her eyes to adjust. There was plenty of light in the room, but it wasn't bright at all compared to the blazing Mississippi sun.

Frances wasn't at her desk, so Arlo went back toward Mads's office.

He had been in there the other day talking to Sam. She had been surprised to see them together. After all, they were old nemeses. But it seemed they had let bygones be bygones.

"I need to get out more," she muttered and knocked on his office door.

"Come in."

She let herself in, then stopped, all her confidence gone. Was what she was about to do going to seal Chloe's ill fate?

"Hey, Arlo."

She nodded. "Mads."

"You need something?"

"I, uh...I've been feeding Chloe's cat, Auggie."

Mads nodded and settled in, as if he expected her story to be filled with unnecessary information and he might as well get comfortable.

"He knocked over some things and I found this." Her hand trembled as she set the little purple box on the scarred wood of his desk. It looked so out of place there next to a natural rock paperweight and a leather blotter. All this masculinity and one delicate velvet box.

One incriminating velvet box.

Mads looked at it, looked at her, and then opened the drawer to his left. He pulled out a pair of latex gloves and opened the lid.

"Where was it?" he asked.

"Under the couch. There was... Auggie knocked over the plant and I used the hose to suck up the dirt. I thought it was a cat toy."

"So you touched it."

She nodded.

"Anyone else?"

She grimaced. "Maybe Camille."

"Camille?"

"Sorry." *Please don't ask me to explain.* "But no one else. Not since I've had it."

He looked up and pinned her with one of those hard stares of his. "How long have you had it?"

"I found it last night."

Mads closed his eyes. "If you find anything else, bring it to me immediately."

"Right."

"And tell those ladies of yours that they need to stop snooping around. No one wants Chloe to be innocent more than I do, but the evidence is the evidence."

"The ladies?" she asked.

"Your little book club thing. They've been asking questions around town. Inna came in today and complained that Helen questioned her incessantly the entire meal at the inn. That's harassment."

Arlo sighed. "I'll take care of it."

"You do that."

Arlo started for the door.

"And, Arlo?" Mads called. She stopped with her hand on the knob. "That no snooping rule goes for you too."

....

Arlo fumed all the way back to the bookstore. Who did he think he was telling her not to snoop into her best friend's case? What kind of friend would she be if she didn't snoop? Not a very good one as far as Arlo was concerned. If she had been accused of murder and she had been the one arrested, she would hope that Chloe would be looking for the truth to buy her freedom.

"What's wrong?" Helen asked as she stormed back into the store.

"Mads," she growled. "He told me to stop snooping around. You too."

"My goodness," Camille gasped.

"I didn't think we did anything wrong." Fern looked to the others for confirmation.

"Apparently Inna complained to him this morning about her supper at the inn."

"I oughta go straighten him out," Helen said, pushing back her shirtsleeves.

"Hold on," Arlo told her. "There's no need for you to do that."

"There most certainly is," Helen argued. "Inna was the one who brought up the subject last night, talking about the reading of the will today and intellectual property. Whatever that means."

"It means the rights to Wally's work," Arlo said.

"Wouldn't that go to Daisy?" Camille asked. "She is his wife."

"It would unless he's designated someone else to get the rights." Arlo tried to explain the little she knew on the subject.

"Like Inna?" Helen said.

"Or Chloe," Camille added.

"Did you know that Chloe's father's business is in trouble?" Arlo asked.

A round of nods went around the room.

"Why am I always the last to know?" Arlo groused.

"Because you only cut your hair three times a year," Camille explained.

Arlo lifted a hand to her waist-length tresses. Her hair was long, dark, and straight, a throwback to the sixties. It seemed you could take the girl out of the hippie commune, but you couldn't take the hippie commune out of the girl. Her hair had looked like this since she was four years old. She saw no reason to change that now. "That's all it needs." But seriously, she needed to hang out at Dye Me a River. It seemed the salon was better than a newspaper. Maybe she should start getting her nails done...

"Mads seems to think that's another piece of evidence against Chloe," Arlo said.

"That she would kill Wally to get her father some money?" Helen shook her head. "She loves that boy. She always has."

And Arlo was afraid that she always would. In jail or out, even beyond the grave. "So what do we do now?"

Helen shot her an innocent smile. "Come to supper tonight. We can talk about it then."

13

"FANCY SEEING YOU HERE." ARLO PASTED ON A SMILE AS SHE MET Sam in the front yard of the Sugar Springs Inn.

Helen had bought the building that housed the inn after her husband died from pancreatic cancer. He worked for the railroad and the insurance payout was good. She overhauled the house, painted it herself, inside and out, and the Sugar Springs Inn was born. To Arlo it was home. At least the home she had known the longest.

Arlo's parents still breezed through Sugar Springs from time to time, and her brother liked to come every year for the strawberry festival, but other than that, Helen was her family.

Family she was going to strangle if she didn't stop trying to set her up with her high school sweetheart. She wasn't even sure *sweetheart* was the right word.

"I think Helen is trying to get us back together." Arlo made an apologetic face. At least she hoped it looked that way. Together they made their way up the walk to the large wraparound porch.

Sam laughed. "I thought I might be the only one who noticed."

Arlo shook her head. "I noticed all right."

"Would that be so bad?" he asked as he opened the door for her.

Would it? She would have to give it some thought, but she was saved from answering as Camille met them at the door. She held a glass of something in one hand and motioned them in with the other. "Come on in. Helen's made drinks."

Arlo eyed her glass. "I thought you couldn't drink because of your heart medication."

"Poppycock," Camille said. "Fern, can you whip up something for Arlo to drink?"

"And Sam too," he joked.

"I don't drink anymore," Fern said, a glass of amber liquid in one hand. Her drink didn't look mixed; it looked lethal. Single malt, aged twenty years lethal. "But I don't drink any less."

Everyone laughed.

The whole group was packed into the front common area of the inn. It was the largest room in the house, connected to the dining room and for the guests to enjoy. And they appeared to be enjoying it all right. Inna was there, along with Daisy, the book club members, and the inn's other guests—Ty Daniels who graduated the year after she and Sam. He'd become a state senator. And Frankie Dell who...well, no one was sure what Frankie did for a living but since it was suspected he had New York and Chicago connections, no one dared to ask.

"Here you go, sweetie." Helen handed her a drink with a quick wink.

Arlo took one look at the dark amber liquid and resisted the urge to pour it into the nearest potted plant. But what had the plant ever done to her? The drink looked like a straight shot of sour mash whiskey. Hopefully nothing higher proof. "I'm not sure—"

Helen patted her arm and put a stop to her. "Oh, you're going to love this."

Arlo eyed it skeptically.

"Drink up," Helen said. She raised her glass in toast.

"*Za vashe zdorovie!*" Inna raised her glass and drained what was inside. Not willing to be outdone by her deceased husband's assistant, Daisy did the same. She winced as the liquid slid down her throat. When Arlo was told to come to supper, she had no idea they meant to have a party.

She took a cautious sniff of her drink, then another. It didn't smell strong.

"Here, Sam. This is a special drink for you." It was amber like the one Arlo had in her hand. So what made it special?

"Take it easy on that," Camille teased. "You don't want to wake up in the morning with a lampshade on your head."

"I don't?" he asked.

Camille patted the side of his face. "So cheeky this one."

He took a sip of his drink and smiled.

"What?" Arlo asked. She still held hers in one hand as if it was about to sprout legs and walk off.

"Try it."

"I'm scared."

His grin deepened. There were those dimples again.

She steeled herself against his handsomeness and the drink and took a small sip. Sweet. "Is this…"

He took another drink. "Yep."

Tea. Why were they drinking tea, pretending it was alcohol?

Because their guests were drinking vodka, toasting everything from Wally and his book to the color of the curtains.

"Are they doing what I think they're doing?" Arlo asked.

Sam nodded. "I think so."

Great. Just what she needed: Inna and Daisy drunk the night before the attorney read Wally's will.

Then again, if it helped them loosen up enough to spill a few secrets…

When she looked at it that way…it was brilliant.

"Have you read it?" Inna asked, her accent even thicker than usual.

"Read what?" Sam was still standing close to Arlo and had been for most of the evening. They had been in the common room for almost twenty minutes. Everyone was laughing and drinking and talking, in general having a good time.

"My Wally's book."

Interesting—that was the second time she had referred to him as "my Volly."

"*Missing Girl*?" He looked down into his glass as if the liquid there had the answers of the universe. "Not yet. But we have a book club now and we're reading it."

"A book club?" Daisy picked that moment to saunter up. She really was pretty in a sexy-girl-next-door sort of way. She seemed to be handling herself well, but Arlo could almost see the thin veneer of composure that kept her looking like the successful author's wife that she was. "How sweet."

"Uh, yeah." Sam stumbled over his words like a person who was learning to walk again.

"We should go," Daisy said to Inna.

The invitation sounded sincere enough, but if one was paying attention—and Arlo was—they would hear that Daisy's words were a little forced, as if she somehow felt obligated to include Inna. Now that Wally was gone, the two of them wouldn't have anything to tie them to one another. At least not that Arlo could see. So either she felt compelled or something else bonded them.

The will?

Arlo supposed they would find that out soon enough.

"Stuffed mushroom?" Helen shoved the platter into the circle of their little group. "Made them myself. Even foraged for the mushrooms."

As far as Arlo knew, Helen had never foraged for anything in her life, except maybe the last almond from the can of mixed nuts. And speaking of nuts, what was she up to?

"Did you know that the most poisonous mushroom known to man looks almost identical to these button mushrooms? The two are practically impossible to tell apart. You know, unless you have the training."

"Thanks." Daisy plucked one of the appetizers from the platter and popped it into her mouth.

Helen held the platter closer to Inna. "Would you like one?"

Inna shook her head and eyed the platter with what seemed to be distrust. Or was it guilt over being presented with the one thing she used to try to kill Wally?

Inna was, of course, on the book club's list of suspects, but Arlo had a hard time understanding why she might kill her employer. Wally was making good with his book. No doubt he had already signed the contract for the next one and was living off a large advance, if the industry reports were correct.

"No," Inna said. "No mushrooms."

"You don't like them?"

She shook her head. "Daisy does. That's what her family makes."

"Grows," Daisy corrected. "We *grow* mushrooms."

Helen looked only mildly interested. "Really? I didn't know that."

Liar. Arlo stuffed one of the mushrooms into her mouth to keep the word from escaping. Helen knew everything about everyone who stayed at her inn.

And someone whose family grew mushrooms for a living would surely know how to tell a death cap from the edible meadow mushroom.

"These are good," Sam said around a mouthful of food. He picked another mushroom off the plate before swallowing the first.

Arlo shot him a look.

"What?" he asked. A bit defensively if she was telling the truth. "I skipped lunch."

Helen smiled at him. "Eat all you want."

He took another.

"Refill?" Camille buzzed up, a bottle of "whiskey" in one hand and vodka in the other.

"It is a party, no?" Inna asked.

"It's Russ's birthday." Helen pointed to the man standing over by the sideboard. Russ England, mayor of Sugar Springs. Next to him, on the sideboard, sat a large white sheet cake, candles sticking out of the top and everything. But it wasn't Russ's birthday. Arlo knew because his birthday and hers were the same and he had teased her about switching their ages for as long as she had lived in Sugar Springs.

"That's a party," Inna said and held her glass up for Camille to refill with the chilled vodka.

"Can I get—" Daisy pointed to the whiskey bottle.

But Camille cut her short. "Oh, no, this stuff is home distilled. You don't want any of it."

"I'd like to try it."

Camille smiled and filled Daisy's glass with vodka. "Locals only," she singsonged and danced away without waiting for Daisy to answer.

"Does it feel strange being at a party so soon after your husband's death?" Fern asked.

"Fern!" Helen chastised. "You shouldn't bring things like that up. Not now."

Daisy stared into her glass, then downed the vodka. "With Wally, everything is strange. Was." She hiccupped.

Helen smiled. "Let me get you a refill, dear."

....

By the time they made it to the cake—after wild mushroom quesadillas with chili verde mushroom salsa—Arlo had no more information about Daisy or Inna than she'd had before they started. The women had put away a gallon of iced tea disguised as moonshine. Apparently neither Daisy nor Inna had seen any of the moonshine shows on television these days. Distilled corn liquor was clear and only got its amber coloring after being aged in oak barrels. But hey, what they didn't know wouldn't hurt them. At least this time. But Arlo suspected that one of them had killed Wally. But which one?

"It's a good thing they are staying at the inn tonight," Sam said as they left the party. "Neither one of them needs to be behind the wheel."

She nodded and was all too aware that he was walking her to her car. It wasn't necessary, but how could she tell him that without appearing uncomfortably aware of his every move?

"Do you think one of them did it?" she asked.

"I don't know."

"I thought you were a private dick."

"And I thought I wasn't supposed to tell anyone that."

Arlo shook her head. "In your expert opinion, is one of them—Daisy or Inna—guilty of killing Wally?"

"You do realize that the evidence against Chloe is stacked high?"

"But she's not guilty."

"That's not up for me to decide."

Arlo sucked in a deep breath. "Let's pretend that Chloe is completely out of the picture. Do you believe that Daisy is capable of killing her husband? I mean, everyone knows that he's been unfaithful."

"Oh yeah?"

"Everyone but you, I guess."

"I guess. Who was the unlucky lady?"

"Inna."

"Ouch."

"I know, right? All the magazines were talking about it. How Daisy caught them together at a hotel. It was sad really. But Daisy pasted on a smile and kept right on going like nothing had ever happened."

"I wonder why." They stopped at her car.

Arlo palmed her keys. "She knows a good thing when she has it. Had it?" She shook her head. "Can you imagine her on a mushroom farm? Have you ever been to a mushroom farm?"

"No, but I take it you have."

"They stink. I mean, literally. It's the worst smell in the world. Think about it. Button mushrooms grow in poop. Manure, feces."

"Stop! I got it." He held up his hands. "So you think Daisy would forgive his affair because she wants the cash cow, so to speak?"

"It's the only thing that makes sense to me."

"What about love?" Sam asked.

"What about it?" Arlo countered.

"Wouldn't that be enough to keep her with him?"

"We're talking about Wally here. Wally Harrison. Class of 2009's Most Likely to Get Punched by a Security Guard."

"That wasn't a real award." Sam pressed his lips together, whether in distaste or to keep from laughing she couldn't tell.

"It was in the underground paper," Arlo said.

"Which you published."

She smiled. "Good times."

A moment of silence fell between them. Around where they stood, the leaves in the trees rustled, an owl called, and the crickets chirped.

It was reminiscent of those early summer nights so long ago. And it would be so easy to lean in and kiss him. Just like she had done back then. Would he remember? Would he kiss her back?

"My answer is yes."

"What?" Arlo drew back, unsure if she had always been so close to him or if she had moved nearer in thinking about the past.

"You asked if I thought one of them could be guilty of killing Wally. My answer is yes. Everyone is capable if properly provoked."

Arlo let out a nervous laugh and opened the car to put something between them. Memory Lane was beckoning, and she had no desire to travel it.

Liar.

"Mads said the same thing."

"That's reassuring." His tone was sarcastic, but his expression benign. She had no idea what to make of it.

"Speaking of Mads," she started. "What were you two talking about the other day? The day Chloe was arrested."

"Nothing."

"Nothing," she repeated. "Now why don't I believe that?"

He smiled. "Believe it or not. That's entirely up to you."

"You know you're a bad liar."

His smile deepened. "Sweetheart, so are you."

She got into the car, and he closed the door behind her. It took two tries to get the key into the ignition and the car into gear.

Sam remained where he stood, watching her until she had backed out into the street. He waved as she put the car in drive and started toward home. She looked into her rearview mirror to see he had moved to his car and was preparing to leave.

She wasn't sure what that was all about, but one thing was certain: she needed to keep some space between her and Sam. It seemed they had a little unfinished business between them.

14

"Lord have mercy!" Frances cried. "What are you doing?"

Arlo lugged the bulky carrier into the police station and set the container, along with its yowling contents, onto Frances's desk. "I can't take it any longer."

"Hey, baby." Frances lifted her hand to the wire door of the carrier so Auggie could smell her fingers.

"This is Chloe's cat and he's suffering from separation anxiety. Because of that, he has destroyed Chloe's bungalow and my couch, given Faulkner anxiety, and attacked two of my customers. He needs to be here with her." At least until Sam could take him.

"Oh," Frances cooed at the beast. "Do you need your mommy?"

Auggie meowed in return. It was the nicest sound she had heard him make since she had stuffed him into the plastic crate for transport. She had never owned a cat before and if she had to go off Auggie's reaction, they really didn't like being in carriers.

"And what are we supposed to do about it?" Mads came out of his office and stood behind Frances. He leaned one shoulder against the wall painted with the great seal of the town of Sugar Springs. He held a coffee mug in one hand, and judging by the dark circles under his eyes, it seemed he might need another cup real soon.

"I've got his litter box in the car," Arlo said.

"Not happening."

"Oh, it is." She turned to make her way back out. The cat was staying with Chloe one way or another.

"Arlo." Mads used that cop voice she had heard before. The one that brooked no argument. But she had known him when he was young, not as large or intimidating as he was now. She had seen him in wet boxers after "almost" skinny-dipping in the large man-made lake behind Lillyfield mansion. She wasn't scared of him.

"You can take the cat, or you can let Chloe go. Your choice."

He seemed to think about it a minute. All the while, Frances babbled nonsense to Auggie who had thankfully stopped yowling. Maybe Arlo just wasn't a cat person.

Mads shook his head. "Fine, why not? Nothing else about this arrest has been ordinary."

"Thank you."

He smiled, and for a moment she caught a glimpse of the Mads she had known way back when. Then he was gone in an instant. "Whatever," Mads growled. He drained the last of the coffee in his mug and stared into it for a moment. "The litter box stays in the cell with her."

....

"I still don't think I should be here," Arlo whispered. They were standing in the foyer of the inn, right outside of the downstairs common room. She checked her watch: 2:55. Beside her, Chloe shifted and pulled on the hem of her shirt, handcuffs clinking as she did so. "And I don't know why Mads insisted on restraining you."

"I think that was the lawyer, and I need you here," Chloe said. "Come to think of it, I'm not sure why I'm here either."

"Maybe Wally decided to man up and take care of Jayden."

Chloe's mouth twisted into a disbelieving frown. "I doubt that."

With Inna and Daisy hovering around and Mads directly behind them, they were keeping their voices low. It also helped since the book club ladies had decided to hold today's meeting at the inn at the precise time of the reading of Wally's will. Sam was moving into the third floor now that it had been rekeyed and was ready for a new tenant. Arlo still wasn't sure if having him so close would be a blessing or a nightmare.

The door to the common room slid open and a small man in a tailored suit stepped out. "Ladies." He nodded at them. "And you, sir." He seemed even smaller as Mads stepped past him into the room.

"He comes to guard you, then leaves you out in the foyer with me," Arlo grumbled.

"Come on, you two." Mads didn't even turn around as he spoke. He settled down in the leather seat in the far corner, his back pressed against the wall.

One by one they filed into the room—Chloe, Arlo, Inna, and Daisy.

They settled down around the common room table where guests at the inn usually enjoyed fresh-baked muffins and coffee for breakfast. Arlo could use one of the muffins right about now, but she didn't need it. Nervous eating was the reason she often carried around five extra pounds.

The tiny lawyer cleared his throat and restacked the papers in front of him. "You know why we are all here. The reading of the will of Mr. Wallace Jerome Harrison."

Jerome. Arlo had forgotten that was Wally's middle name. She had always remembered his arrogant swagger and his overconfident attitude long after he had left town, but his middle name had been forgotten.

The lawyer droned on in legal-speak about parties of the first part and second part, then he turned to Inna. "To my assistant, Inna Kolisnychenko, I leave the desk where I did most of my work and one thousand dollars so she can buy her own computer and tell her own story."

Arlo didn't know what to expect from this decree, but it certainly wasn't the near-purple color that seeped into Inna's face. It rose up from her neck and in seconds was all the way to her hairline. Her hands trembled as she tried to control whatever emotion had taken her over. It almost looked like anger. But what did she have to be angry about? Maybe she was upset that her lover was treating her more like an employee instead of intimate.

"To my lovely wife, Daisy, I leave one third of my estate as deemed by New York state law."

"What?" Daisy was slowly becoming the same color as Inna. But unlike Inna, who wore an ivory-colored dress, Daisy wore green, and the shade of purple now staining her skin was clashing terribly.

The lawyer stopped. "New York law dictates that a spouse cannot be written out of a will. The spouse is entitled to one third of the estate or fifty thousand dollars, whichever is greater. Obviously, Mr. Harrison's estate is larger than one hundred and fifty thousand dollars, and you, Mrs. James-Harrison, are only entitled to a third of that."

"I don't understand." She gritted the words from between her teeth.

"It's simple really," the lawyer started again. "New York law—"

"I understand that," Daisy said, jumping to her feet. Mads sat up, his lazy attention turning alert in the blink of an eye. "I just don't *understand*. How can he cut me out after all we've been through?"

"Oh, you're not cut out," the lawyer cheerfully corrected. "The law won't allow that. So you see, you get one third."

"A pittance compared to what he's worth now." She shook her head, and finally asked the question that was rattling around in everyone's minds. "Who gets the rest?"

The lawyer cleared his throat again and turned his attention back to the papers he held, Wally's last will and testament. But not before his gaze strayed to Chloe.

"Her?" Daisy's voice raised with disbelief. "I'd never even heard of her before we got here. Why would he leave anything to his high school sweetheart?" The last words were spat out like poison.

"Because she is the mother of his son," the lawyer said.

Daisy dropped back into her seat.

Inna braced her elbows on the table in front of her and massaged her temples. Arlo suspected it was a lot of news to digest in one sitting.

"Is this true?" Inna asked.

"Yes." Chloe whispered the word, her tone apologetic. She had never wanted anything from Wally and most likely didn't want this. But she loved her family and she would accept it to help them. It was as simple and as complicated as that.

"Has there been a DNA test? We don't know that she's telling the truth." Daisy scoffed. She turned to Chloe, the girl-next-door gone and in her place a scorned and bitter woman. "Who are you?"

"That's enough," Mads said before anyone else could move. He was on his feet, that lithe grace taking him to the space between Chloe and Daisy. "It's common knowledge around here that Jayden Carter belongs to Wally Harrison. One look'll tell you that."

"You didn't even give him his father's name?" Daisy's voice had lowered in volume but was as shrill as ever.

Chloe sat back, still stunned. She placed her hands in her lap, the cuffs clanking as she did so. "He didn't want anything to do with Jayden. Wally signed all his rights away even before Jayden was born."

"There. That settles it." Daisy turned back to the lawyer.

The man gave a light shrug. "You are welcome to contest any part of this will. But I can tell you that what you received is legally acceptable to the state of New York and despite any agreements between Miss Carter and my client, he is entitled to leave the remainder of his estate to anyone he chooses."

Arlo reached over and squeezed Chloe's hand.

"It's obvious," Daisy said. "That's more reason for her to kill Wally."

Inna shook her head. "That is a mean thing to say."

Daisy grabbed her purse and jumped to her feet. "Say what you want. And enjoy your new computer and desk. Oh, and telling your own story. That should be a bestseller." On that note, she stormed from the room.

"I really don't understand," Chloe said. Her voice was quiet and small, so unlike the vivacious Chloe that everyone in Sugar Springs knew.

"Me either." Inna pulled a slim cigarette case from her purse and a matching gold lighter. She pulled out a cigarette and lit it up.

"You can't smoke in here," Arlo said. It was her teenage home, after all.

Inna exhaled, blowing smoke halfway across the room.

Arlo released Chloe's hand and plucked the cigarette from Inna's fingers. She took it into the kitchen and tossed it into the sink. She ran water over it, then returned to the common room in time to hear Inna say, "You see how she acts. She is guilty of something. I know not why you don't arrest her."

"Daisy?" Arlo asked.

"*Da*, the wife. She is not as innocent as she looks."

They had all received a firsthand enactment of that fact. But as much as Arlo hated to admit it, the evidence pointed to Chloe, and now with this revelation of his will, she looked like she had even more to gain from Wally's death. And that damning earring.

Arlo sat next to Chloe. "Is that all?" she asked.

"For the most part. I'll have some papers for you to sign in a day or so, Miss Carter. Until then, good day." He placed all his papers back into the folder and loaded it all into his briefcase before nodding to them. He started out the door but snatched a cookie off the side table on his way out. Arlo couldn't blame him. Helen was nothing if not a good baker.

"Well, that was interesting." Helen smiled at everyone as she breezed back into the room. The book club had been across the hall the whole time, most probably listening with the door of the living area open so they could hear what was going on inside the common room.

"Congratulations, Chloe."

Arlo could tell by the stunned look on her friend's face that she didn't know how to respond.

Mads stepped forward and grabbed Chloe by the arm. "Come on, girl. It's time to go."

She nodded and stood. "Thanks for bringing Auggie to me," she said to Arlo as Mads started to lead her from the room.

Inna stood, cigarette case in hand. "How do you say? It's been fun and real but not really fun?"

"Close enough," Arlo said.

"Is okay to smoke outside?" Inna asked Helen.

"Yes, there's an ashtray on the porch. I just ask that you don't leave anything burning and move to the side if someone wants to come in or go out."

"*Da.*" Inna nodded, her earrings catching the light as she turned.

"Wait," Arlo called.

Mads and Chloe stopped at the door.

Inna turned around. "What now?"

Arlo could barely see the earrings she wore through the strands of her dark hair. She could only see the right one with any clarity, but she could see it well enough to know. It was exactly like the one she found in Chloe's bungalow.

"Nothing," she said. "I forgot."

Inna rolled her eyes. "Crazy Americans." She tucked her hair behind her left ear, giving Arlo full view of the hidden diamond. It was the same. The. Same. But Inna had two.

She ducked out of the common room, leaving the "crazy Americans" staring after her.

"Did you see that?" Arlo tugged on his sleeve. "Mads? Did you see her earrings?"

"I suppose," he grumbled.

"They were just like the one I found in Chloe's house."

"Inna had both of hers," he said.

"I know but—"

"Those are not my earrings," Chloe interjected. Some of the stupor over inheriting the lion's share of Wally's fortune had worn off and she was getting back to herself. "You know I don't have that kind of money." And like Arlo, the money she did have was wrapped up in Books & More.

"How does Inna have that kind of money?" Arlo asked. She had pondered Inna's salary for what little she claimed to do for Wally, but sheesh.

"She has two of them," Mads repeated.

"Maybe she has two pairs."

"You were just questioning how she had money for one pair, and now you think she has two?" He shot her an incredulous look.

"Maybe the second pair belongs to Daisy. I'd bet anything Wally bought his wife and his mistress—oh, I'm sorry, *assistant*—the same earrings. Daisy could have pushed Wally out of the third-story window and lost one. She wasn't wearing diamonds today because she doesn't have the pair anymore."

"Just because she didn't wear them today doesn't mean that she doesn't have them somewhere else." He shifted, and she could tell that his patience with the whole ordeal had come to an end.

"You know Wally would do something sleazy like that."

"Don't forget her breakfast in the morning." Mads nodded toward Helen and escorted Chloe from the room. Arlo followed uselessly behind.

In the doorway of the living area across the hall, the book club ladies watched with sad eyes as Mads took Chloe away.

"It was that Daisy," Fern said vehemently. "She likes to pretend that she's something, but she's a farm girl under all that makeup and fancy clothes."

"A farm girl that would know death cap mushroom poison takes a while to do its deed," Helen said.

"Nobody said Thursday's attempt with the coffee was the first time." Camille gave an elegant shrug.

Arlo shook her head. "I checked it out, and it doesn't take a lot to kill a person. Half a mushroom cap, according to the internet."

Camille whistled low and under her breath. "That ain't much," she said in her best imitation of a Mississippi drawl.

"You're telling me," Helen agreed.

"But it can take up to two weeks," Camille explained. "That's why people die from it: misdiagnosis. You see, they get sick, sometimes days after eating the mushrooms. When they go to the doctor, they think they have the flu. They get fluids and start to feel better and all the while, the toxins are destroying their liver. By the time that shows up, it's too late." They stared at her with incredulous gazes. "What?" Camille shrugged. "I looked it up on Google."

"Maybe Daisy was tired of waiting for her inheritance," Fern mused.

"Or maybe someone wants us to believe it was her," Arlo countered. "But why give him the poison, then push him out the window? It doesn't make sense."

"Don't forget whoever it was put the mushroom in the coffee Chloe made," Helen pointed out.

"Right." Fern nodded.

"So they wanted Chloe to look guilty?" Camille asked hesitantly.

"Maybe. Or maybe they are trying to keep the attention off themselves," Helen explained.

That sounded more logical, but who in Sugar Springs stood to gain from Wally's death?

Unfortunately, that one was easy: Chloe. But Chloe hadn't known that to be the case until today.

15

THE BELL OVER THE DOOR RANG OUT ITS GENTLE WARNING THAT someone had come into the bookstore. By now Arlo had gotten used to hearing the footsteps in the floor above as Sam organized his office, but she wasn't able to stop herself from looking up and expecting Chloe to walk in the front. A girl had to have hope.

"Hi, Frances."

The police station secretary shot her a strained smile as she lugged Chloe's cat crate, along with its yowling occupant, into the store. "Mads said he was sick and tired of this 'damned cat shedding all over the place.' His words, not mine."

Arlo cast a quick glance toward the floor above. "I'm not sure I have a place for him yet."

"Then he said you had to come get the litter box and it had better be before three." She hoisted the carrier onto the side table next to the reading nook. "I'll bring it as soon as I can."

And he hadn't said any of those things to her when she brought by Chloe's breakfast not two hours ago. Arlo peered into the carrier. "What have you been up to, buddy?"

Auggie hissed.

"Get him outta here," Faulkner screeched, followed by, "Here, kitty, kitty, kitty."

Auggie hissed again.

It was looking like a fun morning. And since it was almost noon when the book club ladies were supposed to arrive, the party just continued. *And* she was four days in to her ten-day reprieve Mads had given her. Almost halfway with no good leads on who really killed Wally. Nothing concrete anyway.

A large boom sounded from the third floor.

Arlo looked up, wondering if the sound was lethal or merely echoed since it was raining in from above.

"Fire in the hole," Faulkner squawked. He was sitting on top of his cage, as if waiting for her to release Auggie.

"Should we go check on that?" Frances asked.

Arlo shook her head. "It's just my new tenant."

Frances gazed at the wooden ceiling above. "You got ghosts moving in? I always heard this place was haunted."

"Tell me one building in this town built before the turn of the twentieth century that doesn't have a reported ghost," Arlo said.

"Good point."

"That's Sam Tucker. He's setting up shop on the third floor."

"I heard about his mama." Frances shook her head. "Sad business, that."

Arlo nodded. Sam's mother had always been good to her, even after Sam left town and broke Arlo's heart in the process. Why was it always the good ones that seemed to go first?

Another loud smack came down from above, followed by a muffled voice, a man's shout. The words were indistinguishable, but the tone unmistakable.

"What kind of business is he setting up?" Frances asked.

Arlo thought about it a moment. "Now that you mention it, I'm not sure. He said he was working as a private investigator." She let her voice trail off. How much PI work was there in sleepy little Sugar Springs?

Frances shrugged, apparently thinking the same thing. "Maybe that's what he was talking to Mads about the other day."

"Maybe," Arlo mused. Was it normal or vain that she thought she had been a topic in that conversation? She would have to ask Chloe. When they got her out of jail, of course.

"I guess I'd better be getting back. Those phones aren't going to answer themselves." Frances turned for the door.

Nor the crossword puzzle supply its own answers.

"The litter box?" Arlo asked.

"I'll bring it ASAP." Frances gave a little backward wave but didn't bother turning around as she left Books & More.

"Come on, buddy," she hoisted the carrier off the side table and ignored Auggie's low growls as she jostled him. "Let's go see what's up with Sam." Hopefully he was ready to make good on his promise to care for Chloe's angry orange beast.

....

One thought kept coming back to Arlo as she climbed the steps to the third floor. Well, two really. Had Sam been talking to Mads about his PI business in Sugar Springs? And had the killer walked these very steps with Wally that fateful Friday morning?

She set the cat carrier on the small landing and knocked on the door. A scraping sound came from inside about the same time, so she knocked again. "Sam?" There was a crash. "Are you okay in there?"

The door swung open and Sam stood there looking a tad disconcerted and even more sweaty. "Arlo!" And then there was the surprise. "What are you doing here?"

She nudged the cat carrier, and Auggie growled. "Chloe's cat."

"Oh yeah." He breathed out as if he had been holding his breath since he had opened the door.

"What's wrong?"

He scoffed. "Nothing."

Arlo planted one hand on her hip. "Now why don't I believe that?"

He sighed. "I'm trying to get moved in and getting everything organized has been a bit of a challenge."

"I see." She shifted her weight from one foot to the other. "So why do I get the feeling you're looking for other clues as to what happened to Wally?"

He straightened, his expression going completely blank. "You don't trust Mads to have gathered every bit of evidence?"

"So you're not denying it?"

"Arlo, seriously?"

"Who are you working for?" she demanded.

"Are you going to bring in the damned cat?"

"Are you going to tell me who hired you?"

"When does the cat get fed?"

"Employer?"

"And the box. Does she go in a litter box?"

"Daisy, right?"

"I'm not telling you. There is such a thing as client confidentiality."

"I knew it!" She pointed a finger at him in triumph. "I knew you were investigating Wally's death."

"Sure." He waved a hand around, but it seemed less like an admission and more about getting her to be quiet. "Now am I keeping the cat or not?"

Arlo shot him a grim smile. "Oh, you're keeping the cat, all right. You promised."

....

"So someone hired Sam to investigate Wally's death?" Helen asked that evening over a late supper. The regular meal at the inn had already been served and cleaned up. Now it was time for a girl powwow.

"And he said that?"

"Well, not in so many words, but he didn't say he wasn't." Arlo checked the doorway to make sure Inna or Daisy hadn't suddenly appeared. "Are you sure the girls are out for the night?"

Helen nodded. "That's what they said. Something about getting dinner in Memphis. They won't be back for hours."

"Okay." Still, Arlo was a little reluctant to talk about this without knowing exactly where Wally's two women were. "When do you think Mads will release them to leave?"

Camille set the basket of cornbread on the table between them and took her seat next to Fern. "Hard to say. But at any rate, I'm sure they'll be here until after the funeral."

"Funeral?" Arlo asked.

"Well, more of a memorial service. Wally wanted to be cremated." Fern took up a piece of cornbread and slathered it with butter.

"So Daisy can take him back to the city," Helen said.

Arlo stared at her godmother. "You knew about this?"

"Of course I did. His widow and his assistant have been staying here for almost a week."

"I'm just surprised. I didn't realize Daisy had shared that fact with you. Has she said anything else that might be useful?"

"You think that's useful?" Helen asked.

"Not really," Arlo admitted. "But something else she said might be."

Camille shook her head sadly. "All they talk about is going back to New York and getting mani-pedis."

"You know what I think," Fern said.

"Yes," Helen and Camille said at the same time. Their voices held notes of resignation and finality.

"What?" Arlo asked. She grabbed her own piece of cornbread.

"I think we should go into their rooms and see if they have another pair of those diamond earrings."

Arlo frowned. "What would that prove?"

"Fern wants to snoop in their rooms and see if she can find anything to incriminate one of them," Helen said.

"Or both," Fern added. "I wouldn't mind seeing both of them take the fall."

"I suppose they could be working together," Arlo mused.

"Absolutely." Fern gave an emphatic nod. "Maybe they decided to kill Wally together and take his money, then they found out that Chloe was going to get most of it."

"Well, she won't get it if she ends up in prison for killing him," Camille said.

"And that's the very reason we should go search their rooms."

"Snooping," Helen said. "That is a completely unethical move. I might even have my license revoked for such shenaniganry."

"Shenaniganry?" Fern asked.

"It's a word," Helen protested.

Fern looked to Camille. The English teacher to the rescue. "It is a word," she said with a nod.

"I still say sometimes snooping is a necessary evil," Fern said.

"An evil is evil, necessary or not," Helen countered.

Arlo sighed. "Elly is right. We can't go snooping around in their rooms. We just have to think of something else to help prove Chloe's innocence."

They all sat quietly for a moment, their suppers forgotten in front of them.

"When is Wally's memorial service?" Arlo asked.

"Thursday," Helen replied.

"Thursday?" Five days away. Her ten days to save Chloe were quickly running out.

"Mads is afraid we'll have a media frenzy on our hands," Fern said. "One of the big Hollywood studios, I forget which one, has offered a gabillion million to make *Missing Girl* into a movie."

"Gabillion million? Is that an industry term?" Camille mused.

Fern waved one hand in front of herself as if to erase the words. "It was a lot of money. I don't remember exactly how much."

Arlo chuckled with a shake of her head. "And Mads is expecting a rush on the town. All the people who want to celebrate Wally's life?"

"Or see where he came from. Who he was," Helen suggested.

Or check out the window he was thrown from, Arlo thought.

"Wouldn't it be better to have the service sooner and not give the rest of the world a chance to find out about it?" Arlo asked.

Helen shrugged. "That's what I thought too, but you know Mads."

That she did. "I'll go down to the station and talk to him tomorrow."

"It's Sunday," Helen said.

Arlo shook her head. "First chance I get," she said. And with any luck that would be sooner rather than later.

16

ARLO STARED AT THE BRIGHT PATCHES OF SUNLIGHT ON THE ceiling of her bedroom. It was time to get up, past time, but she was still lounging, allowing the events of the past few days to get the better of her. She didn't normally wallow, but today seemed like the perfect day for it.

She gave herself a few more minutes of indulgence, then with a groan of resignation, she pushed back the covers and stood. If she felt overwhelmed, she could only imagine how Chloe felt. Depressed, angry, slighted, confused. And hungry. Chloe was dependent on Arlo to get her breakfast, so she needed to get her butt in gear and get her friend some chow.

She pulled on a pair of jeans and a T-shirt, then made her way to the bathroom. She washed her face, brushed her teeth, and pulled her long hair into a hasty braid.

She had washed it the night before after she had come home from work. But she hadn't done anything save brush it out and let it dry. There was no telling how long the braid would last. Her hair was long and thick and as Helen always said, "fine as frog hair." Though when Helen said it, she was referring to her disposition. *How are you today? Well, I'm as fine as frog hair.*

But for some reason that always came to mind. At the thought of her godmother, Arlo smiled. She pulled on her shoes, grabbed her keys and her purse, and headed out to her Rabbit.

"Hi, Arlo," Cindy Jo called from her driveway. Sometimes Arlo felt like Cindy Jo waited for her to come out. Arlo knew it couldn't be fact, but the thoughts came all the same.

"Hi, Cindy Jo." She gave a small wave but didn't stop. She needed to get going this morning and didn't have a lot of time for chitchat. Not since she had lollygagged in bed all morning.

"On your way to church?" Cindy Jo asked.

That was when Arlo noticed Cindy Jo's pastel floral dress and little white purse. It was a miniature version of Camille's bag, but she was certain it wasn't a third as interesting.

"No, uh—"

"Do you want to go with me and Mark?" Mark was Cindy Jo's husband. He was nice enough she supposed, but there was something about him that didn't go with Cindy Jo. Maybe because he was a Yankee. A damned Yankee by definition, since he moved to the South and stayed.

"No. Thank you. I have to take breakfast to Chloe."

Cindy Jo's pink-painted lips formed a perfect, theatrical O. "You don't think she…" Cindy Jo trailed off, unable to say the terrible words. For once Arlo was glad. She couldn't bear to hear them again. Not that she wanted to answer the unasked question. At least she didn't have to hear it spoken.

"No."

"Then why did the sheriff arrest her? He's smarter than that. I voted for him."

"I don't know, Cindy Jo. Perhaps you should call him and ask. I'm sure he would be willing to answer all your questions, especially since you're a concerned voter."

Cindy Jo's eyes grew wide with the possibilities that had just presented themselves to her. "You know what? I'm gonna do just that." She acted as if she was going to pull her cell phone from her purse, but Mark came out of the house before she could accomplish the task.

"You ready to go?" Mark asked. Then he saw her standing there. "Hello, Arlo."

"Mark." She nodded at him, then twirled her keys around one finger, allowing them to slap against her palm. "Y'all have a good day."

"You too," Cindy Jo said with a wave and a smile. "And that invitation is still open. Anytime you want to go to church with us, you just say the word."

Like that was going to happen.

It wasn't that she didn't believe in God, nor did she have a problem with the people who went to church; she just heard them talk about Jesus and their beliefs in God, and Arlo was so painfully aware that she didn't have blind faith in the lessons that were presented. So people had told her that conviction came from going to church and exposing herself to the lessons and faith of others. But for her, all it did was spur on more questions. In the end she decided to forgo church, even while she envied those who could believe without doubt.

So while the majority of the good citizens of Sugar Springs made their way to church, she made her way to The Diner.

If the schedule was in keeping, it was Bill's turn to work which meant omelets. Yum. She could use some eggs and cheese right about now. That sounded like the best thing in the world. Next to her best friend getting out of jail.

With each day that Chloe spent behind bars, they were another day closer to her deadline to prove Chloe's innocence. They didn't have to find out everything. They just had to be able to cast a reasonable doubt on the likelihood that Chloe was the one who killed Wally Harrison. Mads was fair. He would acknowledge it if they brought him good enough evidence. But Arlo wasn't sure the book club ladies would let it end there. They were a little too gung ho to solve the crime. She wasn't sure they would let it drop at reasonable doubt.

Ashley Porter was working behind the counter once again.

"Sit anywhere," she called to Arlo, her face turned down and her thumbs flying over her phone screen.

Must be a pretty important conversation, Arlo thought. Then again, with kids these days, they could be talking about something as mundane as contact solution to as something big as the latest new from the Middle East. Or that a man named Wallis J. Harrison had been killed on Main Street by his high school sweetheart and baby mama. It was just one more "thang."

"I need a to-go order."

Ashley raised her gaze from her phone and settled it on Arlo. She looked a bit stunned, like she was the butt of some kind of prank. "Where's Chloe?" she asked.

Arlo pressed her lips together, then tried to relax. "Jail," she said. "That's why I need a to-go order."

Ashley nodded and slipped her phone into the back pocket of her jeans. "Omelet?" she asked. "Daddy's behind the grill."

Arlo nodded. "That will be fine." She slipped onto the stool closest to the cash register and waited. There were a couple more people in The Diner today besides Cable and Joey. Just a few back-sliding Baptists skipping out on Sunday School, she was sure. They were young. And though she didn't remember their names, she had seen them around town. She thought perhaps they had even come into the bookstore. If not for reading, then for a coffee. They were definitely the specialty-coffee type.

And they definitely knew who she was. They leaned toward each other, heads almost touching across the table that separated them.

Arlo ignored their looks and pretended she couldn't hear their whispers. She also made believe that Cable and Joey weren't doing their own bit of staring and whispering. She tapped her foot while she waited. She was certain this must be the most complicated omelet in the history of eggs. It seemed like it was taking forever. What was he doing? Waiting on the hens to lay?

She took a deep breath. She was too wound up. Maybe it was Ashley's surprised look that she had come to breakfast without Chloe or maybe it was because she felt like she didn't belong any-more. She felt like an outsider in the town she had adopted as her own.

Ridiculous. She was being melodramatic. If they were talking about her, fine. She would just take a tip from Joey and Cable and ignore the whispers and the stares, those surreptitious looks, questioning and condemning. But when the two people talked most about by the town were talking about you...well, that put a different spin on things.

Finally, Ashley came out of the back carrying a plastic bag tied at the top. Inside were two square Styrofoam containers.

Finally. Finally. Finally.

"Here ya go." She set the sack on the bar in front of Arlo and rattled off the total.

Arlo handed over her debit card and waited impatiently as Ashley ran it through the antiquated machine, yet another action that seemed to take a lifetime.

She shook her head. She needed to get ahold of her crazy ideas. But having her best friend in jail was taking its toll. She had to figure out how to get Chloe out of lockup as soon as possible.

Finally, the machine did its thing and Arlo signed the slip.

Ashley folded her copy of the receipt and stuffed it into the top of the bag. With a hasty thanks, Arlo was on her way.

She drove over to the police station with the smell of peppers and onions filling her car. Her stomach rumbled as she pulled the Rabbit into a parking space and got out. This was just what she needed: breakfast with her bestie while they planned a way to get her out of jail.

Frances wasn't at the desk when Arlo came through the glass door. Jason Rogers sat in her place. The change brought her up a little short. But Arlo had never been to the station on a Sunday before, and it only made sense. Frances had to have a day off sometime.

"Hi, Jason. I have Chloe's breakfast." She held up the bag.

Jason nodded and straightened from his slouched position. "Just set it on the desk. I'll make sure she gets it."

Arlo stopped completely. "I usually take it back to her."

"Oh?" The one word conveyed that he really didn't care one way or another, but Arlo wasn't going back.

"Mads lets me eat breakfast with Chloe."

"I understand that." Jason stood and held out a hand for the sack.

Arlo pulled it a little closer to her. She needed this breakfast. Chloe needed this breakfast. "Jason…" His name was a plea.

But he crossed his arms and stared down at her. Damn him for being so tall. "Leave the food with me and I'll make sure she gets it."

"But Mads—"

"Didn't leave instructions that you'd be coming by. I suggest you take it up with him."

....

Arlo spotted Mads's large black pickup truck sitting at the city park entrance. She pulled in next to it and got out, leaving her own breakfast in the car.

Jason wouldn't budge on letting her in and Arlo had no choice but to leave Chloe's breakfast with him. Yet that didn't mean it was over.

She started toward the opposite end of the park. If previous visits were anything to go by, he was playing with his dog somewhere on the field side, and he shouldn't be very hard to find.

Luckily he wasn't. Lucky for her. Maybe not so for him.

He spotted her and waved before throwing the ball for his rambunctious pup.

"Mads," she began before she was halfway to him. "You need to get on the phone right now with Jason and tell him that I get to eat breakfast with Chloe in the mornings. He won't let me in and it's unacceptable. She needs me."

Mads looked at her and blinked. "Hi, Arlo."

She sucked in a deep breath to calm herself. It had really been a trying morning. "Hi," she finally said.

"Did he let her have food?" Mads asked.

"Well, yeah, but I usually go in and visit."

"I know, but this is Jason's day to be in charge."

"And you're not going to tell him what to do." She snorted. "What good is that?"

Before he could answer, Dewey returned with the ball. He dropped it at Mads's feet and pawed at his leg to get his attention.

"Hello, boy." Mads scratched the dog behind one ear, then picked up the ball and threw it. Before the ball even left his hand, the pooch was off and running.

"Arlo, Chloe is only in the holding cells as a favor to you. If Jason doesn't want the liability of allowing you to visit her, that's up to him."

"Ugh!" She threw up her hands. "You're hopeless."

Again, he tossed the ball for Dewey and didn't bother to look at her as he replied. "I think you told me that before."

Arlo turned and headed back to her car. She wouldn't be getting anywhere with Mads today and she was pretty sure there was nothing she could do to change Jason's mind. Not wanting to go home, she headed over to the inn.

There were a couple of cars she recognized in the parking area. Camille's boxy silver Mercedes and Fern's bus...er, Lincoln Town Car. Then Arlo remembered: the book club. They had voted to meet there on Sundays when Books & More wasn't open.

She sighed as she reached for the door handle of the inn. At least Sam's shiny red Ford pickup wasn't in the drive. But the first thing she heard when she stepped into the foyer was his deep laugh.

Even now, after all these years, the sound sent goose bumps racing across her arms. But the first thing she saw was Camille. Apparently, she had heard Arlo's car pull up and had been sent to see who was coming to the door.

"Arlo's here," she called in that lilting way of hers. As always, her big white handbag was hooked over one arm. The sight of the purse made Arlo smile. The only constant was change, but it was comforting to know that something always stayed the same.

Today, Camille was dressed all in peach, or rather pale orange, like a Dreamsicle. True to form she wore a cream-colored shell, her vintage pearls, and pastel-orange Nikes.

Arlo shook her head and looked again. Yep. Nike running shoes the exact shade of orange sherbet. "Camille," Arlo started, wondering for a moment if she might regret the question. Too late to stop, she plowed on. "Where do you get orange Nikes?"

Camille looked down at her feet as if she had never seen them before. Then she cast up an innocent look. "The internet," she said, then turned and went back into the common room.

Of course.

Arlo followed behind her.

The members of the book club were seated on couches that faced each other.

"Arlo." Helen stood when she saw Arlo and gave her a quick hug and a kiss on the cheek. "Sit down. Sit down. We were just talking about this mess with Chloe."

She didn't remind them that they were supposed to be talking about a book, *Missing Girl* or *To Kill a Mockingbird*, it didn't matter either way to Arlo. But a book. That was sort of a requirement for a book club. But it seemed the members of this particular branch hadn't gotten the memo on that.

"Where are Inna and Daisy?" Usually when Arlo came to visit there were several guests lounging in the common area, drinking coffee, chatting, and eating whatever tasty treat Helen had whipped up for them.

"Inna left early this morning," Helen replied. "As far as I know Daisy is still in bed."

Fern *tsk*ed. She was an early riser and swore no good ever came from sleeping in.

"Left?" Arlo asked. She wasn't as worried about Daisy's sleeping habits as she was Inna's wanderings.

"She said something about going shopping in Memphis."

Arlo shook her head. "The airport is there too."

Fern shrugged. "Mads told them both not to leave. I don't think she would go against 'the man.'"

Arlo wouldn't describe Mads Keller as "the man," but she knew what Fern meant. He was an imposing figure and most wouldn't think of crossing him.

"Did you take her some breakfast, love?" Camille asked.

"Inna?" She closed her eyes. Somewhere she had lost the thread of the conversation. "No, you mean Chloe."

"That's right, love."

"Yes." She moved around her godmother and sat on the couch between her and Fern. At least that way she wouldn't have to sit next to Sam.

Camille took the space next to Sam and placed her handbag primly in her lap.

"How was she?" Helen asked. "Did she seem okay? She seemed sort of down when I took her dinner last night."

"I don't know," Arlo said on a resigned sigh. "Jason wouldn't let me in to see her."

"What?" Fern was on her feet in an instant. She might look the part of Sweet Little Old Lady, but she had a streak as tough as cast iron. "Let's go." She motioned for everyone to stand. "Come on. I'm serious."

A pint-sized drill sergeant. That was the best way to describe her. After all, everyone dutifully stood and filed out to their cars.

"Sam, you ride with Arlo. The rest can come with me."

17

"WHY CAN'T HE GO WITH YOU?" IN TRUTH, THEY COULD ALL FIT into the Lincoln. It had bench seating and would easily accommodate six people. But if she pointed that out, she might be stuck sitting way too close to Sam. It wasn't that far to the police station from the inn, but any distance was too far in her opinion.

"Oh, there's no room, love." Camille flashed her an innocent smile. Fern wasn't the only one trying to play matchmaker.

"Aren't you going to help me out here?" Arlo sent her godmother a *please help me* look.

She didn't take the hint. "You and Sam will be just fine." Helen ducked into the car and gave her a small wave.

"If you keep this up, you're going to give me a complex."

"Oh yeah?" Arlo ignored the shiver Sam's voice caused and twirled her keys on one finger, allowing them to fall back into her palm. "Let's get this over with."

"Why are you so against me riding with you?" Sam asked once they were in her car and headed for the station.

"You know why." She shot him a look.

"That was ten years ago."

And yet it felt like no time had passed at all. When she looked at him, she saw a mixture of what he was now and what he had been then. He smelled the same. He still had the same crooked smile and that little chip in his front tooth. With all that working against her, how was she supposed to remember that it had been ten years ago and not last week?

"Yeah." She turned her attention back to the road. It wouldn't do any good to crash the car because she was gawking at her passenger.

"And we're neighbors now."

She nodded. "How did you get to the inn?"

"Camille picked me up. That car of hers." He shook his head.

"It's amazing, huh?" And just like Camille—vintage, stylish, and smooth.

"She told me that she saved her money for eight years to be able to buy it on a teacher's salary."

Arlo nodded. "She said she always wanted a Mercedes. I think it was about ten years old when she bought it. She's had it for at least twenty, if the stories I'm hearing about it are correct."

"It's in mint condition," Sam said.

"Just like Camille."

He laughed, and just like that, the moment turned awkward.

Silence descended upon them. Arlo searched her brain for something to say, but all the things that came to mind dealt with the past.

So they rode that way, neither one speaking until she parked her car in the lot next to the police station.

"Thanks for the ride," he said. She couldn't tell if he was just being Sam or if there was something hidden in the words he said.

"Yeah." She swung her purse onto her shoulder and locked the car. Sugar Springs was a small town with small-town values, but a person still had to be careful. *Small town* and *perfect town* were not synonymous.

"I demand you let us back to see Chloe this instant." Camille was standing in front of the reception desk, one hand on her hip, the other supporting her big white bag. The other women two flanked her, a wall of gray hair and Nike running shoes.

Jason stood and crossed his arms. He had Camille by a foot or more, but the little lady wasn't backing down.

"Remember that B you needed in order to play in the state championship game?"

He blinked, and then a red flush started under his collar and worked its way into his face. He turned a ruddy sort of color, not unlike the red clay dirt that accented Northern Mississippi and the neighboring states.

"You gave me extra credit work to help my grade. I earned it." But his voice didn't sound as confident as it had before.

"You may have earned it, but I gave it to you. I created that work so you could have the chance to make it up. And if I had marked all the punctuation errors in your essay question…" She trailed off with an expressive shrug.

"But the question was on *Hamlet*. Not punctuation."

"Yes, but it was still an English class. Now do be a love and let us through."

To Arlo's utter amazement, he did as she said. Even Sam looked impressed.

"Chloe, dear," Camille called, peering around the corner into the dogleg corridor where the holding cells were.

"Camille?"

"Yes, love, and I've brought a few friends."

Chloe wrapped her hands around the bars and stood on her tiptoes to get a better view. "Oh my gosh." Arlo saw the brief sheen of tears in her eyes before she blinked them away. "I'm so happy to see y'all."

"We're happy to see you too," Arlo replied. "I brought your breakfast, but…"

She nodded. "I know. I got it. Thank you."

"Oh my," Camille exclaimed. "I forgot to get you some lunch." She opened her purse and took out a twenty like a magician pulling a rabbit from his hat. "Sam, go get Chloe something to eat. What would you like, love?"

"Whatever is fine."

"Pizza," Camille said with a definite nod. "Pepperoni or cheese?"

"Pepperoni," Chloe and Arlo said at the same time.

Arlo turned to her friend and chuckled. It was almost a normal moment. Of course it did help that Sam had moved out of her space. Granted, him being within five yards of her these days constituted being in her space. And what was she going to do about it?

Nothing.

That was over and done. But it was different with Mads. She had been around him longer. Once Sam had been in town for a while, say a couple of years, she would grow accustomed to him. Then this crazy attraction she had for him and the past could be put behind her…in a box…with her crazy attraction for Mads…and locked… for all eternity.

Yep. Good plan.

"Here, love." Camille reached into her purse and pulled out a large file. Honestly the thing was so long, Arlo wasn't sure how she got it in her bag in the first place.

"What are you doing?" Arlo asked.

Camille pushed the file between the bars so Chloe could reach it better. Thank goodness she didn't touch the thing. "I'm giving her a file. Isn't that what you're supposed to do when someone you care about is in jail?"

"No." Arlo did everything in her power to keep her voice at a normal pitch. It would do no good to alert Jason to what was going on just outside of Chloe's cell. "Now put that thing away."

Camille pursed her lips, then put the file back in her handbag. "How about this?" She brought out a skeleton key.

"No." Once again, Arlo nearly yelled while Fern and Helen laughed behind their hands.

"I told you," Helen said. "She has everything in there."

"I'm beginning to believe you!" Arlo shook her head.

"I appreciate the sentiment, Camille, but all the jail cells are electronic now." Chloe gave her a sweet smile. Arlo knew she was feeling grateful that someone cared enough about her to try to break her out not once but twice.

"I didn't know." Camille tucked the key back into her handbag.

Crisis averted, Arlo turned her attention to her friend and business partner. "How are you holding up?"

Chloe shrugged. "As well as can be expected, I suppose."

"Are you sure you don't want me to get Jayden?"

"No. I don't want him to see me here."

Arlo nodded. "If you're sure."

"I'm sure."

A movement caught her attention out of the corner of her eye. She turned to see Camille fiddling with the control knobs on a small metal box.

"What is that?" Arlo asked. The thing had to have come out of that near-magical handbag.

"It's an EMP pulse generator."

"A what?" Helen asked.

"Give me that." Arlo grabbed it from her thin fingers.

"What is it?" Fern asked.

Arlo caught Chloe's gaze. Her friend laughed for what could have been the first time since going to jail. It was a welcomed sound, but not perfect. She needed to be laughing on the other side of the bars.

"It's a device to interrupt electronic impulses."

Fern nodded in understanding. "And it will open the doors of her cell."

"Yes, and mess up our phones, the computers out there, even the computers in our cars," Arlo added. "Where did you get such a thing?"

"The internet." Camille gave her an innocent look. About as innocent as the cat with a mouthful of canary.

Arlo shook her head. Ever since the book club had started, these three ladies had kept her on her toes. But she hadn't expected the extra work to come from sweet Aussie schoolteacher Camille.

"Can I have it back please?" Camille held out one hand.

Arlo pulled it close to her chest. "Do you promise to put it away and not use it for…nefarious purposes?"

She raised her fingers in a pledge. "Scout's honor."

"You weren't a scout," Fern interjected.

"Hush, Fern." Camille waved a hand toward her friend but didn't turn around. "Please."

Behind them Chloe laughed again.

Twice in one day, Arlo thought. This trip was totally worth it.

....

Arlo pasted on a smile and entered the police station bright and early the next morning. She had stopped by the supermarket and picked up a couple of pastries, then stopped at Books & More to get a cup of tea for Chloe. She hadn't complained about Arlo's brewing efforts. But Arlo suspected it was only because she was trying to keep her chin up and be grateful. Hard things to do when one was locked in an iron-and-concrete cell.

"Hi, Frances," she greeted the woman behind the desk.

The receptionist/makeshift dispatcher raised her attention from the morning paper and shot Arlo a quick and rueful smile. "How much longer before you can get Chloe out of here?"

"Soon, I hope." Then the worry flooded in. "Why? Did something happen? Is she okay?"

Frances took a sip of coffee from the mug on her desk and winced. "No, I just miss her coffee."

Arlo stumbled with relief but managed to get herself back together in the next step.

"Careful, child."

"Is Mads here?" she asked.

"Who do you think made the coffee?"

Of course.

"Do you need to see him?"

Before Arlo could answer, Mads came out of his office. "Hey," he said by way of greeting. "I thought I heard you out here. You got Chloe's breakfast?"

"I do, but I wanted to talk to you about something."

"Okay."

"In your office, please."

He motioned her in. "You don't want to give Chloe her breakfast first?"

"This will only take a minute." She stepped into his office and turned as he walked in behind her. The place was getting way too comfortable for her. She had been there too many times in the last few days.

"I told the ladies that I would talk to you about this. So here I am." She drew in a deep breath before continuing. "Why are you letting them wait so long before having the memorial service for Wally?"

He crossed his arms and gave her another one of those annoying cop looks. Or maybe it was an annoyed-cop look. "What difference does it make?"

"It's a bad idea to wait too long. It'll give time for word to spread, for people to find out, the media to come." She shook her head. "I'm afraid it's going to be crazy around here."

"And it hasn't been crazy since Wally was killed?"

"Not the same kind of crazy."

"It's done." His words were flat and brooked no argument. "And Jeff at the funeral home up in Memphis can't have the ashes back to us before late this afternoon."

"Why did you send him to Memphis?"

"Inna insisted on it."

"You mean Daisy."

"What?"

"Daisy's his wife. Not Inna."

"I know."

"And Inna insisted that he be taken to Memphis?"

"That's what I said." Mads's patience had come to its end.

Arlo nodded. "I said I would talk to you, and I did." She started to brush past him and out of the office when a familiar voice with an unmistakable accent sounded from the reception area of the station.

"Where is the lawman? I need to speak to head of police here."

"Are we done?" Mads asked.

Arlo nodded.

He left her standing there as he made his way toward Frances's desk. "Can I help you?" he asked.

"I come to tell you that I do not understand why you have blond-haired coffee bar worker arrested. She is not guilty. You should see this when is obvious that my Wally's wife is one who killed him."

"I appreciate your concern, but I feel my team has made the right deduction in this case and the DA happens to agree." He shrugged.

"Did you not find mushrooms in his coffee? Her family owns whole farm of them. You know this, yes? And the earring that belongs to the wife. She is the one who should be in cage. Not coffee girl."

Mads shifted. "Thank you, Miss Kolisnychenko. I'll keep that in mind."

Inna nodded but didn't seem to notice the sarcastic tone.

"How do you know the earring belongs to Daisy?"

"I have same ones. One, two." She showed them. "But Daisy? She bring them, but they are nowhere now. How does that happen?"

A moment passed between them. A moment that was filled with silence.

"You answer now?" Inna asked.

Mads cleared his throat. "I thought it was a rhetorical question."

"No." Inna shifted and propped a hand on her hip while she waited. "The answer will put right women in jail. The one you have now is innocent."

"Thank you," he said. Again.

With nothing else she could say in return, Inna turned on her heel and sashayed out of the building.

Mads watched her as she left. Or should she say he watched Inna's swaying backside.

Arlo stared at him until the sheer force of her gaze turned his attention back to her.

"What?" he said. "You agree with her?"

"You know I do."

Mads nodded. "I know. But you have to understand, I have more evidence than a family mushroom farm and a pair of diamond earrings."

"I guess knowing the accused since grade school isn't a good enough reason."

"You've been watching too much of the *Andy Griffith Show*. Small town law enforcement doesn't work that way. I have to follow the evidence and all the evidence points to Chloe being guilty."

And yesterday's will reading certainly didn't help matters. It gave Chloe a fantastic reason for knocking off the ex-boyfriend. Money. And who didn't need some of that?

Arlo wanted to protest, tell him how that didn't matter. Money was important but not the boss of Chloe, but it was going to take more than words to convince Mads to let Chloe go.

....

"He knows that you met with Wally the morning he was killed," Arlo said when she entered the containment room where the holding cells were located.

"Did he say something?" Chloe asked.

"He didn't have to."

Chloe sighed. "I told him."

Arlo stopped unpacking the croissants she bought at the grocery store bakery and stared at her friend. "Why would you do such a thing?"

"I promised to tell the truth."

"Not that kind of truth." She separated out one of the croissants, set it on the tabletop and stared at the paper underneath. "Wait a minute," she said. "Wait a doggone minute."

"What?" Chloe asked.

"These wrappers. They are identical to the ones we use at the shop."

"And…"

"And he could have gotten the scones at the supermarket, not from you."

"I've already told you," Chloe said. "Piggly Wiggly doesn't carry any scones."

Arlo glared at her. "Really? That's all you get from this? Don't you understand? We don't know one hundred percent that the killer didn't meet him with the pastries. 'You bring the food, and I'll bring the coffee.' And if they stopped at the store, then they will be on the security camera!"

"That's a lot of ifs," Chloe said. "No wonder I didn't make the connection."

"We don't know that Wally didn't stop at the grocery store before coming to the bookstore. Did you notice him carrying a bag or anything?"

Chloe shook her head. "But I wasn't looking. I didn't know to pay attention to every little detail. How many times do you know that the time you're talking to someone will be the last time you ever get to speak to them again?" Her eyes filled with tears.

"I know. I just want to get you out of here."

"The problem isn't with the food they say he ate; it's with the coffee." Which Chloe had made.

"Did he get a second coffee? You know, for someone else?"

"No. I've answered all this before."

"I was just hoping that something else would stand out of the story."

"Like what?"

"Like he got a coffee and two scones because he was meeting someone."

"On the third floor of our building? After he came by to talk to me? That doesn't make any sense. And the only person he would have been meeting there would have been the Realtor."

"Think hard, Chloe. Did he mention anything about that when he was with you?"

"All he talked about was Jayden. I think he'd had him watched or something. He knew too much about him. Too much for a sperm donor who wanted nothing to do with his child for nine years."

"You're sure?" She didn't bother to say anything about Chloe's sperm-donor comment. Chloe hadn't gone to a clinic but essentially that was what Wally had become.

Chloe rubbed her temples. "I'm sure."

....

Arlo was loath to leave Chloe, but what choice did she have? None. She had to open Books & More and pretend like nothing was out of sorts.

Arlo let herself into Books & More and propped the door open without turning on the lights. It was early for the official opening, but late as far as Chloe was concerned.

"Hey, Arlo."

She turned to find Phil from next door standing close. Either he was a quick and silent mover, or she had been deep in her daydreams.

"Hi, Phil."

He shifted. "Can I get a cup of coffee? Chloe always let me buy a cup before opening."

"Of course. Let me get the lights. You don't mind the Keurig, do you? I'm not much on working the espresso machine, and Courtney doesn't come in until three thirty." She led the way into the shop and headed to the back to turn on the lights.

"Keurig is fine." Phil stopped at the bar and knocked his knuckles against the counter while he waited for her to return.

"I can hear you," Faulkner crooned. "You don't think I can, but I can." His echo sounded more than a little creepy.

"Help yourself," Arlo called back to Phil and turned on the lights before going back to the front.

Phil had already filled the coffee machine and had a cup brewing. "Is Chloe okay there in the jail?"

"She seems to be," Arlo said. She went around to the backside of the coffee bar and grabbed her own K-cup for the morning. "She's still here instead of at the county jail, so that's a plus. But Mads isn't going to let her stay here for long."

"Then what?" Phil took a sip of his coffee and waited for Arlo to answer.

It was a question she didn't know how to respond to. What

would happen after the ten days had passed? Would Mads make good on his promise to send Chloe to the county jail? Would she be able to survive if he did? Arlo didn't want to wait and find out firsthand. And the only way to do that was to uncover who really killed Wally.

"Phil," she started, turning to her next-door neighbor on Main Street. "The morning that Wally died. Did you see anything? Anything at all that might seem suspicious."

Phil shrugged. "Not much happens around here."

That was an understatement. Maybe she needed to go about this from a different angle. "What did you see that morning?"

Phil leaned one hip against the counter and sipped his coffee. He was a tall man, thin and wiry despite his age. His sixtieth birthday and come and gone a few years back, but he refused to retire, stating that he felt the good citizens of Sugar Springs needed the unique services his store had to offer. Arlo hadn't yet figured out what those services were exactly. But Phil had always been a good enough Main Street neighbor. "I saw Chloe let him in that morning really early. It was hard to tell how she felt about him. She would start toward him, then pull back as if she wanted to touch him but knew she couldn't. Like a junkie faced with a bag of drugs."

It was a crude analogy—crude but accurate.

"Anything else?"

"Nothing really. I came down to get a cup a little bit later and saw Wally and some man standing outside the other entrance."

18

"ANOTHER MAN? WHO?"

"I dunno. I've seen him before but can't remember where."

Arlo's heart began to thump. "You've seen him here? In Sugar Springs?" This could be the missing link they had been looking for.

"I think so. Maybe. I don't go many other places." Like Arlo, he worked in his shop from open to close six days a week.

"Did they go in the building? Up to the third floor?"

"They went inside. I don't know where they went from there."

"But they were outside? At the door that leads to the third floor?"

"Yes."

"What did he look like?"

"I don't know." He gave a loose shrug.

"Anything," she pleaded.

"He was tall. Kinda bald, with the fringe around the edge."

It wasn't much of a description, but it was a start.

"You've seen him before. Does he live here?" she asked.

"I'm not sure."

"How did he get a key?" The man Wally was with had to have had a key. There were no signs of a break-in, and Arlo and Chloe were careful about keeping it locked.

"How would I know?" Phil shot her a stern look.

"Right," she said. "Maybe from Sandy," she mused. But she was certain Mads had questioned the Realtor. He was thorough that way. But he wasn't perfect. Maybe there was something he had missed.

Green Reality was only a couple of blocks from Books & More. After lunch, when the book club got there, she would head down the street and see what Sandy had to say about this strange man who let Wally onto the third floor just before he was murdered.

....

"Hi, Arlo. I wasn't expecting to see you today."

Arlo smiled at Sandy Green, Sugar Springs's only Realtor—blond hair, brown eyes, with a little extra weight around the middle, but still as cute and dimpled as she had been when she was voted homecoming queen her senior year. "I was hoping I could talk to you about something."

Sandy smiled. "Of course," she drawled. "Everything okay with your new tenant?"

"Sam?" Arlo stumbled over the name as she said it, then composed herself. "He's all moved in." She thought so anyway. There hadn't been much noise coming from up on the third floor this morning.

"Good, good." Sandy continued to smile. "So what did you need to talk about?"

Arlo cleared her throat. She thought that she had this all lined out, but now that she was there... "The day Wally...fell...did you give someone a key to let him into the third floor?"

"No. I already told Mads all about it. I wasn't even in town then."

"You weren't?"

"I had gone over to New Albany to visit my mother." A frown darkened her otherwise chipper features.

"How's she doing?"

"Good, just—" She stopped, and to Arlo's surprise, her eyes filled with tears. "I'm sorry." The trickle turned into all-out sobs.

Arlo moved toward her, unsure of how to proceed but feeling obligated to do something.

Sandy held up one hand and grabbed a tissue with the other. She sniffed as she tried to pull herself together.

"So sorry." Sandy sniffed again.

"Did something happen?" Arlo really didn't want to get involved. She had enough on her own plate right now, but she couldn't ignore the breakdown happening in front of her.

"I came home from my mama's a little early and found my boyfriend…" Tears welled again, and she pressed a hand to her mouth. "Anyway…that's over now."

"This boyfriend," Arlo started.

"Ex-boyfriend," Sandy corrected.

"Right. Ex-boyfriend. Is he balding and tall?"

Sandy stopped. "How did you know that?"

"Does he have the keys to my building?"

"N-no. Of course not, but my work keys were on a hook at my house when I left."

"And where was the boyfriend all the time you were gone?"

"Our—I mean, my house. We were moving in together. He knows where I keep all my business stuff. We were going to be married." She dabbed her eyes again, careful to not muss her makeup.

Arlo hadn't known Sandy's boyfriend…hadn't even known Sandy *had* a boyfriend. Until now. "Do you think he could have given your set of keys to the third floor to Wally?"

"Why would Wally want to see the third floor of your building?"

"Maybe he wanted to use it as an office space or something. That's not the point. Could he have given the key to Wally?" She waited impatiently for Sandy to answer. Instead, the Realtor got out her phone and tapped the screen. She nodded and put the phone to her ear as if the answers to all Arlo's questions were forthcoming.

"Travis, you lying, cheating pile of dog feces. Did you give the key to 309 Main to Wally Harrison last week? Thursday to be exact. That's the same day you decided to throw our love in the gutter and piss on it. Just wondering. Call me when you get this." The dimples mixed with tears as she hung up the phone and took a deep, relieved breath. "He didn't answer." She told Arlo.

"Travis?" she asked. "Coleman?"

"That's right." Sandy harrumphed, obviously still a little wound up.

"Travis Coleman is your boyfriend." It wasn't much of a question.

"Ex-boyfriend."

"Right. And Travis Coleman had access to the third floor of my building."

"I didn't know he was going to use them." A defensive edge had taken over her tone.

"I know. Just making sure I have my facts straight."

Sandy nodded understandingly.

And Arlo had more than enough to go on. "Thanks for all your help, Sandy. By the way…do you think I could possibly get Travis's number? I would like to see if he remembers anything about that day." *Like if Wally had been alone or with someone. Had he already stopped at the store and bought scones before dropping by Sandy's to pick up a key to Arlo's third floor? Or if maybe the grief over his brother's death had finally gotten the better of him and he pushed Wally to his own demise in retaliation.*

"You want his number?" Sandy seemed surprised.

"He might respond…quicker if I call." *And refrain from insulting him.*

Sandy shrugged. "Prank call him a little for me too, will ya?"

Arlo mumbled something that she hoped Sandy took for a yes, then got the number and headed for the door.

....

Arlo dialed Travis's number all the way back to the police station. She knew he wouldn't answer. Even if he was inclined to answer calls from numbers he didn't know, she was sure Sandy's message would turn him off the minute he listened to it.

The line went to voicemail again and again. She hung up. Leaving a message would probably do no good after the butt-chewing Sandy had given him. "One more," she muttered as she dialed the number again.

Voicemail.

But this time she did leave a message, a quick one stating who she was, that she needed to talk to him about something important, and her phone number.

She pocketed her phone as she pushed through the glass doors leading into the police station.

"Hey, Frances."

She looked up from her paper, the beaded chain that held her glasses in place around her neck swaying with the motion. "Hi, Arlo. Here to see Chloe? Go on back."

"Actually, I need to see Mads."

"He's gone."

Arlo stopped. She had drawn even with Frances's desk, intending to walk right past and into Mads's office. "He's not here?"

Frances sat back in her chair and gave Arlo a little smile. "He does get out once and a while. You know, to solve crimes and such."

"I know," Arlo said defensively. Just why did he have to be gone the time she really needed to talk to him? "Can you have him call me? Or come down to Books & More as soon as he gets back?"

"Regarding?"

"I think I know who killed Wally Harrison."

....

"Welcome back. Come on in," Faulkner said as Arlo returned to Books & More.

She ignored the bird and instead turned her attention to the now once-a-day book club ladies. Camille and Fern were seated in the reading nook, while Helen worked behind the coffee counter, no doubt making everyone drinks. No one was holding a book.

"I thought y'all were reading today," Arlo said. She looked at them all in turn, but only Camille braved an answer.

"I can't speak for everyone, but I have a new great-grandbaby on the way and I need to get this blanket done for the little tyke."

The tyke was actually so little that the family hadn't found out the gender yet. But that didn't stop Camille from knitting away in soft pale green. Arlo wondered how she got any knits and purls done around the lump in her lap that was her handbag, but she didn't ask.

"Sam not coming?" She moved behind the coffee bar, taking Helen's place as she came out with a tray balancing three drinks, one hot coffee, one iced coffee, one hot tea for Camille.

"He's got something else today." Fern waved a hand around as if she were shooing off a pesky fly. "But he said he would come tomorrow."

Of course. She took a bottle of water from the fridge and started toward the back office. "I hate to impose, but with Chloe gone…"

"You want us to watch the front?"

"Would you mind?" she asked. "I have some paperwork to finish up and—" *And Chloe being in jail left a big hole*, but she didn't want to say that. She didn't want to talk about Chloe being in jail or that her days of agreement with Mads were running out. They were almost gone and the best clue she had lay with a man who had just been called a lying pile of dog doo. And cheating. Don't forget the cheating.

Helen agreed to come get her in case someone needed something, and Arlo escaped into the office. She wasn't lying; she did have paperwork to do. She had to mark the damaged books from Wally's display out of her inventory. She had to check the orders and see if there was anything new she needed to get for the store. She needed to check Chloe's coffee invoices and see if anything was lacking there. She had done the coffee order once before, right after they first opened, and she was certain she could do it again without messing anything up beyond repair, but she was still a little upset that she had to.

Her best friend was in jail, accused of murder, and here she sat ordering K-cups, coffee filters, and two dozen copies of Stephen King's latest paperback. What was wrong with her? She needed to be out there doing whatever needed to be done in order to prove Chloe's innocence. And she would be, if she had any idea what that next step might be.

A knock sounded on the door and she jumped to her feet. Her first thought was that Mads had come to find out what new information she had.

"Come in," she called, then waited for Mads to appear. The storeroom/office was narrow and windy, and the office part was a little secluded, tucked back in a corner away from all else. It was great in those times when the store was busy, and she needed to get away. So far that had never happened—she had never been so busy that she needed to get away—but she was glad it was set up that way all the same. It made her feel a little more secure to have her business info more than one door from nosy third graders on a field trip.

"Arlo?"

She swung her gaze to Sam Tucker, standing in the entry way to the office. Not Mads.

"S-Sam?" she stammered. "What are you doing here?"

"Can you come look at something with me for a minute please?" His voice was quiet but there was something about it that relayed an urgency.

"Sure." Whatever his issue was, it was most probably better than staring at paperwork she didn't have the concentration to finish, even if she had the mental desire.

She stood and followed him to the interior door that led to the stairway and up to the third floor. The chair that usually blocked the entrance was pushed to one side.

"Did you come down this way?" Arlo asked.

"Yeah. You don't mind, do you?" Sam continued to climb, affording her an intimate look at his tight backside as he moved ahead of her. He must work out. A lot. "It's easier to come this way if I'm coming in to see you or to get a coffee. But I'll use the other door for my business traffic and when I come and go for the day."

"No problem." She was almost sad when they reached the third-floor landing. "What do you need?" *Please don't let it be a leaky pipe.* It was the first thing she could think of. There was a bathroom on both the second and third levels and two on the main floor. It was an old building with old plumbing. She was surprised she hadn't had an issue and she supposed she was due for one. Though she wasn't sure where she was going to get money for a plumber to come in and repair a bunch of pipes.

He paused for a moment, his expression unreadable, then he motioned her behind his extra-large L-shaped desk. Three laptops sat on the mahogany wood, though only one was open. Next to the window a chair had been placed. A tablet sat there, plugged into the wall outlet nearby. He hadn't added much to the large space, other than the desk and the chair. But she saw a box in one corner that looked like it had the word *futon* printed on it and a large-screen TV box propped up against that.

"Here." He gestured for her to sit while he stood next to her, tapping keys on the open laptop.

"What happened to your hand?" Three large angry marks slashed across the back of his hand. The marks were red and painful looking.

He motioned in the air, a noncommittal gesture. "Auggie." He said the name with obvious derision. "He's not very happy with all the moves, I guess."

Arlo stared at the scratches. "I guess." What else could she say? "Where is he now?"

Another vague gesture toward a dark corner of the room. "His carrier is over there. I feed him, then back away. I stay out of his way and he stays out of mine." He ruefully looked at his wound. "Mostly."

He pulled a document up on the screen. "Here," Sam said.

"What exactly is that?" she asked.

"That is a receipt from the store where Wally bought two pairs of diamond earrings."

"Six carats? Those earrings Inna had on weren't six carats." Was it getting hot in there? Maybe she needed to make sure Sam had an extra window unit to combat the Mississippi heat.

"Jewelers categorize the earrings by total weight. So six-carat earrings would be—"

"Three each," she said along with him. And four earrings were twelve carats. Wow. "Wait," she said, the significance of his find dawning on her. "Where did you get this?"

"The jewelry store," he said with a quirk of one brow.

How had she forgotten he was a private investigator? And this piece of evidence just proved that he was still on the case. But working for who?

"He bought two pairs," she mused with a smile. "One for his wife and one for his mistress."

"Assistant," Sam corrected.

"Whatever. Everyone in America knows he was sleeping with Inna." Even though Daisy was beautiful and sexy and quite a catch. Some men just weren't satisfied with what they had and always wanted more. "This proves it," she said, pulling her thoughts back on track. "This proves that Daisy had earrings like the one found at the crime scene and the earring I found at Chloe's belongs to her."

"No. This proves that Wally bought two pairs of identical earrings just before Christmas last year."

"One for Inna and one—"

"Additional pair that could have been for anybody. Including Chloe."

"But—" she protested. She didn't want him to be right, but he was. They couldn't prove that Wally hadn't given the earrings to Chloe, even though Arlo knew she would have told her if he had. That was just the kind of friends they were. Chloe wouldn't have kept them from her.

"He could have just as easily given those earrings to Chloe as Daisy. Or the other way around," Arlo mused.

"He could have just as easily given those earrings to Inna."

"Fingerprints." She snapped her fingers.

Sam shook his head. "There's not a chance of lifting a viable print from those earrings."

"If there's nothing that can be done with this discovery, why are you telling me?"

Sam shrugged. "I just thought you should know."

....

He thought she should know.

The words knocked around inside Arlo's head for the rest of the day. Through all the book club's chatter about mushrooms and poisons, affairs and new books, it was all she could think about.

He wanted her to know. Why? And, even better, why hadn't she asked Sam again who had hired him? And someone had him on the payroll. Why else would he be digging around in an active police murder investigation?

Because he wouldn't tell her who. He might share a piece of evidence with her, but he wasn't outing his client. Not that she could blame him; she hadn't told him about her discovery. But his sort of knocked hers out of the water. Travis may have had access to the third floor of the building and he may have been up there with Wally. But someone else had been there too. Someone who dropped a very expensive diamond earring.

Aside from hacking into the computer at Tiffany's, he could have gotten it from Wally's accountant. Taxes and expenses were one thing that Inna did not take care of. The accountant would have the information. Inna could have it too, she supposed. Or maybe Daisy. She was his wife after all, even though Wally seemed to forget that from time to time.

Or maybe he really did get it from the jewelry store.

Arlo eased behind the coffee bar to the small fridge Chloe kept there and retrieved a bottle of water. She had given up coffee for the day. The caffeine and her whirling thoughts were making her jitterier that normal.

The book club still sat in the reading nook. Camille had put her knitting away and was taking notes. Arlo wasn't sure what she was writing, having tuned out their chatter long ago, but no one held a copy of either *Missing Girl* or *To Kill a Mockingbird*. Some book club.

"Aren't y'all supposed to be reading?" she asked them.

Helen answered. "We called Wally's publisher."

Arlo whirled to face her godmother. "Helen! What were you thinking?"

"We wanted to know if he had any more books coming out."

"And?"

Helen shook her head. "He hasn't turned in his next book yet." Hadn't turned it in? "He's a couple of months late and won't even let them see sample chapters."

"His editor told you this?" Arlo asked. That was valuable and perhaps damaging information.

"One of the secretaries." Helen smiled innocently.

"You can't trust that she told you the truth," Arlo said.

"I guess that's kind of a moot point now," Camille chimed in.

"You would think," Helen said.

Something about the tone of her voice sounded suspicious. "What did you do?"

Fern sauntered up with a smile. "We called his agent."

Arlo pinched the bridge of her nose and moved around the two of them to collapse onto one of the reading nook couches. This was either going to be really good or really bad. "What did he say?"

"She."

"I beg your pardon?" Arlo asked.

"Wally's agent is a she. Veronica Tisdale."

Of course Wally had a female agent. He was just the kind of guy who surrounded himself with beauty. Arlo took out her phone and googled the name. Veronica was African American with high cheekbones and permed hair. She was gorgeous in a Miss America sort of way and Arlo had to wonder if Ms. Tisdale was smart like Inna or a timid, girl-next-door like Daisy. Or maybe she was somewhere in between. But if the sharp light in her eyes was any indication, she had an off-the-charts IQ to go with a body that just wouldn't quit.

"His editor's a woman too."

Fern's voice sounded close to her shoulder.

"What?"

"I read an article in *Publisher's Weekly* about how he insisted that he have a woman editor in order for her to get his female character and his female writing voice."

"Really?" She wasn't sure if she was more surprised that he had demanded any particular editor seeing as how *Missing Girl* was his first book or that the book did have a female voice.

Why had she never noticed before?

But unlike S.E. Hinton, a woman who wrote from a strong male point of view, or J.K. Rowling, who wanted to gently disguise the fact that she was a woman writing books targeted toward a young male audience, Wally embraced his identity. His full name plus middle initial was on the front, his author photo took up the entire back of the book. Yet his female lead was strong, perhaps even stronger than the male. And the surprise twist at the end...well, a person had to be a woman in order to fully understand the perils his female protagonist faced.

Or maybe she was reading too much into it.

"Cheryl Flanagan." Camille smiled. "Look her up."

Arlo wasn't entirely certain she wanted to. But if she had to guess, Ms. Flanagan was redheaded, with green eyes, a killer body, and was highly intelligent.

She missed the eyes. Cheryl Flanagan had blue eyes, but everything else was the same. Top of her class at NYU, graduated a year early, went to work for Davis and Broadstreet Publishing as a summer intern, and became an associate editor two short years later.

It just went on from there. Arlo stopped reading.

"What do you suppose he sees in Daisy?" she mused.

"That girl is beautiful."

"Not that. She just..." She didn't know how to say the words without being unkind. Instead she went back into her browser and printed the pages for his posse of women.

"Look here," she said, holding up the papers. "His editor was a child prodigy. His agent is a member of Mensa."

"What about Inna, his assistant?" Helen asked.

"I couldn't find anything on her. The rest had Wikipedia pages."

"That's weird," Helen mused.

"A lot of people in the industry have wiki pages," Fern informed them.

"No, it's weird that there's nothing on Inna."

Arlo shrugged. "It's almost like she doesn't exist. There are a few connections with her to Wally. You know, at parties and such, but nothing else."

"Facebook," Fern said hopefully.

"Nope."

"Good for her," Helen said. "It's just a time suck anyway, and smart, beautiful, intelligent women avoid such drains if at all possible." She tossed her braid over her shoulder, obviously identifying with this group.

Fern looked unfazed.

"Come here." Camille called them over to one of the store's computers. "Look what I found."

On the screen was a picture of Daisy. The picture was old enough that Arlo didn't recognize her at first. "High school?" she asked.

"Graduation," Camille confirmed.

"That explains the cap and gown," Fern drily commented.

"Not important," Camille said. "Look at this." She highlighted a passage.

"Valedictorian?" Arlo gasped. "Did she go to a small school?"

"Well, yeah, but it was also exclusive. It seems that Mrs. James-Harrison had a scholarship to Camden Prep in Saint Louis."

Behind her she could hear Camille typing something into her smartphone. "A school known for its focus on academics."

"You're saying she went to school that specializes in academics on a scholarship for academics, and she was the smartest one there?"

Arlo shrugged. "Being valedictorian doesn't always mean the smartest, but it definitely means she was dedicated to making good grades."

"But I thought she was…" Camille stalled, too polite to actually continue.

"A ditz," Helen supplied.

"Well, yes." She smiled apologetically.

"We all do…did," Arlo corrected.

"Why?" Fern asked.

"Because that's how she acts," Arlo said.

"Because she wants us to believe that she's an airhead," Helen added.

"Everybody," Camille said. "Not just us."

Arlo looked back at the picture of the young Daisy James-Harrison. Why would someone so smart pretend to be something else, and why would Wally, who seemed to attract smart, beautiful women, allow her to do so? Or had he even known?

19

MADS CAME BY BOOKS & MORE JUST AFTER COURTNEY TOOK UP her place behind the coffee bar. Several teenagers had gathered around. Everyone had a coffee drink and a copy of *The Handmaid's Tale*. This was just what she had wanted from the shop, readers meeting and discussing books. She knew that the kids were reading Margaret Atwood as part of their senior English work, but they were reading and that was all that mattered.

But Chloe was missing it all.

"Frances said you wanted to see me."

Arlo nodded. "I thought I had something about the case for you."

"Why do I hear a 'but' in there?" He leaned one arm against the coffee bar in that lazy way he had. His gaze drifted around the shop, its travels equally as languorous as his attitude, but Arlo knew how alert he really was.

"I just may have jumped the gun a bit." She shrugged as if it was nothing as Courtney brought a steaming to-go cup over to Mads.

"Chief," she said with a smile.

"Thank you." He reached for his wallet but she shook her head.

"It's on the house," she said, then turned to Arlo for verification.

"Of course."

"Now this evidence," he started after Courtney had moved away. "Why don't you let me be the judge of how important it is."

Arlo sucked in a deep breath and let it out in a quick exhale. "Travis Coleman is dating Sandy Green."

Mads blew over the top of his coffee and waited for her to continue.

"He had access to Sandy's keys. And consequently the extra set of keys to the third floor."

She could feel his impatience. Or perhaps she was simply too in tune with him. "Phil saw Travis with Wally the morning Wally was killed."

"Saw him?" Mads asked. His expression gave nothing away.

"Going up to the third floor. Letting him in anyway."

"Are you investigating?" Mads asked.

"No, uh, maybe a little." She backpedaled as he straightened. "I just sort of stumbled onto this."

"And you think Travis could have killed Wally."

"Yes." She let out another deep breath. "He would have motive. His brother's death. Maybe he's been waiting all these years to get his revenge." She nodded. "Yes?"

Mads shook his head. "Do me a favor, Arlo. Start reading romances or self-help books—anything but mysteries—and leave the investigating to the professionals."

"Does that mean you're not going to check it out?"

He started for the door. "I'll check it out," he said. "You sell books. Deal?"

"Deal," she said. Now if she could just convince the book club ladies.

....

"What are you doing?" Arlo asked later that afternoon. It was nearly closing time, and she wanted nothing more than to go home and put her feet up on the trunk she used as a coffee table and do... nothing. Do absolutely nothing. She was pretty sure she could only stand five or so minutes of it. But she wanted to try anyway.

"We're going on a stakeout of Daisy."

"No." Arlo passed the coffee drink off to the customer and was around the counter in a heartbeat. Courtney had been showing her how to make a few of their most popular drinks. Arlo hadn't wanted to learn, since it felt like she was admitting that Chloe might not get out of jail anytime soon, but she couldn't push her own fears off on her coffee-loving customers. She stopped short. "How are you going to do a stakeout when Daisy's staying at the inn?"

Fern was right behind Camille. She tapped her temple with one finger. The gesture pushed up the edge of her cowboy hat. "We overheard Daisy talking about meeting someone at the steakhouse tonight. So we're going over there and seeing what it's all about."

"You *overheard*, huh?"

Camille gave an insignificant shrug. "People talk."

"And in a place like the inn, sometimes people go into the bathroom and talk to other people on the phone so people around can't hear."

"Go on." There had to be more, she just knew it.

"Old houses have large air vents."

"Uh-huh. And I suppose Helen is in on this with you."

"Of course," Camille chirped. "She sent us in here to check the lost and found for disguises."

Arlo resisted the urge to tug the silly stocking cap from Camille's snow-white head and tip the cowboy hat from Fern's. It wasn't a crime to wear inappropriate headwear in the Mississippi summer heat; it simply looked ridiculous. Camille and Fern were past the age of consent—way past—and neither one had been diagnosed with dementia. There wasn't a lot Arlo could do about their planned stakeout. Except maybe try to talk them out of it. After all, she had promised Mads.

Camille waggled one finger at her. "Oh no you don't. I know that look. That's the same look you gave Helen when she said she wanted to get a tattoo in place of her missing breast."

"And when she said she wanted to dye her hair," Fern added.

"You're the reason she only did the ends."

"Which looks fantastic on her, but still," Fern said. She propped her hands on her hips and waited for Arlo to reply.

"That was different," Arlo said. Those times only affected Helen. Now a possibly innocent woman would be involved as well as whoever it was she was meeting. Not to mention everyone at the restaurant, if the ladies ended up making a scene, which with their track record was inevitable.

She couldn't stop them from going—free country and all that—but neither could she stand by and just allow them to waltz into the stakeout dressed like cat burglars and train robbers.

"Fine," she said. "But no hats, and we pretend like it's Camille's birthday."

....

A couple passed Arlo and the book club ladies as they sat in the lobby of the steakhouse. Both the man and the woman gave them a questioning glance but said nothing as the hostess immediately sat them.

"If we have to wait here much longer, we're going to miss everything that happens between Daisy and whoever she's meeting."

Arlo shook her head. "You want to know what's going on, right? Then you have to wait until you can sit close enough you can hear them. Or at the very least see them."

"But—" Camille protested.

"No buts. No one has come in saying they are meeting someone, so she still has to be at her table alone."

"We're at a steakhouse for a stakeout," Fern said. "I'm going to make that my status on Facebook."

Arlo held her hand in front of Fern's phone. "Absolutely not. If Mads sees that, he'll be down here to toss us in jail before we know it. And with five people in the holding cells, he'll have no choice but to send us all to the county jail."

"I don't want to spend my birthday in jail," Camille said.

"It's not really your birthday," Arlo whispered in return. She must have said the words a little too loudly. One of the hostesses shot her a questioning look.

Arlo had never seen the girl before. She probably lived over in Walnut and drove to the Cattle Drive Steakhouse, which sat between Sugar Springs and their nearest neighbor.

"Ladies." The hostess pulled four menus from the holder and waited for them to acknowledge. "Right this way."

As far as tables went in proximity to Daisy, it wasn't bad, Arlo was just glad the waitstaff hadn't kicked them out already or called the police on them for suspicious behavior. People were getting more and more cautious these days with so many shootings and sad things in the world.

Thankfully the hostess sat them three booths away.

"Helen, you sit on that side," Fern ordered.

"I can't see her from here," Helen protested.

"She'll know you anywhere with that hair."

"I told you I should have worn a stocking cap."

"No stocking caps. It's summer."

Camille picked up the menu and started perusing it.

"We didn't come here to eat," Fern protested.

"And if we are made, then how suspicious will it look if we don't have any food on the table?" Camille returned.

"We're not going to be made," Arlo said. "Where did you even learn that phrase?"

"I have cable."

The waitress came by and took their drink orders, and they all turned to their menus.

"Someone's coming," Fern said in an ominous tone.

"We're in a restaurant," Arlo said. There were people all over.

Camille gasped. "Oh my goodness." Her voice was filled with shock and awe.

"What?" Arlo asked.

Helen made as if to turn around. Arlo stopped her. "Don't. They'll see you." She shook her head. Now they had her doing it.

"Kiss a pig," Fern said.

"Who is it?" Arlo hissed.

Camille sadly shook her head. "Our handsome neighbor."

"Phil?" Arlo asked. Not that she would call him handsome. She supposed he wasn't all that *bad* looking. What was Phil doing with Daisy?

Then again, it was Phil who told her that he had seen Travis and Wally together at Books & More. But her blooming theory quickly died as Fern pointed one finger toward the sky. *Not Phil,* she mouthed.

"Sam?" Arlo couldn't help herself. She spun around in her seat and stared at the occupants of the booth three down from theirs. Her gaze met the familiar green of Sam Tucker's sexy eyes.

"You've been made." Camille ducked down, as if she could be seen from the other booth. She was barely tall enough to see over the top of the one where she was sitting.

"He saw me," Arlo said. "But our cover isn't blown. I say we order to keep pretending like it's Camille's birthday and if they come over and say anything, we deal with it then."

"Good plan," Fern said.

It was a terrible plan, but it was the only one she had at the moment. They weren't doing anything wrong. They were eating in a restaurant that anyone could eat at if they were so inclined. And since there weren't a lot of places to eat in Sugar Springs, the Cattle Drive had its share of regular patrons. And that's exactly what she would tell Mads.

"Why is he meeting her?" Fern mused as the waitress delivered their appetizers. Arlo had been so busy thinking about Sam and Daisy James-Harrison that she hadn't been paying attention as the ladies ordered fried pickles and jalapeno cheddar bites.

"She's a beautiful woman. He's a handsome man," Helen said.

"She's a *recent widow* and he's...a handsome man," Fern corrected.

"You really think they're on a date?"

It was the last thing Arlo wanted to think about. She and Sam had had a chance once, if high school love could even be called that. And she hadn't expected him to pine over her. But now that he was back in town, she didn't want to be confronted at every turn with the one who got away and who he was fishing with now.

"He's a PI," Arlo reminded them. And then the connection was made in her own brain. Could Daisy have been the one who had hired Sam?

It was possible, just as it was equally possible that Daisy and Sam were on a date. So much for reconnecting. Not that she and Sam ever would. Despite the little thrill she felt every time he was near.

As she watched, Daisy pulled a fat envelope from her purse and pushed it across the table to Sam. Arlo expected him to thumb through it, but he cast a quick glance in her direction, then slid it under the table.

"What was that?" Camille asked.

"Money," Fern said with a firm nod. "Has to be."

Money for expenses, for services rendered, for whatever job Daisy had hired him to do. No doubt about it—Sam was working for Daisy.

But why?

....

"Are you sure you don't want me to bring Jayden by to see you?" Arlo asked Chloe the following day at breakfast. Arlo only had three more days to prove Chloe's innocence before she got shipped off to the county jail. The mere thought made her stomach hurt.

"No." The word was flat. In fact, everything about Chloe was flat, from her hair to her words to the expression in her eyes.

"He would love to see you, know that you're okay."

She shook her head. "I don't want him to see me like this."

"Speaking of which. I brought you some clean clothes and some gummy worms. I know you like the bears better, but the Piggly Wiggly was all out and I wanted to get here with your breakfast."

Every day that Cloe was locked up, it seemed a little more life seeped out of her. If she stayed there much longer, she would be unrecognizable.

"And Mads said he would take you down to Dye Me a River and let Charlene wash your hair for you. That'll be nice, right?"

"Yeah." Chloe nodded, but her tone didn't change. "That would be great. Walking down Main Street in handcuffs. It'll be someone's best Instagram post of the year."

"Most people who use Instagram will be at school when he takes you down."

"Not helping," Chloe said, then she shook her head. "It doesn't matter. I don't know why Mads just doesn't take me to the county jail."

"I asked him not to. You need the support of your friends and family."

"No one believes me. It's gotten to where no one believes me so much that I'm starting to doubt it myself."

"You don't mean that," Arlo whispered.

"I do." Chloe twisted her hands in her lap and stared at her fingers. "I wanted to hurt Wally for so long. I used to dream about it. Not killing him, but hurting him. Running him down with my car, baseball bat to the head, golf club to the groin. I had a whole Stooges routine in my head. But I didn't mean it. Not really. I just wanted him to feel some of the pain that I felt when he left."

Arlo reached between the bars and grabbed Chloe's knotted fingers. "That's perfectly normal."

"Did you want to do that when Sam left?"

Arlo had wanted to kick her own butt for being so stupid, but she had no one to blame but herself. "No, but I wanted to do that to Wally when he left you."

Chloe smiled. It wasn't the beaming, light-up-the-world Chloe smile that Arlo knew so well, but it was a start in getting her friend back.

"And just because you wanted him in pain doesn't mean everyone is going to think you killed him."

"But see, that's just the thing," Chloe said. "If I heard my story on the witness stand, I wouldn't even believe me. How can I expect anyone else to?"

....

Arlo wanted to climb into the holding cell with Chloe and spend the rest of the day with her, but duty called. A girl had to do what a girl had to do to get her best friend out of jail.

"Has Bill asked the judge to reconsider a bond for Chloe?" Arlo asked Mads after leaving her friend in the tiny little holding cell.

"Judge won't hear of it. I guess his wife was a big fan of *Missing Girl* and the judge wants to make sure justice is properly served— his words."

"That's ridiculous."

"Maybe, but they have all the power."

Arlo shook her head. "I'm not sure how much longer she can take this."

Mads straightened, took his booted feet from his desk, and pinned Arlo with his steady gaze. "Chloe is stronger than you think."

"Maybe, but she's about to crack. Are you serious about taking her down to wash her hair?"

"Yeah, she's in jail, not a POW camp."

"It's just…"

"What?" he asked.

"What if I bring Jayden in to get a haircut at the same time?"

"Okay."

"Would you agree not to handcuff her and march her down Main Street?"

Mads considered the idea. "How do I know she's not going to run?"

"Seriously? She's not and even if she did, you think she can get away from you?"

"I don't like having to chase people." The lazy quality in his voice had a thread of steel inside. He might not like having to chase people, but years of conditioning and weight training meant if he had to run, he would catch whoever was in front of him. And it wouldn't be pretty when he did.

"Mads…"

"Fine. But you owe me."

Something in his voice was almost threatening. Or was it a promise? With him it was hard to tell. "Anything." A shiver slid down her spine as she said the word.

"I'll let you know."

....

Owing Mads would be completely worth it. Or so Arlo told herself as she drove over to Chloe's parents' house to pick up Jayden the following day. What a perfect way to spend a Monday. At least that's how she was going to view it.

Chloe's parents wanted to know how their daughter was doing and Arlo did her best to tell them without alarming them or tipping Jayden off that his mommy was in jail for killing his daddy, even if Chloe hadn't done it.

"Is that guy who died really my father?" Jayden asked on the ride over.

The words took Arlo completely off guard. She bumped the curb but thankfully didn't hit the light pole as she slid her car into a parking space in front of Dye Me a River.

"Why would you say that?" She caught his gaze in the rearview mirror.

Jayden was about as cute as a kid could be. Though he had been a preemie and only four pounds at birth, he had made up whatever he was behind in both size and weight before he started to first grade. Blond curls like his mother's, brown eyes like his father, and dimples that had belonged to both. Arlo knew when he got older he was going to break hearts, maybe even had a few under his belt already. He was nine after all. And nine-year-olds were old enough to understand things, even if the grown-ups thought they weren't.

"Some kids were talking at lunch today. I heard them say that the guy who died, the writer, was my father."

Arlo shut off the car and turned in the seat to look at him directly. "I'm not trying to put you off," she said gently. "But that's something that you need to talk to your mother about."

He sighed. "I knew you were going to say that." Then he caught sight of where they were. "Why are we here?"

"Your mom is coming in and I thought you might like to see her."

"So she's out of jail?" His eyes lit up like the night sky on the Fourth of July. So much for keeping that from him. She supposed his mother being in jail was more lunchroom talk.

"No," Arlo said slowly. "She's coming here to get her hair washed, and I thought it would be a good place for the two of you to meet. She misses you."

"I know."

"Are you ready?" Arlo asked.

"I guess."

"What's wrong?"

"Nothing. Just...I don't have to get a haircut, do I?"

"Do you want a haircut?"

He pulled on one of his dirty-blond curls. "No way. Tasha Anderson said she liked my hair."

"And that's important?" Arlo asked, hiding her smile.

"It is if you like Tasha Anderson."

....

"Hey, buddy." Chloe sat in one of the chairs as Thelma Samuels ran a comb through her wet hair.

Arlo knew she wanted to grab him up and hug him until he had no air to breathe, but she wouldn't.

"You want to get a haircut?" Chloe asked.

He shook his head, those adorable curls bouncing with the movement.

"Good." Chloe smiled. "But you can still sit in the chair next to me. So we can talk."

"That's right." Thelma confirmed.

Jayden climbed into the chair next to his mom. Chloe reached out and took his hand, squeezing his fingers with a small, wistful smile.

Arlo had to leave the bookstore in the hands of the book club with Courtney at the helm of the coffee bar in order to make this happen, but it was completely worth it.

"Hey, Arlo." Nadine Ayers sidled up beside her, smacking her gum to a rhythm only she could hear. Nadine was the owner of Dye Me a River and personally responsible for most of the current hairstyles in Sugar Springs. Minus Fern's of course.

"Hey, Nadine."

"It's a shame, ya know." She nodded toward the chairs where Chloe and Jayden were sitting.

"Yeah." There wasn't much else she could say.

"I was here that morning, but I didn't see anything."

Arlo turned to look at her, wondering if she was hearing her right. "You were here that morning? The salon doesn't open that early."

"I've been training." Nadine ran a hand down her flat stomach. Now that she mentioned it, Arlo could tell that she had trimmed up. Not that she was ever overweight. "I'm going to run me a 5K in October."

"You were running?"

"I didn't see him fall or nothing, but he went up the stairs with Daisy."

"His wife?" Arlo's heart began to thud in her chest. Could this be the information she had been searching for? If Daisy was with Wally, then how did Travis fit into all this?

Nadine shrugged. "Maybe it was the other one. I can't tell them apart."

And just like that, the bubble burst. Daisy and Inna were about as different as two women could be. "They look nothing alike."

"I don't know which one is which. Plus, she had a scarf on. Or a hood. Or maybe even one of those A-rab coverings."

A hijab? "Was she short? Tall?"

"She had on those tall shoes. With the thick soles and the high heels."

The type of shoes they both wore. "But you're sure that it's one of them, Daisy or Inna?"

"Yeah, pretty sure."

"And not Travis Coleman."

Nadine drew back and gave her a strange look. "Not unless Travis is going around in drag."

"I suppose not,"' Arlo murmured. "But you don't know which one—Daisy or Inna."

"Because her hair was covered. Other than their hair, they look alike from a distance."

She supposed that was true.

"Is that important?" Nadine asked.

"Yeah," Arlo replied. "Whoever he was with most probably pushed him out the window."

....

Arlo pulled her car into the empty spot in front of the police station and got out. What a day it had been, and it wasn't over yet.

Chloe managed not to cry when Mads came and took her back to the police station. After that, Arlo loaded Jayden into the car and drove him back to his grandparents' house. She hadn't had a chance to talk to Mads until now.

She pushed inside the station. Frances had already gone home for the day and Arlo made her way past the desk and down the hall to Mads's office.

She knocked and entered the open door.

"I was wondering when you would show up." Once again he was seated behind the desk with his feet on the blotter and his baseball hat pulled down over his eyes. He looked half asleep but she knew better. The man missed nothing.

"Nadine said she saw Wally and a woman go up to the third floor. It was either Inna or Daisy."

"Do you realize how that sounds?"

"Mads, this is big. Huge. This means one of them killed Wally."

He straightened, his booted feet hit the floor with twin thuds. "It means he was seen with one of the two women he is normally seen with."

"Nadine said she saw them go up the stairs."

"I've already talked to Nadine. She was so far away she couldn't tell which one of them it was and if she was wearing a hood or a scarf. For all we know it was Sam dressed as a woman."

Or Travis.

"Why would you say that?"

He shrugged and looked at her appraisingly. "Are you worried Sam might be changing teams?"

Arlo flushed. "Why would you bring him into this conversation?"

"First name that popped into my head." He smirked.

Arlo shook her head. "You're just determined to keep Chloe in jail."

"That's not true. But as of right now, the most evidence I have is against her. Why would Daisy or Inna kill Wally? He was their meal ticket."

She knew what he was implying. Chloe was the one with motive. Chloe and Travis.

Mads stood. "If that's all, I hope you'll excuse me. I'm late for supper."

20

THE FIRST BAPTIST CHURCH ON THE CORNER OF MAIN AND Troost had never been as full as it was the day of Wallace J. Harrison's memorial service. It was standing room only when Arlo made her way into the sanctuary. Even the Presbyterians showed up.

"I didn't know this many people lived in Sugar Springs," Arlo said to Nadine, the owner-stylist from Dye Me a River.

"Some of these folks are from as far away as Memphis. Probably farther if we asked more of them."

It was sad, really. People were scheduled to come out and see him when he was alive, but he got his best turnout at a time when he wouldn't even be able to enjoy it.

The murmur in the crowd dulled as Inna stepped forward and took the microphone from the pulpit. "I want to thank you all for coming to here today. Wally would be glad to see all your faces, all people who loved him."

"What is she doing up there?" Nadine asked. "Doesn't the pastor normally do all that stuff?"

"Inna is something of a control freak." That was putting it mildly. Half an hour with her and everyone in the room would know as well.

"Maybe even his wife," Nadine continued. "I mean, it's a eulogy."

But after spending the evening watching Daisy dig around in her salad while Inna threw barbs about mushrooms and farm girls in the big city, Arlo wasn't sure Daisy was up for eulogizing.

"She's just so...polished," Nadine said, her head tilted to a critical angle for studying the woman as she made her way from one side of the stage to the other. "And yet not."

Inna appeared polished on the outside, a shiny diamond glittering like those earrings that mocked Arlo. Inna knew what to do and when to do it. Her English wasn't perfect, but it was a heck of a lot better than Arlo's Russian. There weren't many people in Sugar Springs who spoke more than one language—if any. So Inna was alone on that front.

She talked about Wally and what a pleasure it had been to work for him. The words seemed to hold a double entendre, but Arlo wasn't sure if half the people in the sanctuary even realized the implied meaning. She spoke about how hard he worked and the efforts it took to produce *Missing Girl*.

She moved from side to side as if working the crowd. A shiny black urn sat on a pedestal in the center of the stage. A picture of Wally was balanced on an easel at one side.

A few other people got up and spoke, but none for as long as Inna.

"Is his wife not going to say anything?" Nadine mused aloud.

Arlo shrugged. Daisy was down in front, seated in the place reserved for family. She wore the perfect black dress with just the right amount of matching lace to make it elegant and sophisticated and sexy all at the same time. For a farm girl, she sure knew how to dress.

Behind her in the pew sat Chloe, Mads on one side of her and Jayden on the other. Her parents were on the other side of him. Arlo wondered what they thought. After all this time, Wally had finally decided he wanted a relationship with his son, then Wally died. That relationship would never be.

Arlo's gaze snagged on Daniel, Chloe's father. Mr. Carter had been more than a little upset when Chloe had come home and told him and her mother that she was pregnant. Ten years and Arlo could still remember the anger in Daniel Carter's eyes whenever someone mentioned Wally's name. And when Wally disappeared without so much as a word goodbye…well, it wasn't good. Mads had questioned Daniel and Liz, Chloe's mother, after Wally's death, but Chloe had been the one arrested.

Wally's parents, Sue Ann and Dave, had stayed on in Sugar Springs for a while, but after Chloe had the baby, they moved over into Alabama somewhere. They never once saw Jayden. Perhaps they thought Chloe was trying to trap Wally. Or maybe that she wasn't good enough for their poetic son. Today they sat on the other side of Daisy. How did the Harrisons feel about their golden child marrying a mushroom farmer's daughter?

Once everyone had their say, Brother George, the pastor of the First Baptist, invited everyone to the fellowship hall for a time to "celebrate Wally's life."

It was ironic really, to celebrate someone's life once they were gone, but even more so when the town where they were celebrating was the last place that person would want to be—alive or dead.

....

"Try the spinach dip. It's amazing."

Chloe whirled around, her eyes filling with joy as she saw Arlo. "I'm so glad to see you." She gave Arlo a one-armed hug. The other hand was firmly chained to Mads.

"Seriously?" Arlo said.

Mads shrugged. "It was the only way Wally's other women would allow her to come."

"But handcuffed together?" Arlo shook her head.

"It was that or handcuffed in front. We figured this way would look a little more natural. Maybe not draw so much attention."

Like everyone in the room wasn't talking about Chloe, Jayden, Wally, and the triangle that he'd built between them.

Or maybe that was the triangle between him, Inna, and Daisy.

Arlo allowed her gaze to roam around the room. She found Inna standing amid a group of men, all hanging on her every word. She held a drink in one hand, nonalcoholic unless someone had snuck something in. Since it was a Baptist Church, that was entirely possible.

Inna was talking, her eyes sparkling. She was in her element as the center of attention.

Across the room, Daisy was standing, quietly talking with the pastor. Brother George was a good man, on the soft side for a Baptist preacher, but hearty and full of vim all the same. Arlo had never heard the man preach, but she had heard that he could shake the rafters when he wanted to. Being raised by hippie parents had both advantages and disadvantages. She had never been introduced to any sort of organized religion. That was good because it left her mind open to read the works of all the prophets and decide for herself. Bad in that she lacked the faith of most those around her. Most days she was fine with it. But there were other times when she wished to have the comfort that religion, prayer, and a network of believers could provide.

"Which one do you think he really loved?" Chloe asked.

"Chloe! Seriously? What kind of question is that?"

She shrugged one shoulder, pulling on Mads's sleeve with the motion. "I don't know. I'm just thinking out loud."

"You shouldn't be thinking about that at all," Arlo said.

"Inna's so dark and mysterious. And that accent."

"She sounds like Natasha from *Rocky and Bullwinkle*."

"I know, right? Sexy."

It wasn't the word that Arlo would have used, but if she was being fair—and she wasn't—Inna did have certain exotic qualities that could be considered attractive. But Arlo didn't trust her. It was nothing but a gut feeling. Inna seemed too comfortable with the entire situation. It was almost as if she thrived off Wally's murder. As if there was some satisfaction in his demise that made her blossom like a night-blooming flower.

"I'm going to get another lemonade," Arlo said. "You two want anything?"

Mads shook his head and went back to talking with the mayor, Russ England.

"A hacksaw?" Chloe joked.

"I'll see what I can do." She moved through the crowd to the counter next to the kitchen. The fellowship hall was just a fancy term for Sunday School rooms and a kitchen, but she knew they used it all the time for church meetings and other such events. Like now.

"Hey, Arlo."

"Hi, Sandy." Realtor turned lemonade dispenser, Sandy poured Arlo another cup of the sweet yellow liquid, then wiped off the counter with a damp rag.

"Did the rat fink ever call you back?" Sandy asked.

"I was about to ask you the same thing." *Though maybe not in those words.*

"Yeah, he called this afternoon. I was going to call you then, but I figured I would see you here."

"And you figured right." She waited for Sandy to take her turn in the conversation and tell her what Travis, aka the rat fink, remembered about the day Wally was killed. "So what did he say?" she prompted.

"Oh, right. He said that he gave Wally the keys. He didn't say much—Wally, not Travis—but he mentioned maybe using the third-floor space as an office. But the person who was meeting him would have the final say."

So Wally was meeting someone, and that person was either Daisy or Inna, according to Nadine. Which cleared Travis somewhat. And none of it mattered, according to Mads, because Chloe probably killed him anyway.

"He told Travis that he was meeting someone?"

"But he didn't say a name. Or if he did Travis doesn't remember. I think he does, but he won't tell me unless I promise him the vinyl copy of *Abbey Road* we bought together."

"Not worth it," Arlo said. After all, it was just a woman's life hanging in the balance.

"Exactly what I thought." Sandy's dimples creased as she smiled, and Arlo couldn't be mad. They were all doing what they had to do.

"Thanks for talking to him for me," Arlo said.

"My pleasure. It was more than worth it to tell him John, Paul, George, and Ringo would forever be mine."

Arlo started to move away when she was flanked by Fern and Camille. "Where's d'Artagnan?" she asked.

Camille patted her arm. "He wasn't a musketeer in the story, you know."

"That would make you d'Artagnan." Fern laughed, obviously deciding this was the funniest thing in the world.

"Your godmother is over talking to Daisy and Pastor George."

"About?" Did she really want to know? Yep, it was painful, but better that way.

"Taking Wally back home."

"Is she really leaving tomorrow?"

"Helen is trying to talk them into staying for a while longer. Resting before heading back into the hustle and bustle of the city."

"But Daisy said she wanted to go back," Arlo guessed.

Camille shook her head. "She's just grieving, love. She only wants the pain to stop and something different than what she has now has to be the answer."

"What about Chloe?" Arlo asked.

Fern shook her head. "I don't think Chloe wants to go to New York City."

Arlo sighed. "One of them is guilty. I just know it, so we can't let them leave tomorrow."

"I don't see a way to stop that from happening," Camille said.

"If you ask me, it's Daisy. She's grieving just a little too much, don't you think?" Fern quirked her head toward the widow.

They all looked over to where Daisy was. She daintily dabbed at her tears and sniffed. Though they were inside, she wore black gloves and dark sunglasses. To Arlo she looked a little like a blond Jackie Onassis. For the daughter of a mushroom farmer she cleaned up well and knew her stuff. She was as elegant as, if not more than, anyone else in the room. Including Inna.

"That's the shame of it all," Camille said.

"What?" Had she been talking out loud?

"Daisy could hold her own with the finest and most elegant the world over. She has class and style."

"I see that."

"But Inna, she relies on her accent and her exotic nature to lure people to her."

They all took a minute to study Inna. She was still talking, but this time to a different group of men. Arlo had to wonder if they were taking turns or if their wives had come over one by one to get their men and take them away. Then, like sharks' teeth, another set popped up to fill the space and adore the woman who stood before them.

"You're right." Why had she never noticed it before? Maybe because like all the adoring men fawning at her feet, she had been too caught up in Inna's act to do much more see her for more than what she allowed them.

But Daisy had a style about her—grace, Helen would have called it.

And grace was something Inna didn't have.

Arlo shook away those thoughts. Like it mattered. Maybe when they got back into their normal social circles something like that couldn't be overlooked, but here in Sugar Springs, breeding was for horses and pedigree for hunting dogs. Everything else was inconsequential.

....

Another day, another breakfast, Arlo thought as she breezed through the door of the police station just after eight. She had been hopeful yesterday after Wally's service that Mads would change his mind about keeping Chloe locked up, but she knew she was laying more blame on him than he was responsible for. Still, it would have been nice to have her best friend out of jail.

"I have a steak-and-egg biscuit from The Diner." Arlo lifted the sack to show Chloe, but her friend was lying on the cot, her face turned away from the door.

"Chloe?"

She didn't move.

Arlo stood as still as possible, watching to see if she was still breathing. When she saw the even rise and fall of her back, she knew her friend was at the very least taking in air, even if she wasn't fit for company.

"Chloe?" Arlo asked again.

Chloe rolled over onto her back and flung one arm over her head. "I'm just not in the mood today, Arlo."

"That makes two of us, but if you eat, I can promise that you'll feel better."

"Pinkie swear?" Chloe asked.

"Pinkie swear." Arlo hid most of her smile and waited for Chloe to come closer to the bars before pushing the sack through to the other side. "I put a file in there as well. I'm not sure exactly what it's used for, but that's what they always do in prison break movies."

"Is that what this is? A prison break?" Chloe took her sandwich, then crawled into the middle of her cot before unwrapping it and taking a big bite.

Arlo did the same, perched on the hardbacked chair Frances had brought in despite Mads's protests. "I wish."

Chloe shook her head. "I'm going a little bit nuts in here," she finally said.

"I know." She did, but she didn't. All she could do was imagine what it was like and that was hard enough. "I'm doing everything I can to get you out of here."

Chloe sighed. "I know. It's just…"

"It's just what?"

"If I was out there, I would be able to help you."

"If you were out here, I wouldn't need any help."

They each took a bite and thoughtfully chewed.

"They're leaving town today," Arlo said.

Chloe nodded. "I know. Frances told me."

"I can't think of one reason to make them stay."

"Other than one of them is guilty?"

"But which one?"

"My money's on Inna."

Arlo drew back a bit. "Inna? Why?"

"Because like me, the evidence is all pointing toward Daisy. So she can't be the one. It has to be Inna. She engineered it all."

"That is the most twisted logic I have ever heard."

Chloe laughed, then immediately sobered. "Yeah, I suppose. It's just I got nothing but time in here. Time to think."

"Have you asked Mads if you can have your phone? You could play *Candy Crush*."

Chloe laughed, then the sound changed and became sobs. "Promise me if I don't get out of there that you'll take care of Jayden. My mom, she means well, but he needs someone young and happy that can help him through this modern world."

"Chloe, I—"

"Promise me," she begged.

"I promise," Arlo said.

"And pinkie swear."

"Pinkie swear." And she knew it was something she could keep because she couldn't stand the thought of raising Jayden without Chloe there and she wasn't giving up without a fight.

21

"Do you know who did this?" Inna stormed into Books & More just before noon with her cell phone in one outstretched hand.

"What?" Arlo asked. She squinted at the screen, like that would help her see it any better. It would have been more beneficial for Inna to keep the phone steady, but there was a deeper fire about her today and Arlo was smart enough to know when to talk and when to shut up.

"The memorial service," she said. "Someone at the service put this up on YourTube."

"YouTube," Arlo corrected.

"Whatever. It is up there, and I do not like it up there. They put my name." She shook her head. "The people in this country have such great freedoms and this is what they are used for?"

Arlo felt the need to apologize but bit it back. She wasn't responsible for YouTube any more than anyone else. And though it was a free country and she feasibly could tell someone how to live their life, it was a free country and they didn't have to do it.

"You look great," Arlo said by way of consultation. Thankfully in the part of the video that she watched, there was no sign of Chloe or Mads or their matching wrist wear.

"We will have a media uproaring storm now."

Arlo shook her head. "It won't be all that. The Kardashians fired another maid, wrecked a car, and had another surgery. I give it to the end of the day and it'll all be settled down by then."

Inna shook her head. Her earrings flashed. "I bet it was that Daisy. She's always trying to hurt me."

Interesting. Arlo knew that the women got along under the public eye but figured the pair wouldn't be all buddy-buddy in private. Seemed like she wasn't far off the mark.

"Why would Daisy do that?"

Inna shot her a look. "Are you really so full of naïve?"

"I…guess…"

Inna sniffed, took one last look at the video on her phone screen and tossed her dark hair behind her. "Daisy always has hate for me. She knows Wally loves me more. Loved me," she corrected herself. "And she has hate enough to know this would hurt me."

Arlo looked to the phone even though the picture was gone. "The video was just you talking about Wally at the service. How will that hurt you? I'm sorry I don't understand."

Inna stiffened. "If you do not, then I do not tell you." She lifted her chin to a superior angle. "In my country we would use the YourTube for something useful. Not hurting others."

Arlo watched her walk away, not bothering to point out that they had "YourTube" in the Ukraine and "something useful" didn't include launching civil unrest.

Inna tossed her dark curtain of hair over to one side, then pushed her way out of Books & More.

This really wasn't happening, Arlo thought. But it was. Her best friend was in jail and the woman responsible was leaving town that evening. The more she had thought about it that morning, the more she knew in her heart of hearts that Daisy was responsible for Wally's death. She had all the motives—cheating husband, finding out about his high school love child, missing earrings. Well, that wasn't motive, but it was a damn good clue. And Mads just couldn't see it.

That left her no choice but to do something. What? She had no idea. She glanced around the store to check on the customers and the book club.

Only Fern was seated in the reading nook.

"I thought y'all were still meeting every day."

Fern looked up from *Missing Girl*. "We are. Camille went down to pay her electric bill, then she was going to take Chloe something to eat. Helen wanted to talk to Dan the grocer about something or another. I think bad tomatoes. Or was it potatoes? They'll be back."

"How's the book?" Arlo asked.

"Strange. You know, I knew Wally his whole life. I didn't teach him like Camille did, but we lived across the street and two doors down."

Arlo made her way to the back of the couch and leaned one hip against it. "I had forgotten that."

Fern nodded. "He was an imaginative child, but this?" She stuck one finger between the pages to hold her place and lifted the book for emphasis. "This is just weird. It doesn't sound like him at all."

Arlo gave a small shrug. "Just because they think it doesn't mean the writers believe it all. It's just a story."

Fern sighed. "I suppose you're right. Readers do get caught up and think of authors by their books."

She shifted, maybe even exhaled a little too loudly.

"What's wrong?"

"I just can't believe Daisy James-Harrison gets to come to town, wreak havoc on Chloe's life, then leave again, like nothing happened."

"She is a widow now."

"By her own hand most likely." Arlo straightened. "I can't stand by and do nothing."

"Then go do something."

It was that simple.

"All right then, you've got Books & More. Think you can handle it?"

Fern smiled. "In my sleep."

....

"Hey, Frances. Where's Mads?" Arlo asked as she walked into the police station. She had no time to waste.

"Office."

"Thanks."

Frances never once looked up from her crossword puzzle.

"Mads?" She gave a courtesy knock, then stepped through the partially open door.

"Damn it."

Arlo jumped as a golf ball rolled toward her. It wasn't going fast; it was merely unexpected, and it startled her. "What the—"

"If you want to storm in here and ruin my short game, then I suggest you make it important."

"You have to let Chloe out of there."

He propped one hand on top of his putter and waited for her to continue.

"Did you see her this morning? She's about to lose it, and I can't say I blame her."

Mads tucked the club under one arm. Then he rubbed his eyes and pinched the bridge of his nose. "It's not up to me."

"You're the chief of police."

"And as such it's my job—my duty—to arrest anyone I need to. I can't make exceptions because I like a person, or I went to school with them. Or because I loved their best friend once upon a time."

Arlo took a step back. He had never mentioned their shared past, and frankly she preferred it that way. The best plan was to pretend it never happened because when she let the memories in, they had a tendency to stick around. She didn't need that kind of distraction right now.

"You can't—" she started.

"Evidence," he said. "And I can. I have to."

"I'm not going to let this rest. I can't—we can't—let two strangers come to town and allow our own take the blame for a murder one of them committed."

"You don't know that."

"Daisy is about as guilty as a person can be. You may have

some evidence against Chloe, but she doesn't have the motive that Daisy does."

"Before they read the will, I might have agreed with you, but now that Chloe gets the bulk of his estate…" Mads shook his head. "Don't go poke a bear, Arlo. They can be really dangerous."

She stared at him for a heartbeat more. When he said nothing else, she growled in frustration and stalked from his office, out of the police station without even bothering to say bye to Frances.

If Mads wouldn't help, someone would. Someone had to. Maybe someone with a little more stroke. Who was the most powerful person in Sugar Springs? The mayor.

With a triumphant smile starting on her lips, Arlo turned and made her way from the police station the courthouse.

The courthouse was the oldest building in town except for Lillyfield mansion and the old Cathouse over on Fourth. It smelled old, like dust and floor wax, and the scent made Arlo anxious. Somehow, when she was younger, she had associated that smell with power, or maybe the fact that she had none. She and her parents had come here in order to sign the papers that would give Helen guardianship of Arlo until she turned eighteen. Until her parents had actually signed, she had worried they would change their minds. They could be flighty like that, just one of the many reasons that she wanted a stable home. She had felt small and insignificant as she waited with her fate balanced in the hands of the people who made her and the one person she could depend on. She had breathed in that odor and had never forgotten.

"I need to see Mayor England," she told Joanne, the woman behind the reception desk. Joanne had been a couple of years ahead of her in school. And if Arlo was remembering correctly, she had dated Mads's older brother until he joined the army and left her behind. She had never married.

"Concerning?" Joanne eyed her carefully.

"Chloe Carter, and it's important."

"It always is. Do you have an appointment?"

"Joanne," Arlo sighed. "Please." Why was it that people in positions of small power wielded it like a sword?

The woman heaved an exasperated sigh, then motioned her back. "Oh, whatever. It's people like you who jam up the system."

"Thank you." Arlo walked past without another word. She wasn't to blame. That was on the Daisy James-Harrisons of the world.

Arlo marched to his office and tried to figure out what she was going to say to him. She figured demanding that Mads release Chloe would be a lost cause. No, she had to be smart about this.

She entered the half-glass door to find another reception area. At least that's what she thought it was. Cardboard boxes, the kind that were used for paper storage and had lids, were stacked higher than her chin in crooked rows that looked like a dangerous game of Jenga. Some had lids, but still more seemed to be missing them. But they could be quickly found in a stack by the overflowing trash can. A wooden statue of an Indian, the kind that used to be in smoke shops, guarded the spot between two doors. A large desk with papers scattered across its top dominated the space. The chair behind the desk was empty and the door behind, the third door in the room, was open. Arlo wasn't sure if she should check the room or call the police. Maybe both.

"Mayor England?"

"Come on back. My secretary had an emergency."

It appeared so. Arlo stepped around the desk and entered a room that was as pristine as the room before had been junky. Not a paper seemed out of place. No boxes, just tall oak filing cabinets, a matching oak desk, and a leather chair that creaked as its occupant moved.

"Arlo Stanley. How are you doing today?"

"Not good." She shook her head and realized she was being overdramatic. It was one thing to stop and talk to the mayor in The Diner and quite another to go into his office with an official request. "Do you know Chloe Carter?"

"Of course."

"Then I'm sure you also know that she's been arrested for the murder of Wally Harrison."

"Go on."

"I have good reason to believe that Chloe is innocent, and Daisy James-Harrison, Wally's wife, is the actual murderer." Or Travis Coleman. He still hadn't been one hundred percent cleared. At any rate, it wasn't Chloe.

The mayor smoothed a hand down his tie and leaned back in his seat. The chair creaked as he shifted. "You do."

"Mads won't listen to me. I know he's just doing his job, but he's wrong this time and I need your help."

"My help? What can I do?"

"Something. Anything. We can't let Daisy just leave tonight and go back to her life. Not if her leaving is going to destroy Chloe's life. And Jayden's too."

"That's her son?"

"He's nine."

Russ England paused for a moment, and she knew he was thinking about her request. He was taking her seriously and that was definitely a step in the right direction.

"I wish I could help you."

"W-what? You won't do anything?"

"How can I? I don't have the authority to detain someone. Not when regular law enforcement already has someone else in custody."

"He's wrong. And he doesn't believe she's guilty either. Chloe wouldn't hurt a fly. We share a business together. I know this firsthand. She…she won't even kill spiders." But they all knew that Wally was worse than a spider.

"I really wish there was something I could do."

"You pretended it was your birthday at the inn."

"A favor for an old friend." He smiled in remembrance and Arlo vaguely recalled a little something between Helen and Russ during her senior year. At the time she had been too caught up in Mads to pay much mind. It seemed now like she ought to have been paying attention. Ah, the selfishness of a teenager.

"So what am I supposed to do?" She really wasn't expecting him to answer.

"If you need her to stay in town longer, then find some excuse to make her want to stay."

As far as advice went, she couldn't say it was the best. But it certainly wasn't the worst.

Arlo thanked the mayor and made her way out of the office, then down the large stone steps and onto the open concrete plaza with its statue of General Lee on horseback. She looked up at the bearded face etched in bronze. "All right, Robbie, old pal. What's my next move?"

Find an excuse to make her stay.

Arlo really wanted Daisy, but she had a feeling if one of them stayed, the other would too. And she remembered the attention that Inna received at the wake. She adored being adored. And people like that loved nothing more than a party.

"What are you doing out here?" Camille walked by carrying a paper sack from The Diner.

"Thinking. Is that Chloe's dinner?"

"Yes, poor love. She was feeling so down. I went to The Diner and got her a chicken-fried pork steak."

Nothing like breaded and fried pork to lift the spirits. "We have to do something," Arlo said. "I went to talk to the mayor, but he couldn't help. Mads says he can't do anything. And a killer is about to get away!" She blew out a frustrated breath. "A killer is about to leave town and the only thing I can think of is a party. A going away party. Inna would want to come, and Daisy seems to do whatever she says."

"A party is a lovely idea. A big party, even bigger than the wake."

"We only have a couple of hours." To plan the party of the year? "Didn't we already try this?"

Camille waved a dismissive hand. "Amateur hour. This time we get the whole town involved."

"I don't know."

"I'll get Helen and Fern."

"Fern's manning Books & More, and Courtney doesn't get out of school until three." There was no way this was going to work.

"Maybe if her grandmother signed her out." Camille batted her eyes innocently.

"You're not her grandmother."

"They don't know that."

Betty Sanders who ran the attendance desk at the high school knew everybody and everyone. "Yes, they do."

"Don't worry, love. I got this. Now get back in there and see if Russ can let us have the gym for the night."

"He can do that?"

"He is the mayor, and his brother is the principal, so I would say yes. And if that doesn't work, tell him we're sending in Helen."

That might have been her best course of action from the start. "Are you sure about this?"

"Absolutely."

"I don't know." Arlo bit her lip.

"Well, love. Right now it's the only plan we have."

....

Arlo could hardly believe it. Camille managed to get Courtney out of school so she could work in the store while the four of them planned the party. Lesson learned: Never underestimate the power of little old ladies, no matter how innocent they looked or how sweet and musical their soft Aussie accents made their words.

Mayor England let them have the gym without a threat. Then Arlo started on the south side of Main Street and went door to door asking for help, inviting people, telling them to tell their friends. Books & More would supply the coffee. Neddie at The Diner promised hors d'oeuvres. Joyce from Blooming Blooms said she would bring flowers, and Delores at Diamonds Galore talked Frank the owner into giving away a diamond tennis bracelet as a door prize. Shelly at Let's Party said she would bring all the party supplies and decorations they could handle. Courtney knew someone who could play music and the strobe light they had at the class reunion mixer was still in the gym.

Somehow the four of them, with the help of the entire town, would throw the party to end all parties. Now they just had to convince Inna and Daisy to stay in town long enough to attend. And before that they had to find out who made the pink punch for the reunion mixer. They needed a barrel full of that—stat.

22

"It was supposed to be a surprise, but since you're leaving we have to tell you."

Arlo stood on the bottom step at the inn, blocking the way for Inna and Daisy. She hadn't meant to be so aggressive, but when Helen started talking about the party, neither one seemed interested.

"You have to tell why?" Inna said.

"So you won't leave," Camille added.

"It's the least you can do," Fern said.

Daisy set her suitcase down on the step below the one where she stood. She pinched the bridge of her nose. "I want to go home. I'm getting a migraine and I left my prescription medication at home."

"Our local pharmacist, Doug, will be at the party and I'm sure he'll float you a couple of pills." Helen's expression didn't change and her mouth barely moved as she lowered her voice and continued. "You did invite Doug, didn't you?"

"Can't remember," Arlo whispered back.

"I'm on it," Fern said.

"Why do you whisper?" This from Inna.

"We're…we're just trying to think of a way to get you to stay."

Inna crossed her arms and harrumphed.

"Listen," Arlo started, "You're celebrities to these people. I know you live in New York and half the people there are stars. But we don't get a lot of that around here. The town wants to thank you for coming. They want to throw you a send-off. They want to be around celebrities."

"We didn't get to have Wally's book signing," Helen said. "Give them this."

Inna looked back to Daisy. They whispered for a moment, then Inna turned back to Helen, Arlo, and Camille.

"Fine. We will go to this party. You will get Daisy her headache pills and tomorrow we leave."

Arlo almost melted with relief. They would come to the party. Now all they had to do was get Daisy to admit to killing Wally. After that, they were home free.

....

"I can't believe you did all this in just a few hours." Chloe turned around in a circle, the strobe light flickering across her chambray sundress. It was her favorite and that was the exact reason why Arlo had snagged it out of the closet for her to wear tonight.

Talking Inna and Daisy into staying had been a piece of cake compared to trying to convince Mads to let Chloe come to the party without handcuffs. In the end, as always, Mads did the right thing and there they were.

"Have you seen Sam tonight?" Arlo asked casually. Perhaps too casually.

"What's up with the two of you?" Chloe asked. She sipped her punch and twirled from side to side, her skirt brushing around her legs.

Arlo frowned. "Nothing. Well, he's our tenant."

"That didn't sound like a landlord voice."

"How much of that have you had?" She peered into Chloe's pink cup.

The theme for the party was pink. Pink napkins, pink plates, pink streamers, pink tablecloths, pink balloons. Pink everything. Shelly had told them that since pink tended to sell well year-round, especially in the spring and October, she had stocked up with plenty to spare. Arlo liked pink well enough, but the amount in the gymnasium was a tad overwhelming.

"One. Like it's any of your beeswax."

"I'm pretty sure this is stronger than what we had at the mixer, so proceed with caution."

"Yes, Mama."

"Have you seen them tonight?"

Chloe waved a hand toward the dessert table. "Inna was over here a bit ago, but I haven't seen her since then. I think Daisy is hiding from me. I have kind of 'the other woman' vibe with her."

"Which one of you is the other?"

Chloe took another drink of her lethal punch. "Not sure."

"Well, I'm going to go find her. I've got to figure out a way to make her admit that she killed Wally."

"Good luck with that." Chloe's tone was light, but her eyes held a pleading look.

"Thanks." Arlo snatched up a pink cup of the pink punch and started to wind her way through the crowd. Courtney's friend whose dad had a "ton of records" ended up being related to Phil from next door to the bookstore. And ton of records was correct. He had everything from "The Purple People Eater" and Chuck Berry to Maroon 5 and Meghan Trainor. And most of the town showed up for the party.

Now it was time to get down to work. Though she wasn't sure how she was going to get Daisy to admit that she pushed Wally from the third floor of Arlo's building.

But first she had to find her.

Arlo danced her way through the crowd and across the gym floor. That was where the bathrooms were located, and she figured at some time or another Daisy would have to go pee. Standing outside the ladies' room door to wait for the woman seemed a little stalkerish, but it sure beat winding through the ever-moving crowd for hours, searching but not finding.

And there was a crowd. It seemed as if the majority of Sugar

Springs had turned out for the party. Maybe she needed to offer spiked punch at the book club meetings in order to get a bigger crowd. Then again, the crowd she had right now was difficult enough to deal with sober. She smiled a little. Fern, Camille, and Helen might be a handful, but she didn't know what she would have done without them during all this time.

Arlo allowed her gaze to wander around the gym. Just as last time, little groups had formed, Cable and Joey and a couple of other men were standing against one wall, drinking punch and assessing the crowd. Mayor England, his brother, Jimmy, who was also the principal of the school, and Leonard the school custodian where in a heated discussion. She didn't know for certain but it looked like they were talking about the floor. And a few of the Main Street merchants had gathered together. Even Sandy Green and Travis Coleman seemed to have made up. She saw them on the dance floor staring dreamily at each other.

As much as she wanted to find the killer and free Chloe, she knew Travis wasn't her man. That earring! It mucked up everything. Travis didn't wear earrings, wasn't a cross-dresser, and couldn't afford to purchase such large diamonds. He might have let Wally into the building, but she was certain he couldn't have been the one to push him out the window. No, someone else was around.

Like the woman of the hour. Daisy James-Harrison. It took only fifteen minutes for her to show up at the entrance to the locker rooms, a.k.a. where the only bathrooms in the gym were. Arlo followed her inside.

The girls' locker room smelled like every locker room all around the country—like wet mold and gym socks. The only differences were the details. The Lady Blue Devils' locker room had white walls and royal blue stalls. The paint was chipping off in several places, and if Arlo wasn't mistaken, that smear of lipstick had happened on her prom night. But that was over ten years ago and surely… She shook her head.

"Excuse me." Daisy came out of the stall and headed for the sink where Arlo stood. Never mind that there were four others; for some reason Daisy wanted the one she was in front of and that was okay with Arlo because it gave her an excuse to talk to Daisy.

"Sorry. Hey, I've been wanting to ask you about Wally."

"I really don't want to talk about him." Daisy's voice was quiet. She washed her hands, dried them on the industrial paper towels, then checked her reflection in the mirror. She really was a pretty thing. Wholesome and graceful, but in a sexy way. And like most of America, Arlo had to wonder why Wally had strayed.

"I'm sorry. I just know I'll never get this opportunity again. I sat behind Wally in English class senior year. He was always cheating off Danielle Owens's paper." Arlo laughed. Until this moment, she hadn't realized that fact. Wally was always cheating off Danielle. She was the smartest person in class. Sort of like Daisy and her academic career. "In fact, I think I made better grades than he did."

"It's not always about grades. It's about voice and timing. Not just in the writing but in the publishing industry. The world has to be ready for your book."

"Interesting."

Daisy tried to move but Arlo stepped in front of her. "How many times are you going to do this today?"

"Sorry. I just know that I'm not going to get another chance like this."

"I believe you already said that."

Arlo let out a nervous chuckle. "Did I?" Perhaps she should have thought through her strategy before blocking Daisy in the bathroom.

"Can we finish this someplace less stinky?"

No! She wanted to scream. *I don't want you to be able to get away once I get you to admit that you killed Wally.*

"Sure. Sure." She turned and slowly made her way out of the locker room. She didn't want to walk too fast and give Daisy an opportunity to lag behind and escape.

Back out in the gym, the music was still playing, and everyone was milling around, eating, drinking, and she supposed being merry, but she still had a job to do.

"Tell me about his process," Arlo said. "Does he only work in one room? Or have to have certain music playing? Did you know Victor Hugo used to write naked?"

Daisy pinned her with a cold stare. "I did not. And I'm finding this conversation a little annoying."

"I don't mean to be a pest," Arlo said. "I...I want to write a book too." Not exactly the truth, but at least the lie stopped Daisy from tapping her foot. The woman turned to Arlo. Her expression was still one of annoyance.

"You want to write a book," she scoffed gently, not enough to be rude, but enough to get her point across. "Everybody wants to write a book. But there are only a few who actually have what it takes to stare at a computer screen for hours on end and live someone else's life."

Arlo had never thought about it that way before. She supposed writing would be a little like living a different life. But this wasn't about her. It was about Wally. "Is that what Wally did?" she asked. "Just stare at the computer until something came to him?"

A small, derisive laugh escaped the pretty young widow. "Wally spent many, many years staring at his computer screen while I worked to put food on the table. But I wanted him to live his dream." To Arlo's horror, the woman's eyes filled with tears. "And do you know what it took?" She sniffed and nodded to a spot across the room to where Inna stood, talking to the mayor and the school janitor. About what was anyone's guess. "She became his inspiration, and I was left out in the cold."

"And you hated that."

"Of course." She turned her attention back to Arlo. "Anyone would feel the same."

But would anyone kill because of it?

"So he wrote with Inna."

Daisy shook her head. "I need a drink."

"Let's get some punch." Arlo led Daisy to the refreshment table. She couldn't let Daisy out of her sight. Not when she was this close to getting to the truth.

Arlo poured two cups of punch and handed one to Daisy. "So, Inna," she prompted.

Daisy took a big gulp of the punch. "Always Inna. Every day. All day long."

"That's got to be hard on a marriage."

Daisy shot her a derisive look. "Seriously? You don't have to pretend that you don't know Wally was having an affair."

"I'm sorry."

Daisy drained the rest of her punch and scooped up another serving. Arlo almost felt sorry for her. In all of this, she seemed more like the victim instead of the bad guy, but there was too much evidence to believe anything else.

"Then he up and gets himself killed and leaves me a third of everything. A third." She shook her head. "I stood by him. Always, and I only get a third."

Arlo thought it best not to mention that the rest went to his son, a worthy recipient. But Daisy had a point. A third of his estate wasn't a pittance, but a slap in the face nonetheless since it was the bare minimum of what he legally had to leave to his wife. It was an insult, and Arlo had the feeling, if he could have left her less, he would have.

Daisy sighed, a defeated sound. "He started shutting me out years ago." She shook her head and smiled a little into her cup. "I don't know why I'm telling you all this."

Arlo shrugged. "I've got one of those faces. People tell me all kinds of things."

"I suppose."

Arlo waited.

"You want to write a book?" Daisy asked.

"Uh, yeah." She had almost forgotten her own lie.

"Well, if you want to know about Wally's process," Daisy said after another gulp of punch, "you'll have to talk to Inna."

....

"How did it go?" Fern sidled up to Arlo fifteen minutes later. She'd had fifteen minutes to stew over what Daisy had said and the weird feeling she was getting about her innocence.

"She seems…sad," Arlo said finally. It was the best word she could use to describe Daisy.

"Of course she's sad. Her husband was murdered, and she knows that if she doesn't get out of this town soon, she'll be arrested for killing him." She punched one fist into the palm of her other hand. "I knew we shouldn't have tipped her off."

Arlo shook her head. "I don't think she suspects anything, but I got this really weird feeling that she's not our guy." One of those gut feelings like when she was a kid.

"Of course not." Camille joined them. "She's a woman."

"That's not what I mean."

"Oh?"

"Arlo thinks Daisy's innocent," Fern interjected.

Camille's eyes widened. "What?"

Arlo wrung her hands. "She's hurt about his affair with Inna, not angry. And jealous and sad. I believe she really loved Wally." What was it about that man that gave him such devotion from not one but two ladies?

"Jealous, hurt, and sad can push people just as far as angry."

Arlo watched Daisy from across the room. She was still drinking punch, but she had slowed a little. At least she wasn't gulping it down like it was the last drink on earth. She was standing in a small circle of people, all Main Street vendors. Joey the dry cleaner, Delores from the jewelry store, and Cable from the menswear shop. Daisy might live in a high-rise in New York City, but there was a little bit of the Missouri farm girl still in there somewhere.

"She would know, don't you think?" Arlo asked.

"Know what, love?" Camille returned.

"About the mushrooms. Daisy would know that the poison wouldn't take affect right away. She would know."

"Perhaps," Fern acquiesced with a small shrug. "So?"

"So why would she even bother with it?" Arlo asked.

"Maybe she wanted time to convince him of something?"

"So she would convince him and then he would die?" Arlo asked.

"I don't know," Fern grumped. "Why would she kill him if she knew she was only getting a third of his estate? She could have bided her time and tried to get back in the will for more."

"Exactly!" Arlo snapped her fingers. "She didn't stand to gain all she could from his death. And if she really loved him…" *Think, Arlo. Think!* She only had a few more hours before her number-one suspect would leave town. Then what would she do?

"Why is everyone over here in the corner looking all serious?" Helen asked as she approached.

Arlo glanced back to Daisy, then let her gaze drift over to Inna. "I tried to get Daisy to confess, but she wasn't having any of it."

"And now your goddaughter thinks the killer is innocent," Fern's tone was almost accusing.

"Daisy?" Helen asked.

Arlo's gaze drifted back to the blond. She didn't look like a killer. But was that a prerequisite? Ted Bundy didn't look like a killer, but everyone knew how he was. But it was more than a look. Somehow she just knew that Daisy was innocent. It might not be something she could explain, but it was there all the same.

"She didn't do it," Arlo said emphatically.

"You're sure?" Helen returned.

"I am. I don't know who killed Wally, but it wasn't his wife."

....

Arlo eased down onto the bleachers and wondered where the night had gone wrong. She'd had such big plans to bring Daisy to justice, to free Chloe, and set everything right. She had failed. Miserably.

"Your party did not go so well." Inna stopped just in front of Arlo and propped one hand on her hip.

"I thought it went great. Didn't you have a good time?"

"*Da*, but that is not what you want. I know."

Arlo leaned back. "What do you know?"

"You want your friend out of jail. And you want Daisy to go into the jail, no?"

"Yes." Arlo shook her head. "No."

"It has to be one or the other."

"I just want my friend out of jail." It was the truth. "She didn't kill Wally."

"I know." Inna's voice was flat, resigned almost.

"You know?"

"Of course. She is not the type. She's a sweet person, no? Sips her tea from dainty little cups, her marmalade cat curled at her feet. *Da*, I know the type, and she is not it."

"I wasn't aware murderers have a type."

"Oh, but some do."

....

Inna's words stayed with Arlo long after she had gone home. Everyone left the gym in a mess, vowing to meet tomorrow at lunch to clean it all up. The only thing anyone worried about was the food.

Arlo looked to her right. In the passenger seat was a foil-wrapped paper plate, covered edge to edge in appetizers—cheese pinwheels, artichoke dip, and stuffed mushrooms. It wouldn't help with the five pounds she would like to shed, but it would make a great snack tomorrow. Or even tonight.

Thankfully Cindy Jo wasn't out when Arlo pulled into her drive. She wasn't up for another conversation about appetizers, the freezer section at the wholesale club, and the "sheriff." In fact, she didn't want to think about Mads at all. Come to think of it, she could add Sam to that list as well. She didn't want to think about anything really, but Inna's words kept playing in her head over and over. "She's not the type."

Arlo wasn't sure there really was a type that were the only ones capable of murder. But even this stranger could see that Chloe was innocent.

She turned off the engine with a sigh, then she gathered her purse and the plate of appetizers and headed into the house. It was dark and quiet as it always was, but tonight she didn't enjoy the peace. It only made the words in her head echo even louder. *She's not the type.*

Arlo set her midnight snack on the kitchen bar, tossed her purse onto the nearest chair, and kicked off her shoes. She wiggled her toes a bit, then eased toward her bedroom to change. Maybe she would feel better once she put on her pajamas. Or maybe not. Nightclothes would signify that the day was over, the last day she had to prove her friend was innocent.

Or maybe she had been going about this all wrong. Why was Wally killed? Maybe this was about something completely different than cheating husbands. Maybe a person from his past. Someone who knew all his secrets.

And once again she was back to her best friend.

"I know Chloe didn't do it," she said to no one. But she wanted the words out in the world.

She isn't the type, Inna had said. *She sips her tea from dainty little cups with her cat curled up at her feet.*

It was the perfect mental image of Chloe.

A stranger could see it. Why couldn't everyone else?

Arlo pulled on a pair of cotton shorty pj's, then dumped her clothes into the hamper. She should put the food in the fridge and go to sleep. There was nothing she could do now. Nothing but pray that the jury could see through all the BS evidence to who Chloe really was.

She slipped the foil covering from the plate and picked up a pinwheel. It was good of everyone to pull together for Chloe. Too bad it was a bust.

Her cell phone rang. She wiped her fingers on a kitchen towel and then fished the phone out of her purse.

"Hey, Elly."

"Hello, sweetie." If nothing else, it was good to hear the familiar voice once again. "Just wanted to check on you."

"I'm fine." Her voice was flat.

"You don't sound fine."

"I will be. It's just…"

"It's just what?"

"I don't understand how it is that a person who's innocent can look guilty enough for the police—good police like Mads—to arrest them."

"Looks are deceiving."

"But…" Arlo wanted to explain how she couldn't let it go. It was important. But Helen knew that. She wanted to explain that it wasn't fair. Helen knew that too. And if they didn't find the real killer, then Chloe didn't have a prayer. But Helen knew that as well.

She doesn't look like the type.

"Oh my gosh!" Arlo almost choked on one of the stuffed mushrooms. "That's it."

"What is it?"

"The tea. It all makes sense now. I'll be right there."

"Honey, it's late."

"First thing in the morning, then. I'm coming over to talk to Inna."

"Inna?"

"Yes." Her heart pounded. How could she have been so blind?

"Well, that's why I called. Inna and Daisy are leaving."

23

"What?"

"They're coming down the stairs as we speak."

That explained the thumping sound she heard in the background, or maybe it was the blood pounding in her ears.

"Don't let them go anywhere."

"I can't keep them here."

"Yes, you can. Call Fern and Camille. Do something to stall them. I'll be right there."

....

Arlo didn't bother to change clothes. It might look strange going out dressed in her pj's, but she couldn't risk taking the time. She had to get to the inn and fast.

She grabbed her car keys from the bar, slung her purse over her shoulder, and headed out the door.

The only shoes in the room were her high heels from the party and the shoes she wore when she cut the grass, so she left on her slippers and hopped into her car.

"Please," she begged all the way to the inn. "Please let her find a way to keep them there. Please let their rental car not start. Or have a flat." That was almost as good. But she had a feeling she was going to arrive at the inn to see Helen and Camille performing charades as Daisy and Inna walked out the door, taking the truth with them.

She stopped at the light at Main and Sixth but only because someone was coming. *Please don't let it be them.* The last thing she needed was a speed-limit car chase all the way to Memphis International.

The truck turned, slowed, then came to a stop beside her.

What now?

The window rolled down, and Sam propped one hand on the steering wheel as he stared at her.

"Nice outfit, Stanley."

"I don't have time for this, Sam. I've got to get to the inn. I know who killed Wally."

He sat up straight. "You do?"

She nodded.

"You're sure?"

"Yes!"

"Have you called Mads?"

She hadn't even thought about it.

"You go on. I'll get him on the line and be right behind you."

"'Kay. Thanks." The light turned green, and she hit the gas. She wasn't positive, but she thought she heard him call out, "Be careful!" as she sped away.

....

"It was working this afternoon," Daisy said.

"You were the last one to drive it," Inna accused. "What have you broken?"

"I haven't broken anything."

Arlo could hear the argument before she even got out of the car.

Camille and Helen stood on the porch watching, while Fern was off to one side looking entirely too innocent.

"Good job," Arlo muttered to herself. "Going somewhere?" she asked a bit louder.

Inna looked up, those blue eyes sharp with anger. "I guess not, as you have parked behind the car."

Arlo looked at her own vehicle. "I suppose I have."

"No matter. It will not crank. Daisy broke it this afternoon."

"Are you sure you're not framing her for that too?" Arlo asked.

"Too?" Inna shook her head. "I do not frame."

"Yes," Arlo said quietly. "You do. You tried to frame Daisy for killing Wally."

Daisy got out of the car, sputtering. "Inna?"

The woman planted her fists on her hips. "And if I do?"

"Oh, you do," Arlo assured her. "I know. But they arrested Chloe instead. You forget. I was at the police station when you asked Mads to arrest Daisy."

"You what?" It was clear that Daisy thought she and Inna had a more amicable relationship than really existed between them.

"I was merely suggesting that he look into things."

"Like the mushroom poison that you put in Wally's coffee. You figured that would look like Daisy was trying to kill him. Am I right?" She took a step toward Inna, but the woman held her ground. Honestly, Arlo had forgotten how tall she was. Or maybe she seemed larger than life since Arlo was at a height disadvantage in her pink terry slippers.

Helen and Camille came down the stairs. Strength in numbers.

"You cannot prove a thing."

"Yes," Arlo nodded. "I can. See, I found the earring you dropped in Chloe's bungalow. Just what were you doing in there?"

"I was not."

"Then how do you know that she drinks tea from dainty little cups with her marmalade cat?"

"I have seen this cat, yes? He has been in the store and in the place above and in the police station. He is a well-traveled beast."

"But Chloe's teacups aren't. They're displayed on her counter. She has a whole collection depending on the day of the week or her mood. But you would only know that if you had been in her bungalow. Where you dropped the earring you were going to use to frame Daisy."

Daisy gasped, and her hands flew to her ears. "I thought you said I left them at home."

Inna shrugged. "That's what you get when you treat people around you like servants. I am not servant."

"You're not even an assistant, are you?" Arlo asked.

"No," she admitted. Arlo could see the burning light of truth in her eyes. "I am author."

A collective gasp went up around the ladies.

"You wrote *Missing Girl*," Arlo said "That's why it reads like the person writing only knows English as a second language. Because they do. But why?"

Inna shifted, seemed to debate how much to tell her. Finally she inhaled and let her breath out slowly. "You know how hard it is to get green card?" She shook her head. "No, of course you don't. It's hard. Very hard and I work and work and can't keep my visa and no green card. And Wally he comes to me and says I will publish your book for you and split the money. We will make the big bucks. You won't have to have a green card because no one will know it is you." She shrugged in that elegant way she had. "It seemed like good idea at time. Not so much now." She shrugged again.

"Because he kept all the money." It was beginning to make sense now. "But what about the earring? Why were you in Chloe's bungalow?"

"Because of the will."

Arlo frowned. "You knew about the will?" What was she saying? Inna seemed to know everything about Wally. She might not have been a good assistant—or even an assistant at all—but she was an expert when it came to all things Wally Harrison.

"Of course. He was supposed to will the money to me. But instead he gave it to that brat."

"And you wanted to see who Chloe was?" So Inna and Wally's connection was more than just the book. The affair was real after all.

Again Inna did that shrugging thing that she did so well. "I wanted know who this person was who could bewitch my Wally, even ten years after."

Bewitch? Arlo wouldn't say that. But Inna had an odd perspective for sure. "Well, it's over now."

"No. It is not." She dashed to the side and around Arlo, sprinting for her car. Well, as much as a woman wearing four-inch platform heels could sprint. Arlo's slip-on house shoes weren't much better for running. Still she managed to catch Inna before she could duck into the car. But she only got her by the hair.

It must have hurt. Bad. Inna swung around and flung a hand out, connecting with Arlo's left cheek. Pain shot all the way though her head and into her brain. Teeth were rattled, stars danced, but somehow Arlo managed to hang on. Without Inna, they had no proof that Chloe was innocent. There was no way she was letting her escape now.

The sound of a police siren split the night. Just one big whoop, then it disappeared amid the blue-and-red flashing lights.

Inna wilted, like a starched hanky in the noonday sun. She was limp, but Arlo couldn't let go. Her fingers were entwined in the silky dark hair of the woman who had killed Wally J. Harrison.

....

"Ouch." Arlo pressed the bag of frozen carrots to her cheek and winced. "This hurts."

"You're lucky it's not worse."

"It's going to be." She frowned at the bag of vegetables. "It's supposed to be peas."

"Hush," Helen said, though the word held no malice. "The main thing is that it's cold."

"That's another thing." She shrugged out of the cover that someone had draped around her shoulders. "It's sweltering out here." May in Mississippi was no joke.

"It's to protect you from shock." Camille said.

"I'm not in shock."

Camille moved to place the blanket around Arlo, but she shifted before it touched her shoulders. Thankfully Camille took the hint.

It had been less than an hour since Mads had pulled up with Sam right behind. They'd grabbed Inna, who was kicking and yelling in Russian or Ukrainian. Arlo didn't know. Maybe both.

She told them all how angry she was, how much she hated Daisy, and how her adoration for Wally had pushed her too far. He had laughed at her when she told him that she had poisoned him with mushrooms. It took weeks for the poison to take effect and if a person knew that they had ingested the mushrooms, there was an antidote. That was when she pushed him.

"So the scarf that Nadine saw was really just Inna's hair," Helen mused.

Arlo nodded.

"That girl really should wear her glasses more," Camille added.

"The one reason you won't see me in her chair," Fern said.

"I thought that was because you were too cheap to pay someone to do it."

"Pah." Fern waved a hand as if Helen's words held no weight. "I'm an old woman. Who cares what my hair looks like?"

"I do," Camille and Helen said at the same time.

Arlo laughed. "Get your hair done on your own time. Let's go get Chloe out of jail."

....

"Are you going to tell me who hired you?" Arlo asked as she rode with Sam back to the police station.

"Wally."

Maybe the last person she had suspected. "Wally?"

"He knew something was up with Inna, and he was starting to wonder if Daisy was having an affair."

"So he changed his will," she mused. "That way she wouldn't be able to get the majority of his money. Inna's money."

"If what she's saying is true."

"Have you read the book?"

Sam chuckled. "I've tried. It's a little over this country boy's head."

But she knew: Sam was a lot smarter than he let on. Always had been.

"I don't doubt what she says, but there's no proof. Now she's going to prison, and Jayden gets the money." She stopped. "Why now? After all this time?" She didn't have to explain further. He knew what she was saying.

"I don't know. Guilt maybe. Premonition. Sometimes it takes people a while to see where they've messed up. Maybe he just wanted to make things right."

"Maybe." But Wally was gone, and they would never know his reasoning.

Sam pulled his truck into the parking lot behind the police station and cut the engine.

"Thanks for driving me."

"It was the least I could do since Helen wasn't going to let you drive after your... What was it again?"

"My traumatic encounter."

"Right."

They got out of the truck as Helen pulled up in her Smart Car. Fern hopped out and shook herself like a dog shaking off fleas. "Arghhh. That car. Makes me feel like a giant."

"Hush," Helen countered. "It's a great car."

"But not the least bit smart."

Camille had stayed at the inn with Daisy, who was still in shock over learning the true nature of a woman she had lived with for the past two years or more. Arlo couldn't blame her. It was jarring news.

"You didn't have to come out here," Arlo protested. She knew they wouldn't turn around and go home. They were there to see this through. Arlo wasn't sure that was a good thing or bad.

"We're here for you," Helen said with an encouraging smile. Arlo wasn't sure what it all meant, but she didn't ask.

Together they walked into the police station.

Things worked a little differently in a small town. Mads had brought Inna in and had her in the holding cell. Tomorrow she supposed he would call the sheriff to come pick her up.

Arlo stood with Sam, Helen, and Fern as they waited for Chloe to be released.

"Come by tomorrow when you can. We'll need you to sign a couple of papers. Frances will have them."

"Okay." Chloe's voice sounded hesitant and a little worried, as if she was wondering if Mads was going to take it all back before she could get out the door.

Her face broke into a sweet smile as she came around the corner and saw them standing there.

Arlo rushed to her friend and hugged her like there was no tomorrow. For a while there, she had been worried there might not be.

Then Chloe began to shake.

"Shhhh…" Arlo smoothed a hand down Chloe's blond curls. "It's okay now. You're free."

She said something, but the words were lost in the tears and sobs.

"Come on," Arlo said. "Let's take you home."

....

In the end, they all wound up back at the inn. Everyone but Mads, who stayed at the station with Inna. He felt she needed supervision through the night.

"You didn't have to do this," Chloe said with a small nod at the blueberry-lemon coffee cake in the middle of the table. They had all gathered in the dining room, drinking coffee and eating. It was late, but they needed to add a normal moment to the night to help get everything back on track.

Daisy twisted her hands together. "I bake when I get upset. Well, I want to. I usually don't. Sometimes I bake and give it to the neighbors. I don't know why I'm saying all this." She shook her head.

Helen covered her hand with her own. "You've had quite a week yourself."

She nodded. "I suppose. It's just…" She looked up to Chloe. "I'm sorry about what I said at the reading of the will. I didn't know Wally had a son. He never mentioned it. Not once in all these years. But your son, he deserves the money that the book's brought in."

"Thank you," Chloe said. She wrapped her hands around her mug of tea as if she needed to absorb all the warmth she could.

"Make sure he has money for college," Daisy continued. "Please."

"Of course." With the money Wally had brought in on *Missing Girl*, there would be money for college and beyond.

"I guess I'll go home in the morning, if that's okay."

Helen smiled. "Okay? It's fine, but you know you don't have to leave at all."

Daisy frowned. "You mean stay here, in Sugar Springs?"

"Yep. Why not?"

There was no reason except small-town life wasn't for everyone. And a person like Daisy seemed to belong in the city. Though Arlo had to remind herself, she had come from humble beginnings.

"I'll think about it."

"I could always use help here and with your baking skills…"

"Everyone who bakes in town is going to want to hire you," Arlo added.

"Hey." Chloe pretended to be hurt. "Seriously though. This is a great cake. You whipped it up like a ninja."

"I suppose I could bake." The idea seemed completely foreign to Daisy. "I'll think about it. But for now." She stood. "I'm going to bed. Thank you for being so kind to me even after everything."

Fern frowned, or maybe it was a smile; with her it was hard to tell. "It ain't your fault. And Sugar Springs could always use another resident."

Daisy nodded and moved toward the stairs. Arlo wondered if she would take Helen up on the offer or even go to work for the grocery store bakery. With the money she got from Wally's death, she might even be able to open a bakery of her own right there on Main Street.

"Good night," they called, then turned back to their warm drinks and cake.

"I hope she stays," Fern said.

Everyone turned to look at her.

"What? A person can't be nice to a down-and-out stranger?"

"Sure they can," Camille said.

"We just didn't expect it from you," Helen finished.

....

"Is there anything you want to tell me?" Chloe said the following morning at ten. Arlo had told her that she didn't have to work the day after she had been released from jail, but she said she wanted things to go back to normal as quickly as possible.

"Hi. Yes, it is a beautiful morning."

"Sam is on the third floor. He said he was renting it from you for his business. My cat is up there with him, but the poor baby is so scared he won't even come out for me."

Arlo started to answer, but Chloe plowed on. "Helen called and said she was bringing magic bars and one-pot spaghetti. When I asked her for what, she laughed and said, 'book club.' Like that was supposed to mean something to me." She stopped polishing the cups and glasses she had rewashed that morning. "So?"

"Yes, I leased the third floor to Sam. He agreed to keep Auggie, but the cat has been a bit traumatized since you went to jail. It may take him a little time to adjust. And the Friday night book club has decided to meet here every day for lunch. Oh, and Sam comes down for that too." Arlo smiled. "Welcome back."

EPILOGUE

"NOW THAT I KNOW THAT INNA WROTE THIS BOOK, I LIKE IT better," Camille said.

"You like it better because a murderer wrote it?" Fern pinned her with a hard stare.

"Not that, but I can see Inna in this book. Wally, not so much."

"There's a town in there just like Sugar Springs," Helen pointed out. "Do you think he meant to set up this town as in the one in the book?"

Arlo shrugged. "Who knows?"

"Inna," Fern said.

"Probably, but you are not writing her a letter to find out." Helen set her mouth at an angle that brooked no argument.

"I guess that means Wally did have some influence on the book."

Camille cast a quick glance at the staircase leading to the third floor. "I guess Sam is too busy to come down."

"He has no problem being here at ten," Chloe threw in. "Every morning."

"Seriously," Arlo said. "He's coming down for coffee. Not to see me."

"You just keep telling yourself that."

"Do you remember that girl who disappeared a while back? The piano teacher? They never found her car or any trace of her." Camille's voice took on wistful tone. "Just like the girl in the book."

"You don't think…" Helen started.

"*Pah.* What would Wally, or Inna, know about that girl?" Fern demanded.

"Writers do research," Arlo pointed out.

"But how do you do research in a small town? Everyone knows that you're in town."

"You hire someone else to do it for you," Camille said.

"That's ridiculous." Fern sat back with a frown.

"Is it?" Arlo asked.

They sat in silence for a moment, each mulling over the possibilities of a decade-old missing person case.

"There's only one way to find out," Camille said.

Fern and Helen nodded. "Agreed."

"No." Arlo shook her head. "Absolutely not."

"Oh yeah." Fern smiled—at least it was a smile for Fern.

Chloe stood behind the coffee bar and shook her head. She hadn't been a part of solving the last mystery of who killed Wally. If she had, she would understand the gravity of their plan.

"Please," Arlo said, but the ladies were already gathering their things.

"We hit Lillyfield first," Helen said.

"Good plan." Camille adjusted her handbag strap on her arm.

Just then Sam appeared at the opening to the third-floor staircase. He frowned when he saw everyone getting ready to leave. "I just got here," he protested. "What did I miss?"

ACKNOWLEDGMENTS

At the end of writing a book, there are always so many people to thank. So many that inevitably someone is left off the list. Thank you to all those not mentioned.

Thank you, thank you, thank you to my agent, my editor, and everyone at Sourcebooks for helping make this book a reality.

I have to give a shout-out to my bestie and assistant and all-round "Girl Friday," Stacey Barbalace, for always being there when I needed something read. Even at two o'clock in the morning.

And a big thanks goes out to my son for not running for the hills when talk turns to things like poisons, death, autopsies, and gun-shot residue. All in a day's work when your dad is a cop and your mom a writer! And thanks for being so patient when I say, "Just let me finish this thought," and it turns into two hours.

And thanks to my husband, Rob, for answering question after question even when you're off duty and done with police work for the day. Your love and support mean so very much to me!

About the Author

Amy loves nothing more than a good book. Except for her family…and homemade tacos…and maybe nail polish. Even then, reading and writing are definitely high on the list. After all, Amy is an award-winning author with more than forty novels and novellas in print.

Born and bred in Mississippi, Amy is a transplanted Southern belle who now lives in Oklahoma with her deputy husband, their genius son, and three very spoiled cats.

When she's not creating happy endings or mapping out her latest whoduni-t, she's usually following her teen prodigy to guitar concerts, wrestling matches, or the games for whatever sport he's into that week. She has a variety of hobbies, including swimming (a.k.a. floating around the pool), any sort of crafts, and crochet, but her favorite is whatever gets her out of housework.

She loves to hear from readers. You can find her on Facebook, Amazon, BookBub, and Goodreads. And for more about what inspires her books, check out her pages on Pinterest. For links to the various sites, go to her website: AmyLillardBooks.com. Or feel free to email her at amylillard918@gmail.com.